THE FIRE WITHIN

by Joe David

BOOKS FOR ALL TIMES, INC.

A Virginia Publishing Company

Alexandria, Virginia

He who has done his best for his own
time has lived for all times.

— Schiller

Limited First Edition

Library of Congress Catalog Card Number: 81-65447
Printed in the United States of America
ISBN — Hard: 0-939360-00-4 $10.95
ISBN — Soft: 0-939360-01-2 $4.95

Jacket and cover designed by

Richard Garza

BOOKS FOR ALL TIMES, Inc.

A Virginia Publishing Company
Post Office Box 2
Alexandria, Virginia 22313

The characters in this story are fictitious. No attempt was
made to model them after anyone living or dead. Instead,
the characters are symbols of ideas popular in education
which I have attempted to personify.

The Author

Joe David spent over 18 years being conventionally "educated" at some of America's "better" schools, including two years of graduate study in journalism. After the military service, he studied in France and Switzerland between teaching jobs in the public schools. During the past ten years, he has written many articles and books. His writing assignments have taken him into many remote countries of the world where he has had the opportunity to observe the evil effects of government out of control. He is currently on the editorial board of *Reading Improvement* and at work on more stories which expose schemes to undermine individual freedom.

Those who corrupt the public mind are just as evil as those who steal from the public purse.
— Adlai Stevenson
Speech, Albuquerque, New Mexico
September 21, 1952

To Anne Harte and others like her

Audiovisual Teaching Can Create Push-Button Freaks, Warns Dr. Steele

Acting school superinten- dent, Dr. Marshall Steele, last night warned parents at Kennedy High School that the audiovisual center, as propos- ed by the recently elected school board president, Richard Lathan, "would dis- courage students from lear- ning to interrelate and could cause their demise as humans by making them push-button freaks."

Last night's meeting was Dr. Steele's third attempt this month to warn parents about Lathan's controversial audiovisual-proposal. Once again Dr. Steele stressed that the best way to reverse the declining interest in learning would be to spend that seg- ment of the $10 million federal grant, reserved for innovative programs, not on an audiovisual center, but on the salaries and expenses for a student panel which would settle disputes over all major school issues.

"Students aren't lear- ning," Dr. Steele went on to say to a packed auditorium, "not for the reasons Mr. Lathan thinks, because teachers aren't teaching, but they aren't learning, because the impersonal schools which the huge bureaucracy has created are frustrating students by not giving them a voice in their education."

Designate Urges   OMB

Chapter 1

Anne Harte gasped at the sight of the wall painting behind the large mahogany desk. The painting, done in an abstract-expressionist style of fragmented images, was of a woman either bathing or masturbating. Because the images lacked clear definition, one moment the painting appeared to be innocent, the next moment pornographic. Sitting beneath the painting, leaning over the desk and massaging his temples was a man who without looking up asked Anne to sit down. As she approached a red-leather armchair to the left of his desk, he dropped his arms and stared at her like someone with blurred vision who hadn't had enough coffee or sleep to sober him after a night of drinking.

Despite the lines undulating across his forehead and shooting from the corners of his eyes, he could've been either in his late thirties or fifties, prematurely old by dissipation or freakishly young by good luck. By popular standards he was quite handsome, the type who would appeal to a vast majority of women Anne's age as a sensual father type. To Anne, though, he was just the personnel director for the Board of Education.

At least this was her first thought of him. More specific thoughts came to mind while watching him awaken from his stupor and stare at her legs, her figure, and finally her face. As she sat in what appeared to be a sturdy armchair, she felt her body sink into the soft, featherlike seat almost to the floor. Before she could pull herself up, she was buried in the chair with her legs in the air, exposing herself for him to study. For one violent moment she hated him and his innocent-looking chair. Without expressing this hate beyond her look, she pulled herself up, then sat on the front edge of the chair.

His questions, as he casually interviewed her, were as cleverly worded as the chair was cleverly designed. If she answered one way, she was saying yes to a sexual overture, another way, no. While questioning her, he was leaning back in his chair, tilting it toward the painting, and was staring at her legs. She knew by his smile that he saw more of her legs than she cared to show. Yet she made no effort to change her position. She merely answered his questions appropriately and conveyed, when their gazes met, a polite but firm no to his overture.

Without appearing discouraged by her attitude, he pulled his chair forward, cleared his throat, then began to tell her about the job opening at Church Junior High School and about the six teachers who quit the all-black school, one after nearly being raped.

"Of course," he said with the suggestion of a smile, "the student never really tried to rape her. It was just one of those misunderstandings . . . a simple case of over-reaction on the part of the teacher."

"What about the other five?" she asked. "What were their reasons for quitting?"

"To be honest," he said, "they just didn't see eye to eye with the principal on certain key issues."

"I see."

"Do you?" And he was now leaning back in the chair again, glancing at her legs. "Well, in that case, I have another opening in a nice white school district. But, it requires a little experience." He began to free his smile. "Do you have any experience, Miss Harte?"

"I do. But not the type that will qualify me for that job."

"Then in that case the best I can offer such an attractive white woman as you is a teaching job at Church."

"I'll take it," she said.

A row of stores, gutted by fire during the riots, lined the street like a block-long brick wall ready to fall forward. Covering the faces of these stores, in lieu of display windows, were sheets of plywood. Painted on the plywood were black-liberation murals of angry-looking black men with raised rifles, leading an army through a city ravished by fire and looting.

Anne crossed the street with her back to this brick wall and stared ahead at Church Junior High School. An American flag, hanging from a pole attached to a second-floor window sill, and a museum-of-modern-art sculpture by the entrance, resembling a 20-foot flame of twisted metal, were all that distinguished the school, a shoebox of glass and stone, from all the other newly built shoeboxes in the city.

As Anne approached the school, the flame seemed to be consuming the building. When she paused in front of the school to study the sculpture and push aside several strands of her long, blonde hair which the wind had blown across her mouth, several black teenagers, strolling lazily to school, pointed at her and called her a honky. They then began hurling stones at her. Without running, without revealing her fear, she walked briskly past them and three teenagers climbing the twisted-metal flame and entered the school through a green door which was spray-painted with obscenities.

Inside the school against one wall was a gold-frame photograph of the former U.S. President, Alexander Church. He was sitting in a wing chair by the fireplace, meditating like someone deeply troubled by an America which didn't conform to his standards. Written across the wall above the picture was his famous quotation: "My dream for a New America is for all freedom-loving Americans to give their best selflessly to their country."

Anne grew sad thinking about his dream for a New America. She remembered his military support for an undeclared war which ultimately resulted in millions of Americans dying uselessly protecting a "friendly" dictator in Africa while he ignored the systematic overthrow of Caribbean and Central American countries by Marxist terrorists. She remembered his successful anti-trust action against three major corporations which finally had to dispose of some holdings in order to be in compliance with the law and, in the process, throw hundreds of thousands of Americans out of work. She remembered his New America Program to spend billions of dollars on America's needy which shamelessly turned out to be not the indigent, but the politically connected bureaucrats administering the food, housing, and medical assistance program. And she remembered his threat to use legal force of all types from anti-trust action to Senate and House Committee investigation against any industry which didn't "voluntarily" lower prices in his fight with big business to curb an inflation that he caused by his generous printing of paper money to support his welfare programs and undeclared war.

Protecting his name from being tarnished by these "achievements" was his Black Rights Amendment which newspapers forced through Congress after arousing hatred and violence among the races with their inflammatory articles. Such flagrant means to such ends *might* have been justified to Anne if it had succeeded at reducing the tension between the races. Instead, the Amendment merely increased racial tension by making it now legal to discriminate against whites rather than blacks. In this way the first significant step was taken toward using violence rather than justice as a means to settle future racial unrest. With "achievements" like this, she thought ruefully, what kind of New America would freedom-loving Americans be helping to create by giving their best to their country? One look at what was happening at Church Junior High School revealed in microcosm exactly what that might be.

Her sadness deepened, when she looked ahead . . . beyond the screaming and shoving teenagers rushing through the hall . . . toward a teacher who was telling a boy to clean the mess he made in her room. Several teenagers, standing near the teacher, were leisurely scribbling obscenities on the wall, while one girl, hopping past them like a kangaroo, was knocking loose tile blocks from the low-hanging suspended ceiling. Beyond them . . . at the furthest end of the narrow hall . . . was a broken window facing the jungle outside. By the way the floor-to-ceiling window was broken, it looked as though someone had flown through it with outstretched arms like an airplane.

Anne leaned against the door. For a moment she felt weak and helpless, and wondered how she would ever teach here. But her self-doubts passed when she remembered something Dr. Maria Montessori had once said: "When a child has disruptive tendencies, some great need of his isn't being met." Almost immediately she recovered her poise and stood perfectly erect. She then walked briskly to a door marked office. Somehow she would meet that need, she assured herself, and as successfully as she once had at the university.

A long, high counter divided the office into two unequal sections. The smaller section where Anne was standing was for the teachers and visitors. The larger section where the desks, filing cabinets, and office equipment were kept was for the office personnel. Atop a filing cabinet was a percolator and a doughnut box. Office personnel, looking important and busy, hurried out of the rooms to the left and right of the main office. They then suddenly paused by the filing cabinet long enough to pour coffee or grab a doughnut. Afterwards, they quickly disappeared into another office where they engaged in loud conversation.

Anne waited for a woman to finish her phone conversation before approaching her. The woman was chatting gaily about a date last night when a bell rang. After glancing at the clock over the filing cabinet, she told her friend she'd call back later, then quickly hung up.

"I would like to see . . . " Anne started to say to the woman.

The woman sprung to her feet. "Could you wait a few minutes, please." She then grabbed her styrofoam cup and a doughnut and disappeared into a room to Anne's right.

When she didn't return within a reasonable time, Anne called to a woman nearby. The woman, munching on a doughnut, strolled past Anne into another office without responding.

A little later another woman left the inner office and walked to the counter at the opposite end to where Anne was standing. She glanced at Anne as though she were an object which required no greeting, then lifted a paper from the counter and forming each word on her lips began to read. Anger welled up in Anne and rushed out in her stare. She marched to where the woman was standing and said firmly: "Would you tell the principal I'd like to see her?"

The woman delayed looking up just long enough to be impertinent, then in a bored voice said: "Your name?"

"I'm Miss Harte, Anne Harte, the new English teacher."

The woman flipped on the intercom. "Mrs. Daniels," she said into a microphone, "the Mrs. Park's replacement is here."

"Send her in," a voice answered.

The woman, before resuming her reading, pointed to a closed door by the teachers' mailboxes. Since the door was locked, Anne had to wait after knocking for the sound of the buzzer.

The principal's office looked like a typical school office, all gray-metal cabinets and furniture. On the desk were two phones, one red (a hot line to where?) and another black, next to an elaborate intercom system. To relieve the gray-metal look and to give the room some warmth, a collection of pictures were arranged attractively on the wall. Each one had a picture of the same white woman with the same charming smile. One picture was with the mayor, another with the superintendent of schools, still another at a ground-breaking ceremony. Next to these pictures were degrees, awards and membership certificates from various civic and honorary organizations.

The same woman as in the pictures, minus the charming smile, had just extended a green line on a large attendance chart next to the wall and was now stepping back a few feet to study the irregular lines. She was an attractive white woman who wore a dress with a pleated skirt. She would've been stunning in that dress, if she didn't have on such heavy-looking orthopedic shoes. The incongruity of the dress and shoes was so disturbingly obvious that it detracted from her stylish appearance.

Turning, the woman removed her glasses, attached to her neck by a chain, and let them bounce against her chest. But when she saw Anne, she lifted the glasses to her eyes and, without putting them on, examined Anne with what seemed to be the care of a jeweler studying a rare stone. "My," she said, generously emphasizing key words for dramatic effect, "you're a very attractive woman!" She then smiled a smile which undoubtedly photographed well but which in person was held just a little too long, was just a little too broad, to be anything but just a little too artificial. The artificiality spread after Mrs. Daniels sat behind the gray-metal desk. Almost miraculously the gray-metal desk transformed itself into a status symbol endowed with a special power to bestow on anyone sitting behind it an air of importance. Even her voice, which was just a little too deep for a woman, deepened slightly, giving it a more authoritative ring. It almost seemed that Mrs. Daniels was deliberately trying to create a psychological barrier between herself, the cultured educator, and Anne, the novice teacher. She might have been successful in her efforts if a boy hadn't come to the window behind the desk and started to entertain Anne by making grostesque facial expressions.

Mrs. Daniels was in the middle of a sentence in which she was elaborating on "how a student learns, not by thinking, but by doing" when the boy appeared and started to amuse Anne with his buffoonery. At first Anne wanted to ignore the boy, but was unsuccessful. The boy's behavior seemed too fitting in view of the nonsense Mrs. Daniels was gushing.

Startled by Anne's inattentiveness, Mrs. Daniels stopped talking and turned toward the window where Anne was staring. At that precise moment, the boy stopped clowning and made a vulgar gesture with his hips and arm at the principal. Without rising from her chair, the principal yanked the shade down, then muttered something about those disrespectful savages.

In the hall, several teenagers were overheard arguing, calling each other four-letter names. Mrs. Daniels cocked her head toward the wall to the hall and listened with a look of weariness. After a pensive pause, in a voice with none of the artificiality of before, she asked: "Tell me, Miss Harte. Have you taught before?"

"Yes, for a year at the university."

"Oooh," she said, leaning forward, impressed. "Were you *fulltime* faculty?" She once again underlined key words, made them jump from the sentence.

"No, I just taught several remedial English classes."

"I see," she said flatly. "Well, you'll find *here*, Miss Harte, that the work will be challenging . . . just what a young teacher needs."

"I know. That's why I came."

"Have you read any of Carl Blanc's books?"

"A few."

"*Only* a few? Oh, Miss Harte, you must read *all* of him. In fact, I *insist*. Working with so many new students isn't easy for inexperienced teachers.That's why I urge that all my teachers read Blanc. This way we can unite ourselves with a common philosophy."

"Are there many inexperienced teachers on the staff?"

"Oh yes. *Many*."

"You mean downtown staffed this school with mostly inexperienced teachers?" Anne asked, surprised.

"Unfortunately it's true, Miss Harte. Occasionally such mistakes are made in staffing. But then, *isn't* that how we learn?" she said with lady-like emphasis on important words.

"It's a pity that the school had to lose six teachers to learn such a mistake."

Mrs. Daniels, obviously startled by such a remark from

a subordinate, became a little defensive, as if Anne were blaming *her* for the teachers' decision to quit. "There will always be *those*, Miss Harte, like the six who just quit, who don't realize how *lucky* they are to be part of such a *wonderful* school." Mrs. Daniels smiled charmingly, ignoring the swearing in the hall which grew louder, and said casually: "Did you know our school is a candidate for *several* awards in *original* design?"

Anne wondered (as she shook her head) if Mrs. Daniels ever left her pedagogic vault long enough to notice Church's unimaginative shoebox design.

"Why teachers like you will be the *envy* of the system," the principal continued. "Some of the most *innovative* ideas in education are being encouraged here. And to think, Miss Harte, you'll be part of all this."

"What type of innovation are you considering?"

The principal leaned forward, obviously *thrilled* at the opportunity to tell Anne everything. "It isn't official yet, but there is talk of establishing a panel of students for evaluating teachers, curriculum, and school policy. As you probably know, it's the *latest* concept in education, and it is sure to guarantee *total* involvement of every student here."

"Do you honestly believe that such a panel is wise?"

"*Absolutely!* In fact, as Carl Blanc once said." Mrs. Daniels continued in a voice of an administrator trained in the illusions of education, "the *only* way to prepare a student for life is to let him perform those *relevant* activities so important to *democratic* America."

"I disagree."

Mrs. Daniels looked incredulously at Anne. "You disagree?"

"That's right. I believe our responsibility is to educate students, to teach them to integrate ideas and prove them logically, to think about ideas and understand them conceptually, and not to waste intelligent minds on limiting life experiences."

"Well," she gasped, unable to hide her shock with a smile, "you *certainly* are a woman of opinion."

A voice over the intercom interrupted them. "There's a Mrs. Jones to see you, Mrs. Daniels."

Mrs. Daniels' pretty face wrinkled into annoyance as she pressed a button on the intercom. "*Which* Mrs. Jones?"

"Calvin's mother."

"Is *that* the boy who started the fire yesterday in the cafeteria?"

"That's right."

"Well, send her to Mr. Slaughter. You know I don't handle *those* problems."

"But Mr. Slaughter isn't in his office."

"Then page him." Mrs. Daniels paused, then added as an obvious warning: "And Miss Brown . . ."

"Yes, Mrs. Daniels?"

"Don't disturb me again unless it's important." She then released the button and turned to Anne. "Now let's see," she said. "Where were we? Oh yes, we were discussing the student panel."

For thirty minutes, while teenagers ran and screamed through the hall, Mrs. Daniels tried to convince Anne that she was mistaken about the educational value of the student panel. To make her point, she generously quoted Carl Blanc and stressed through continuous repetition of key ideas that education had to be relevant to a student's interests, his spontaneous impulses, and his instincts, which were best expressed through action. She then named prominent psychologists, philosophers, and educators who agreed with Blanc, and repeated their main arguments which reinforced Blanc's point of view, and dared Anne by her tone to refute them. After thoroughly exhausting the subject, certain that she had driven her point into Anne's brain like a wedge, she said: "So you see, Miss Harte, man learns...not by thinking...but by doing! Therefore," she concluded in a voice of someone convinced of her victory, "the schools mustn't be a place to teach a ready-made universe of knowledge or intellectual skills . . . but a place where students can perform relevant *life* experiences."

"That," Anne said, unimpressed with her argument, "is nonsense."

Loretta Daniels' education career began 20 years ago during the period which Superintendent Fritz Spender recently popularized (before being fired for payroll extortion and being replaced temporarily by Dr. Marshall Steele) as the Repressive Era in Public School Education Like others aspiring to one of the few careers open almost exclusively to women, Loretta Daniels had to pass difficult oral and written exams which were conceived to uncover her philosophy of education, or, as Loretta laughingly told friends, her philosophy on the state controlling minds.

Since Loretta Daniels was taught by her high-school-principal father from early childhood to think like an educator, she understood the philosophy of public school education completely and passed her exams with ease. Her probationary period as a teacher was also no major challenge for her. Unlike other teachers, Loretta never had to be indoctrinated by supervisors on what and how to teach. From the beginning she knew that it was her responsibility to turn her students into non-thinking, charm-school personalities who would follow the leader on faith, cling to racial and social prejudices, sacrifice themselves for altruistic ideals and in short, master all the characteristics, deemed necessary by big government, to be ruled easily. This Loretta Daniels did, and well. In fact, she did it so well (so painlessly, as her principal once said) that supervisors came to her for suggestions on teaching.

Although teaching was dull and standardized, and the subjects and textbooks rigidly selective in language and point of view, schools were orderly and safe. Most important, everyone quickly learned the rules. If a student were too bright, if a teacher were too original, or if an administrator were too honest, he would be swiftly re-programmed. It was, as Loretta often remarked with nostalgia, the Golden Era of Public School Education. The government's control of the mind through propaganda was so complete that many of its victims weren't strong enough to free themselves. But this Golden Era to Loretta's chagrin ended when a few articulate citizens began to organize successfully a civil-rights movement.

The federal government, motivated by the huge amounts of money it could squeeze from taxpayers, suddenly became "morally" interested in the civil-rights movement and began a large-scale campaign to make the public feel guilty for the infraction of rights for which the government was originally responsible. To persuade the school system to become also interested, huge grants were offered by the federal government as an incentive to any school system which could prove a need. Eager for a share of these grants, schools created this need by implementing new programs as though they were a panacea to all social and racial problems. These new programs, abandoned shortly after being implemented for newer programs, were selected carefully with one view in mind: to create chaos by breaking down teaching standards.

To speed this decay, large and impossible-to-teach ability mixes of frustrated and angry students were placed in one class without providing teachers with methods and tools to educate them successfully, and students were passed from grade to grade without being taught anything in order to spread illiteracy on all levels. During this period of Planned Destruction, most of the competent teachers deserted the system and were replaced by unqualified teachers, and the few students from white, middle-class homes who weren't rushed off to private schools, were bused into hostile, inner-city school districts in order to set off racial tension. For the school system's success at creating a need, the government awarded the system almost $50 million in grants a year.

Loretta recognized the problems which the passing of the Golden Era would bring from the start and wisely went on for a Master's to escape the turmoil. Her husband who remained in the classroom after the pendulum swung from the repressive to the permissive era died of a heart attack during a student riot while foolishly trying to hold back the swinging pendulum. A few teachers like Loretta wisely avoided similar fate and bribed friends downtown to give them coveted appointments. Loretta, more fortunate than some teachers, was sent to a high school which somehow survived the turbulence of such change with reasonable dignity.

Her relatively uneventful and comfortable career, first as assistant principal and later as principal of Washington High School, would have probably continued un-interrupted until retirement if she hadn't learned that the school would be closed soon because of dwindling enrollment. To avoid an appointment to an inner-city school where the need was the greatest, she decided to take a leave after the school closed and start work on her doctorate. She knew with a doctorate she would have a better chance for a promotion downtown where she could defend her career against the capriciousness of bureaucrats.

While working on her doctorate, she began to publish research papers in respected journals. These published papers, read by a small group of influential educators, quickly established her as an authority on permissive education. Talk shows, eager to exploit her growing fame, asked her to appear on television periodically.

During one such appearance, she met Dr. Marshall Steele who at the time had just been temporarily appointed superintendent of schools. Dr. Steele, impressed with what he called her ability to make "bullshit look like caviar," immediately asked her after the television show for her support in promoting a student panel which he was using as an issue to win public support for his appointment as the next permanent superintendent. For her cooperation, he promised her a job downtown. But before he could offer the job, she would have to end her leave and for a year work at Church where she would be expected to sell the staff and community on the student panel. If she succeeded, he would personally see to it that she was promoted the following year to the job of assistant superintendent of personnel. At first Loretta wanted to refuse. She had taken the leave to escape the possibility of being hurled into an inner-city school, and now suddenly she was being asked to do what she energetically tried to avoid. But when she gave his offer some serious thought, she realized that it was an exceptional opportunity. If she succeeded at selling his panel to the staff and community, she knew she would never have to worry about her future again.

During her first few weeks at Church, she laid the foundation for her future by reminding her staff and her students' parents of the basic goodness of teenagers. This goodness, she told them, could only grow by allowing students to satisfy their needs, their instincts, and their impulses through action. To convert skeptics on the staff, she promised them special favors for helping her spread the Word. The others, mostly young and innocent teachers, were kept innocent by overwhelming them with quotations from famous educators, psychologists, and philosophers whose theories agreed with Loretta's.

Despite the monumental problems caused by defiant teenagers, no one on the staff seriously questioned the validity of her philosophy. Most teachers blamed themselves whenever anything went wrong in their classes. Mrs. Daniels had made certain to this by making them feel guilty whenever they tried to discipline students for any violent and evil behavior.

Then, on the third week her philosophy was dramatically challenged when one teacher, respected by the staff for her tact, was almost raped by a student. This teacher along with five other teachers, angered when Mrs. Daniels put the blame on the teacher and not the boy for the near rape, quit to demonstrate their view that, though teenagers might be basically good, students still needed moral and intellectual guidance. "Refusal to provide this guidance by allowing students the freedom to act out their impulses," the teachers said in a letter to the principal and the superintendent of schools, "would only reinforce the evil these students learned in their environment."

Other teachers, less intelligent than the six, began to question the truthfulness of the premise that teenagers were basically good. None had accepted the principal's argument that the teacher, through shamelessly provocative action, had encouraged the boy to try to rape her. Their own experiences with students who tormented them for no apparent reason now convinced them that teenagers were evil and needed strong discipline. Loretta knew, if she didn't end the spread of such thinking, the teachers might strike. If that occurred, they might win public sympathy and turn the community against a student panel. Since she had to prevent this for the sake of her future, she told the teachers at a meeting that the only way to end student rebellion at Church was to give students the right to govern themselves which they were demanding by their revolt against teachers. To make her argument convincing, she appealed to their selfless social concerns, planted in their fertile minds at liberal colleges, and exploited these concerns emotionally by mentioning all the pertinent details of the boy's background leading up to the near rape which influenced his actions. In this way she was able to create guilt in them for their anger toward the boy, when their anger toward him and the administration was justifiable, and swiftly take control of their minds once again without any real protest.

But now with the arrival of Anne Harte, she had the feeling that maintaining this hold on their minds would be difficult. The new English teacher, unlike the other teachers at Church, was too bright to be manipulated. During their get-acquainted talk, Anne's computer-like brain . . . so dangerously programmed to accept only reason . . . seemed quick to grasp the madness behind Loretta's philosophy. For those thirty minutes, while Loretta talked about the student panel, she observed the principal with the cold, blue eyes of someone staring in judgement at an adversary. Loretta knew that she would have to watch Anne and make certain that the blonde beauty with the brown mole in her dimple learned to believe the bullshit was caviar. Failure to do this could force the teacher with the strong, tamper-proof mind to turn the staff against the principal and ruin her chances for a job downtown.

Lathan Accuses Steele of Gestapo-like Plans

School board president, Richard Lathan, angered by Dr. Marshall Steele's growing support among board members to use federal-grant monies to finance a student panel, today accused the acting superintendent of trying to create a "federally funded Gestapo".

According to Lathan, Dr. Steele is worried that without board members' support for his "Gestapo," Lathan's recommendation to fire him for his long history of incompetence will be approved, unchallenged. "That's why he is so determined to defeat the audiovisual-program proposal," Lathan told reporters. "He knows if he succeeds at this, he will not only undermine my influence to fire him, but he will also protect himself against any future criticism by using his paid pack of student thugs to intimidate his critics."

After briefly summarizing what he believed were the advantages of an audiovisual program to a student panel, Lathan ended his press conference with another jab at Dr. Steele's character. "Therefore," he said, "I can only conclude by Dr. Steele's opposition to such a sterling program that he is a power-mad dictator who, if not fired, will turn his so-called "student panel" into mercenaries against anyone daring to block his move to take control of the schools."

Several board members who have expressed strong support for a student panel, vehemently disagree with Lathan. "It seems that Lathan forgets one thing in his smear campaign of Dr. Steele," a board member said confidentially. "Which is best for the students: an audiovisual program that doesn't permit independent thinking or a student panel that does?"

In its November 24 issue, News reported on the results of a

Chapter 2

Tom Slaughter honked his horn, then shot his sports car into the heavy traffic on Bradley Boulevard, cutting in front of a station wagon. To avoid a collision, the station wagon swerved into the opposite lane of traffic. Because of some miracle of timing, it thinly missed another car and skidded to a stop, blocking traffic.

"You stupid ass," Tom said angrily, glancing at the station wagon in his rear-view mirror. "Why don't you learn to drive!"

He then shifted into fourth gear and drove through the morning traffic, dodging cars as though they were basketball players trying to prevent him from making a basket. Each turn of the wheels brought him in near-collision course with other cars, but his skill spun him free. When he finally passed all obstacles, Tom flattened the accelerator and sped along the freeway to work. Behind him . . . like players on the court . . . were the exasperated motorists.

Once his whole life had been basketball. He played it in the school yard, in the alleys, even in the classroom behind the teacher's back. He walked and talked and lived basketball, for basketball was going to lift him from the inner city to the pinnacle of success. A basketball scholarship got him through college, and he was just about to spring to national fame when he became arthritic.

Jobs were scarce for black arthritic basketball players with light skin and green eyes. White employers saved their token jobs for those who fitted the black stereotype. So he accepted the only decent-paying job offered: teaching physical education in an inner-city public school. Once again he found himself in the same environment he had struggled so hard to escape, this time seemingly for life. Then, at the annual teachers' meeting he heard Dr. Marshall Steele speak of the need for young, black administrators downtown.

The following year Tom returned to the university for a Master's in school administration. After graduation, he applied for a comfortable office job downtown, among the Great White Thinkers of Education. But the only job he was offered, after months of interviews and promises, was at Church. He accepted the assistant principal job, hopeful that with a little hard work and politics, he would someday earn his place downtown. Yet he sensed by accepting the job that he would never rise out of the inner city despite his determination, because he just wasn't black enough to please the White Lords of Education.

Mrs. Loretta Daniels, though, felt differently. During a conference before school opened, she expressed optimism about his future and assured him, if he were a cooperative administrator, she would personally see to it that he was well-rewarded. Her appointment to Church was temporary, she told him. As soon as the assistant superintendent of personnel retired next year, she would replace him, and she would be in the perfect position to help her friends. Tom, realizing how useful Mrs. Daniels could be, pledged his full cooperation.

That evening he celebrated his arrangement with Mrs. Daniels by visiting his favorite disco, popular with the Beautiful White People of the City. While sitting at the bar, scanning the women, a white model whom he recognized as the Easy-On Hairspray Girl, approached him. In person she was smaller than the television blow-ups had led him to believe and, for this reason, he doubted at first that the two women were the same. But when she smiled the same photogenic smile as on television with its promise of fulfillment, his doubts passed. As he watched her walk toward him, looking as beautiful as she had looked on television, running in slow motion with her luxurious hair dancing behind her, he experienced a wonderful awakening which lasted all night with her.

For several days, floating in the memory of his awakening, he began to believe that the Great American Dream would be his at last, first the promise of the job, and now . . . if he continued to be lucky . . . the woman. But by the end of the week, his hope of seeing Sue Whyte again began to fade. None of his calls left with her answering service were ever returned.Then, on the second week, when he was sure it was useless to call again, he started to receive calls at strange hours of the day and night from other models who claimed to be Sue's friends. From the start their interest was clear. Although he never saw these models more than once each, he didn't object. Attracting such a parade of beautiful white women pleased him and left him feeling special, even though they often exhausted him without ever really satisfying him with their insatiable sexual demands. Sometimes in their company, he would think of Sue whose passivity by comparison was more satisfying. But he quickly stopped thinking about Sue . . . about the American Dream Girl whose love he so joyously stole like some forbidden pleasure . . . when one model said, after an hour with him, that he wasn't as good as Sue had promised. The cold, matter-of-fact way she had said it made him suddenly realize that he was a convenience to her (to all the models) during her (their) experiment with something *black*!

Bitter, he called Sue and told her answering service that he was no longer available as a 24-hour stud service. Afterwards, he made a date with Joy Franks, a black teacher whom he knew at Church, and stayed with her at a hotel until his bitterness passed.

He was thinking about last night with Joy ... especially the cockroaches and urine-stained sheets at that run-down hotel ... when he parked his sports car behind the school. As he locked the car, he wondered how he would discourage Joy from taking last night seriously. Seeing her every day at school would make it difficult. But his thoughts cleared of Joy when he entered Church and saw the new English teacher leave the principal's office.

Almost immediately he found himself responding to her ... to her hips which gently broke the straight lines of her raincoat with its light, yet rhythmic side-to-side swing. Poetry, he thought, could be written about the way her hips so effortlessly moved without even faintly resembling Joy's burlesque swing. For a moment he merely stood firm and watched her walk down the hall. Then suddenly with the skill of a basketball player in motion, he hurried after her, dodging teenagers scattered throughout the hall. If a fight hadn't delayed him, he would've done or said something impetuous to the woman.

Ten minutes later he saw her again, this time outside her classroom, standing in a mist of lemony-scented perfume with her back to him. When he greeted her, she turned and looked up at him. Long gossamer-like strands of silky blonde hair fell straight to her shoulder and over her forehead in bangs, drawing his attention first to her blue eyes, then her slightly upturned nose, then her almost-too-thin-to-be-noticed lips, and finally, when she smiled, a dimple which had a small brown mole in the center. Like the models she was beautiful. Unlike them she didn't need dramatic makeup and clothes to create this beauty. Instead, her beauty was a gift of nature.

Although the new teacher was friendly and talkative, she was a little aloof, not enough to disturb him, but enough to convince him winning Anne wouldn't be easy. Unlike the models, she would take time to make. Since she was free that period, he invited her for coffee in the teachers' lounge where he hoped they would be alone, so he could dazzle her with his charm. To his annoyance, Joy Franks was in the lounge, dancing to the polyrhythmic sounds of some African tribal music. The French teacher, Ernest McQueen, sitting near the window, was watching her dance. He was fascinated, it seemed, by the ease with which she made every part of her body (from her shaven head to her barefeet) respond to a different rhythm of the music. As Joy leaned backwards, in what was obviously the frenzy of the finale, shaking her abundant breasts freely under her brown-and-white, ankle-length batik dress, Tom walked to the phonograph and shut it off.

"Hey, leave that on," she said, springing erect with one beautiful motion.

But when she turned and saw Tom, she smiled and forgot the dancing. She approached him, then encircled his neck with her arms and pressed her thighs against his. "Well, how's my big headhunter this morning," she said with a graceful movement of her body that seemed to start at her ankles and sneak upward, snarling him in one sensuous embrace.

"Bored," he said, removing her arms.

. She stepped back and looked at him, obviously hurt. "What's wrong, Tom? Don't my drum beats raise your body temperature anymore?"

He walked to the coffee pot. "Your drum beats . . . like that shaven head of yours . . . have the same effect on my body temperature as an impaled shrunken head!"

Joy laughed. It was a loud, angry laugh. Then she noticed Anne and stopped laughing. She now smiled, but coming through her smile was the same loud anger. In an effort to be friendly, Anne said hello. But when Joy didn't acknowledge the greeting, Anne shrugged her shoulders and sat down.

Tom walked toward Anne with two cups of coffee, spilling one and leaving a trail behind him. After he handed the coffee to Anne, he sat next to her. Joy sat next to Ernest at the opposite end of the room. Like always Ernest was wearing skin-tight levis, a blue t-shirt and heavy construction boots. In his right ear was a small gold earring and attached to his wide-leather, black belt, also on the right side, was a chain with a bunch of keys. He would've looked tough in his truck-driver-like masquerade if his clothes weren't always so just-laundered clean and if his gestures weren't always so unconvincingly masculine.

Anne like everyone else meeting the white French teacher for the first time was amused by the sight of him which she tried to conceal by sipping her coffee. Ernest didn't seem to notice this or, if he did, didn't seem to reveal it, and he asked by speaking from the side of his mouth: "You gonna be teachin' here?"

"That's right," Anne said, as she struggled to hold back a smile.

"Like it?"

"Ask me that in a few days after I recover from the shock."

"Let-me-tell-you-something, you've got it easy here. I've worked at eight different schools in the city and believe me, this here school is the best compared to them."

"How long have you been teaching to have so much experience?"

"This is gonna be my third year."

She jerked her small-frame body to attention and in the process nearly spilled her coffee on her skirt. "You've been to eight schools in two years?"

"That ain't many," he said. "One teacher I know was transferred every month for two years."

"How does she teach?"

"Who teaches?"

Anne's neck suddenly rose from her high-collar blouse, lifting her head proudly into the air. "Well, I hope to."

"Good luck." He then looked up at the wall clock. "Guess I better mosey back and collect them test papers."

"Do you have a class now?" Anne asked.

"Sure, but I gave 'em a French exam, so I thought I'd take a break."

"You *leave* the class during examinations?"

"Why not?" he said, rising. "Hell, they cheat whether or

not I'm there. So why watch." He then walked from the room like a self-conscious adolescent imitating a man while a red handkerchief, dangling from his right back pocket waved goodby.

Tom noticed that Anne became pensive and out of reach after Ernest left. His hope of having a relaxed, easy conversation with her now evaporated. He was angry, not with Anne, but with Joy and Ernest for ruining what could've been a pleasant break. He turned to Anne, even though he knew drawing her out would be difficult with Joy present, and said: "Don't look so worried. Not all the teachers here are like him."

"For a moment I was concerned."

"Personally, Miss . . . Miss . . . " Joy began.

"Anne," she said. "Anne Harte."

"Thank you," Joy said with what seemed to be unexpected sweetness. "Personally Miss Anne, you should be *extremely* happy with the staffing here. We have some very devoted white missionaries in our native quarters and some are even successfully converting the savage children to their white religion."

Anne glanced at Joy with the bored indifference of someone undisturbed by her rudeness, just startled somewhat by its blatancy. "Well, I wasn't quite thinking of joining a mission."

"What were you thinking of?"

"Teaching here."

"But that's what I'm talking about," Joy flashed a smile. "Teaching here!" Joy rose, undulating her body in the process, then swung her hips toward the percolator. Anne rose also, thanked Tom for the coffee, then after a I've-got-to-prepare-for-class excuse left.

Tom watched her leave. Once again the same excitement which he had experienced seeing her walk through the halls returned. Joy, while holding a coffee pot in one hand and a cup in another, stared at him, but she stopped staring, when he turned toward her, and, pouring her coffee, said casually to him: "I see by that bonfire in your eyes that you find her bewitching."

"I'd have to be blind not to see her charms."

"That's what I like about you, Tom. All a woman needs for you to do an African tribal dance is to grow blue eyes and blonde hair."

"When a woman looks like Anne . . . blue eyes and blonde hair aren't even necessary."

She added cream, then sugar to her coffee, and stirred it a little more vigorously than necessary. "Providing," she said, a little too sharply to be casual, "she wears *white* war paint!"

He leaned back in the sofa and smiled, amused by the current of hostility in her voice. "That's right, Joy. That's all it takes . . . just a little white war paint."

"Why don't you give her a leopard-skin dress, trimmed in monkey fur and a few colorful beads. Then you can tell everyone she's a soul sister."

"You sound jealous."

"I *am* jealous, Tom. That's why I'm a cannibal and go after flesh."

"So that's why you tried devouring her."

Joy turned quickly toward Tom, her breasts swinging almost independently as if too heavy to be in total harmony with the rest of her body. "Let's just say I protect what's mine by scarring off the white competition."

"What could Anne possibly want that's yours?"

"You!"

"Me?" he said, bathing luxuriously in his amusement. "Honey, you done blown yer mind."

She stiffened in self-defense as though by stiffening she could minimize the pain of his amusement. "What about last night?"

"Well, what about it?"

"Now don't tell me that Miss Pretty White Missionary Lady has shrunk your fuzzy head and made you forget already?"

"It sounds to me like your head's shrunk if you take one night stands in cheap hotels seriously."

Joy's eyes swelled into huge protrusions, blazing. "You'll never change," she said. "There aren't any drum beats in your soul."

"Look, Joy," he said. "When I want to get serious about some African aborigine I'll go to the Congo and get the real thing. I don't need no bald-headed caricature like you to get all hung up on."

She stood arrow straight, looking down at him proudly, her eyes jetting flames from out of the calmness of her poise. "I should've known how you felt. Worshipping that principal's white Mumbo Jumbo for so long has turned that brain into stone."

He laughed good-naturedly. "What's wrong with being practical?"

"You'd know the answer to that if you were black," she said, "if you resisted white sorcery like my dad did."

"Yeah, but look what happened to him."

"At least he died for a cause."

"Shit," he said. "Who are you kidding? He stood up to that honky with a gun, not because of any black cause, but because you pecked at his manhood until he had to do something desperate to protect his self-respect."

"You know, Tom," she said calmly, almost too calmly for her mood, "I'm going to make me a doll tonight, dress it in your nice Brooks Brothers' clothes, paint its face tan and its eyes green." Then she added, releasing all her anger: "And stick pins in his eyes, heart and ass!"

"The only way that'll work, Joy, is if someone believes that stupid nonsense."

"Maybe that's why voodoo doesn't work on whites any more than your charm worked on those models, because they don't believe either!"

"Oh, why don't you run a bone through your nose!" he said, then stomped from the lounge.

Smoke from a fire puffed from the bottom slits of a wall locker and drifted like morning dew over the tile floor in the hall. Tom, ignoring the fire, marched through the smoke to his office.

Anne Harte's curiosity of life had ignited a fire within her for knowledge, a fire which her mother had wisely kept alive with the right kindling during Anne's pre-school years. In the first grade, while Anne's classmates played with toys, Anne sat by her desk with her feet together and her long blonde pigtail resting on her right shoulder and wrote rhyming poems with sophisticated meters or read detective stories which she solved ahead of the storybook sleuth. She would have probably continued like this, progressing to more difficult and challenging material at her own speed, if her second grade teacher, resenting Anne's independence, hadn't demanded Anne's complete conformity to class routine.

The teacher without respecting Anne's abilities made her do simple subtraction, read books with monosyllabic words, and write "Last-Night-I-Saw-On-T.V." compositions. Interspersed among these "basics" were such activities as visits to the toilet, song time, juice breaks, naps, and recess. If Anne and her classmates did all these things to the teacher's liking and sat straight and quietly in their seats while the teacher talked in a monotone for 15 or 20 minutes about rat control or good citizenship, they would be allowed to go home on time at three.

Bored by the regimentation, Anne bombarded the teacher with whys. Why must we all march to the toilet at 10 a.m. and 2 p.m. when we don't have to go? Why must we play with kids we don't like? Why do we have to learn songs that make no sense? Why can't we work at something until we finish it, instead of until our time is up? And why do we all have to take naps when some of us rather read or write or learn fractions?

The teacher, annoyed at having her authority questioned, tried to silence Anne by sarcastically referring to her as the Why Girl. Her classmates, following the teacher's lead, also called her the Why Girl, but in a vicious voice which Anne would attack with angry retorts.

For the next six years until graduation, school was uneventfully dull for her. Teachers would overload her with conflicting ideas from history, literature, science and the like, and would make no effort to integrate them intelligently. When she attempted to integrate these ideas for easier retention, her teachers would crush her effort by talking down to her as if only someone retarded would attempt such an absurdity. Then they would praise a dull student for repeating verbatim what he often learned without understanding.

Instead of finding relief in high school as she had hoped, she discovered that her teachers (as tenanciously as those in elementary school) demanded conformity by pounding un-integrated "basics" into her head with their sledge-hammer-like wills. To discourage her from forming the wrong concepts, they graded her by some secret, subjective method which totally mystified her. Whenever a teacher returned a test paper, Anne seldom understood why she received the grade she had. She always had the feeling when she did poorly that she had left out some important detail, some final step to her argument which would make it intelligible, and when she did well that she had accidentally hit upon some new and brilliant "truth" which would solve life's mysteries. Yet if she clung to this "truth" and carried it with her to another class, she would find it a handicap because each of her teachers, even within the same department, had different and often conflicting "truths" for her to master. In desperation, she studied harder, searching among the boring detail, taught to her by rote, for understanding. But instead of finding understanding, she found mental fatigue and confusion. Exhausted, she finally let the fire once consuming her burn out, and she did what all the other students did: She memorized irrelevant footnotes to important concepts and formed erroneous conclusions, based on her limited knowledge of the facts.

Unable to soar to the limits of her reasoning powers, she learned to find contentment in her almost encyclopedic knowledge of the "basics" (ecology, rat control, excerpts from major writers, dates and names of events and people in history, and the like). She would have probably remained frozen for life on this intellectual level, if she hadn't decided to join the debating team.

With an enthusiasm almost forgotten, she researched the subject of each debate methodically and armed herself with enough documented information to annihilate her opponent. In no time she gained a reputation for exposing the fallacy in her opponent's argument with swiftness. One day while debating the importance of strong government to freedom, her opponent pompously quoted Alexander Church ("My dream for a New America is for all freedom-loving Americans to give their best selflessly to their country"). With lightning speed, she asked him what his education didn't prepare him to answer: "How long would we be free if our government expected all freedom-loving Americans to give their best selflessly to their country and not for their own self-interest? Would America then be different from communist countries preaching similar self-sacrifice to the state?"

Before her question could penetrate the minds of the listening students and do havoc to the years of being taught never to question the concept of loyalty to the government, the school principal sprung to her feet and interrupted the debate. She said that Anne's question was irrelevant and dangerously un-American, and that if Anne persisted in asking such questions, she would have to stop the debate. Instead of being intimidated by the principal's critical tone, Anne stood as perfectly erect as her hair was perfectly straight and boldly eyed the principal. By asking her opponent those questions, by going through all the reasoning necessary to understand the dangers of such self-sacrifice to the state, Anne had taken the first important step toward breaking free and gaining intellectual insight. With the confidence of someone who knew she was right, she said to the principal: "You're quite mistaken. In fact, if I may be permitted to say so, you are being dangerously un-American for trying to suppress the relevant."

After high school graduation, Anne decided to prepare herself for a teaching career. She was convinced that good teachers were a scarcity and that their conspicuous absence in her life was a major cause for her boredom and frustration in school. If she had had one good teacher dedicated to truth, she might have learned something in school besides irrelevant footnotes and might have become a different person by now (maybe a poet or writer or even a sleuth). She knew her experiences weren't unique. There were other students like her, waiting impatiently for the right teacher to lead them to some mountain summit. Convinced that she could be such a teacher, she enrolled in a private university. But to her shock she discovered a major obstacle facing her.

Most of her professors assumed a certain accumulation of knowledge as a prerequisite for understanding their subjects. Since she lacked this knowledge (wasted as she was, memorizing obscure or irrelevant footnotes during her important learning years), she was now confronted with the herculean task of mastering what she should've mastered years ago in order to understand what was being said by her professors. At first she was angry and bitter with the public schools for depriving her of an education. But she overcame this bitterness and anger by refusing to accept defeat passively. Instead of quitting as some of her classmates had done, she stayed and struggled, even after sometimes failing, until she finally began to succeed.

With each success she slowly emerged from her anger and bitterness and left behind the memory of her high school years. In the beginning her successes at mastering her subjects were modest, faint rays of light squeezing through minuscule cracks in a dark enclosure. But as she studied and persisted, the cracks widened until finally she could see . . . see the unclouded mountain summit ahead.

Once again after years of neglect, the fire slowly began

to burn. Then upon graduation it burst into open flame when she ambitiously decided to go on to graduate school. That summer she began work on her Master's, and a year later she graduated with honors. While working on her doctorate, she lost interest in obtaining a terminal degree in literature after accepting a part-time job teaching remedial English. The students assigned to her were like reflections of herself once. Most of them were honor public school graduates, misled by inflated grades into believing themselves scholars. The shock of learning the truth upon entering college left them bitter. Like many public school graduates, they were unable to integrate and prove logically, to think and understand conceptually. Teaching these students . . . guiding them through their bitterness . . . became an obsession for Anne. During the first weeks of class, she identified with their struggles, understood their bitterness, and reminded them by her example that they too could succeed despite their deficiencies. As they began to turn their bitterness into energy to master their studies, she became exhilarated. The knowledge which had taken her so many years to master was now joyfully dispensed, and she refused to stop dispensing it until they had learned what they should've learned in high school.

Two straight A public school valedictorians dropped out during the first semester, discouraged by the challenge despite Anne's efforts to stop them. The other fifteen, though, remained and in their first year after intensive help from Anne were able to pass all their subjects. One boy, Jeremiah Lee, did more than just pass his subjects. At the end of the second semester he made the honor roll.

It was her success with these students that was responsible for her decision to return now to the root of the problem, to the public schools where all the damage was being done.

Like many other classrooms at Church, Anne's classroom was painted gay carnival colors, very much in keeping with the philosophy of making the school room a happy place. At first sight, the greens, reds, yellows and blues of the walls, desks, and chairs were all that caught her attention. It wasn't until after she had adjusted to the excitement of color that she began to notice the depression which filtered this brightness. First, there was the exposed live wire protruding from an outlet which once was for a thermostat or an electrical switch. Then, there was a smashed glass showcase patched by wood and generously covered with graffiti. And after crossing the room and observing the broken windows, singed bulletin boards and knife-scarred desk tops, there was . . . to her disgust . . . a grotesquely large, circumcised phallus drawn on her chair with almost photographic accuracy.

Since no one came to class, she used most of the morning to wash away the abscenities and cover the bulletin boards with construction paper. She then spent the remainder of the morning setting up a library in one corner of the room for students to use for studying or reading. Along one wall of this small library were shelves which she lined with books. Most of these books were old and had broken backs and torn pages. She had found them scattered about the room and jammed into her locker. In the school book room, she obtained other books, also in the same condition. Some were in sets of 20, others less. Since she didn't have enough books for all her students, she requested a supply from those on order and hoped, if the books ever arrived, that they would be useful.

By early afternoon the room was beginning to hide its war scars and attract a few students. Although she wasn't ready to teach, she did have some think questions for them to answer.

One of her concerns while teaching her remedial classes at the university was the students' inability to think. Most of them were familiar with the basics. They knew how to punctuate, to spell common words, and to use acceptable grammar. They could quote lines from famous poets, match major authors with their book titles, and even remember scenes from plays. But they learned most of this by rote. No attempt was made by their teachers to organize the subject around principles which students could understand. Instead, the teachers organized the subject around meaningless detail which the students had to memorize for exams. When important ideas were discussed, they were usually mixed with the irrelevant. Because of this, her university students showed no real grasp of the subject. They had learned to accept all ideas as valid with none having more validity than others.

The Federation of Educators deepened the problem for them by its successful campaign to persuade schools to teach "the colorful language of the street" rather than middle-class English. The Federation's basic reason for this clever campaign against a strong, language-base curriculum, according to newspaper articles, was because of its "concern" for minorities who found "the complex language and obscure vocabulary of middle-class English archaic." This "concern", Anne believed, was widening the inequities among the races through the use of language and was making it impossible for minorities to interpret difficult material. To cripple them further, many schools still taught students to read, not by the sensible phonetic method, but by the Look-Say method, which required readers to memorize new words rather than to discover them by learning the sounds of letters. For these reasons, most of her university students lacked a mature grasp of the language.

Anne knew that to succeed at Church, she would have to devise a teaching plan which would overcome her students' deficiencies. She also knew ... by the large number of students running the halls all morning, spreading terror ... that trying to teach students totally discouraged by the schools would require a great deal of skill, perhaps more skill than she had. She was thinking about how she would try to interest them in learning again, when six teenagers entered her room. One of them approached her, while the other five remained by the door, observing Anne.

"You a teacher?" the girl asked.

"That's right."

"What-cha teach?"

"English."

"Is you like them other teachers?"

"I don't know," Anne said. "What are they like?"

"Dumb."

"Dumb?"

She then told Anne about the science teacher who never completed an experiment correctly, about a history teacher who always forgot key facts, and about a math teacher who added numbers on his fingers.

"You ain't like them," the girl asked, "is you?"

"No," Anne said, reassuring her with a smile. "I know my subject a little better than that."

"Good," the girl said with relief. "Me and my friends here wanna go to college. But we don't see no way how we gonna do that with dumb teachers teachin' us. I mean some of them teachers is DUMB!"

One boy who was standing by the door stared at a wall poster which had four pictures of blacks set in triangles. The first picture was of a teenager painting a city skyline. His painting of the skyline was free of all irrelevant detail and, for this reason, it had a greater visual impact than the actual skyline in the background. The second picture was of a young man sitting at a desk. He was completing a complex mathematical equation on paper with the intense interest of one who derived pleasure from thinking out and solving a problem for himself. The third picture was of an intelligent-looking man in cap and gown, delivering a graduation address. He had the self-confidence of someone who had the ability to say well what he believed. The fourth picture was of a distinguished-looking executive studying a chart which his young assistant interpreted for him. The executive who was listening attentively had a look of total respect for his assistant. Written across the top was "Journey to Success".

"Did-cha put that up?" the boy asked Anne.

"'That's right."
"You know," he said. "I think I gonna like you."
The six students then gathered around Anne, asking questions almost all at once.

Facing Joy's classroom was a poster of a white policeman and a black youth. The policeman, built like a stevedore, was clubbing a kneeling youth who...while bleeding...was feeling blindly past the scattered books for his broken glasses a few inches from his fingertips. In blood-red letters across the top of the poster was: "Equality for all!" Surrounding the poster was a pictorial history of the blacks from the slave trade in early America to the overcrowded tenements of modern-day Harlem. Interspersed for contrast were pictures of while colonial America, enjoying the leisure activities made possible by slavery.

Joy stood in front of the class with the wall as her backdrop and watched the students, after sitting in their seats, react with a tremor of hate to the message the wall screamed to them. Everything she said, standing there, sounded suddenly urgent and, as Dr. Amos Williams, a black scholar, had pointed out, after using a similar method to arrest attention, *relevant!* It was his way . . . as it was now hers . . . to dramatize the importance of black history to the class. "Take away our history," Dr. Williams had told his college history class, "and you can control us in the present. But give us our history and you will give us a deadly weapon to defend ourselves against the attack of white lies!"

Like so many blacks educated in the public schools, Joy understood what Dr. Williams had meant. Without black history, it was easy for cunning teachers to mold her in their image. All they had to do to transform her into an imitation white girl with pigtails and pretty little-lady dresses was to teach her to associate black with prostitutes and hustlers and white with great statesmen and executives. After a few years of such programming of her mind, she was ready to interpret the black experience exactly as her teachers had wanted her to do: completely out of focus!

When a black man was harassed by the police for "eyeballing" a white woman or was arrested for being too poor to carry money, she would interpret this to mean that they were lecherous or worthless and deserved to be harassed or punished. When the white precinct worker pressured blacks to vote his way on election day (threatening to evict them from public housing or cancel their welfare checks if they refused), she would interpret this to mean that he was trying to make them good citizens. When someone talked about companies which paid whites more than blacks for the same work, she would interpret this to mean that the blacks were lazy and didn't work hard enough. When women compalined that their welfare checks didn't cover basic expenses, she would interpret this to mean that they were alcoholics who spent most of their money on liquor. And when the pastor in church preached about the glories of America and her bountiful love for all mankind, she would smile and shout: "Amen, brother. Amen!"

But it wasn't until high school that she broke free from these white distortions and lies. This occurred suddenly after reading a book in the public library on the cruelties of slavery. One of the stories which brought about this sudden change was about a black man and woman who were caught after trying to run away from their sadistic white master. For punishment (and a lesson to all his other slaves), the man was nailed through his feet and hands to the ground and burned, and the woman was stuffed into a barrel with nails driven through it and rolled down a steep hill. For several days after reading the book, Joy was unable to think about anything else and repeatedly asked herself: How could a country so full of human kindness allow itself to be so cruel?

At school when a teacher romanticized the South before the Civil War and made the plantation owners sound kind and cultured, Joy found herself filling with anger. In the middle of the teacher's lecture,she jumped to her feet and corrected her by telling her some of the stories she had read. At first the teacher looked stunned, as if overpowered by the sudden assault of truth, then after recovering, said contemptuously: "Really, Joy. You must learn not to believe everything you read."

Other teachers, by telling her the same thing, successfully planted doubts in her mind about the truthfulness of what she read. But she abandoned these doubts when a white man with violent-looking blue eyes grabbed her, while she waited for her father outside a drugstore, and dragged her to a car with two other men in it. As she tried to free herself, her abductor looked at her contemptuously ... almost exactly as her teachers had when challenged by the truth ... and said: "What's wrong, baby? 'Fraid we white boys ain't got enouf cock for you?"

Her father who was approaching her at that moment suddenly froze and stared, obviously too terrified to stop them from driving off with Joy. After exhausting themselves raping her in a wooded area near the city limits, the men left her ... with only a man's long-sleeve shirt for cover ... in the business district of a lower-middle-class white neighborhood where she had to find her way home past name-calling, stone-throwing anti-blacks.

For months afterwards she never spoke to her father. She couldn't forgive him for his lack of courage. But it wasn't just that that disturbed her. It was deeper: the entire system of conditioning blacks to a status of inferiority. Determined to lead blacks to freedom, Joy organized a movement among her classmates to demand reparations from the whites for years of enslavement, and she planned rallies at school to protest the racially biased lessons. Sometimes for spite she would leave newspaper clippings of her demonstration on the table for her father to see, and with her look ask: What about you? What are you doing for the blacks?

Then one day, after drinking liquor to fortify his courage, her father unexpectedly changed. All his docility, conditioned by years of economic enslavement to the white establishment, disappeared. That morning he led a civil-rights march into a white, blue-collar neighborhood of the city and was shot. White authorities blamed their inability to solve the murder on the confusion caused by the riot after the shooting. Outraged by their excuses and the injustice, she swore that she would dedicate her life to the black cause. She knew the best way for her to be effective was as a teacher in an inner-city school.

As she now stood in front of her class with the wall as her backdrop, she was obsessed with implanting in each student that deadly weapon of knowledge which Dr. Williams so often talked about: black truth! Holding her shaven head high and proud like an unconquerable black princess, she said to her students: "Let's hear those war drums!"

"Black is beautiful," the class said in unison.

"Louder!"

"*Black is beautiful!*"

"LOUDER!"

"BLACK IS BEAUTIFUL!"

In the silence which followed she could still hear their voices ring in her ears. When the ringing stopped, she walked to her desk to the left of the wall and sat down, then in a soft voice said: "Today, brothers and sisters, I'm going to tell you an African folk story. It's called 'Uncle Tom and Miss Pretty White Missionary Lady' . . . "

ext
on,
to
he
e
ard
ty
ill

tee
rd
am
as
t,
of
ic
in
a
al
il
or
h
n

N
D.
thi
rep
co
me
sta
dia
m
pl
b
op
d
dis
me
m
is
ri
all
of t

10 Students Disrupt
School Board Meeting

Ten high school students, chanting "We don't want to be push-button freaks," disrupted a school board meeting yesterday during a heated discussion over the audiovisual program and sprayed red paint on the board president, Richard Lathan, when he told security to "toss the thugs out!"

At a news conference later, Lathan blamed the demonstration on a bulletin, circulated in a half-dozen area high schools, which, he claims, was written to turn students against the audio visual program.

Although no evidence exists to verify Lathan's charges at this time, the incident has successfully brought into focus once again what Acting Superintendent Dr. Marshall Steele has been saying for months: "Students aren't learning, not because teachers aren't teaching, as Lathan believes, but because students aren't given a voice in their schools."

The Enormous Power

Chapter 3

Most boys whom Anne knew during her high school years thought of her as a sex object with no rights of her own, placed on earth by God for their sole pleasure. Since she was attractive, they were eager to convince her of this, and through "manly" force tame what some regarded as her "unnatural" resistance to them. These boys didn't realize that her "unnatural" resistance to them was caused by their attitude of her as an object. A few of the brighter boys, on the other hand, did, and they wisely concealed their intentions by spending weeks and in several cases even months preparing her with gifts, dinner, and attention for their advances.

Occasionally a boy with persistance and experience would break through her defenses and bring her to that delicate brink of madness in which her body screamed for his. At such times, she believed that being a sex object for predatory males was the fate of all girls, and it was madness to resist. Despite this growing conviction, she still fought to save herself and fiercely clung to the notion that someday she would meet a boy who wasn't interested in just making conquests, a boy who genuinely admired and desired her (as she would admire and desire him) for what she was: a girl of virtue!

But finding such a boy seemed unlikely. Most of her dates (in spite of careful selectivity) thought of her as someone to conquer, a sexual whim to be used, then afterwards to discard. Since she was a stubborn adversary who would scratch, kick and bite her way to freedom, several boys out of malice began to spread false rumors about her being "easy". Indifferent to these rumors, she continued to date . . . more out of boredom with her life than interest in any particular boy . . . and learned to regard her struggle as a game in which to survive without losing she had to be coyer than her opponent. So instead of fighting them off in parking lots, at parties or in movie theaters, she would flirtatiously invite them home and, after being brought to the door, would hurry inside the apartment to safety. Sometimes a boy would plead with her to let him in "just to make it look good" for the couple they double-dated with, waiting in the car outside. Instead, she would go to the front window and time the boy's departure from the building. If he left immediately, she would date him again. If he didn't (and waited in the hall "to look good"), she wouldn't.

For awhile in this way, she was able to avoid being pressured into a compromise. But all this changed during a junior-senior picnic when one boy dropped something into her Coke and during her semi-conscious state that followed raped her.Out of anger over this ruthless seizure of her body she reported him to the police. But when the case came to court, she lost the case because several of his friends testified that she was "easy". After that, she avoided boys entirely, even through college. Then in graduate school she met Jeremiah Lee.

Jeremiah was one of the black students assigned to a remedial English class which she taught. At the time of their meeting, he was still depressed over his poor performance in college. Like most honor high school graduates, he had assumed repeating his high school success in college wouldn't be difficult. But when he discovered how unprepared he was academically for college, he became quite sensitive and introspective, and blamed his poor performance on his stupidity.

To encourage him (as well as the other students in her

class) she told him that what he now faced wasn't any different than what she had faced five years ago. She explained to him what she had to learn for herself, that his poor college record was no reflection on his intelligence. Instead, it confirmed what university professors had always known, that the public school system had blatantly neglected its responsibility to teach. Consequently, he had a choice. He could either quit and accept defeat or he could stay and overcome his academic deficiencies.

Several of her students dropped out, discouraged by the amount of work they had to master. But Jeremiah . . . like the majority of her students . . . remained, inspired by Anne's success. He directed his energies to his studies with herculean determination, never pleading for pity or never giving excuses for occasionally failing. His only thought during that first year of college seemed to be: "I *will* succeed!"

Because of this success-oriented attitude, she identified with him and saw in his struggle to achieve a man who was determined to triumph over the evil influences bent on destroying him and shape his own destiny. To guide him in this direction, she would have coffee with him after class and hasten his success with special help and encouragement. In the beginning, it was a restrained teacher-student relationship which, after the first month, became more personal and friendly. At first she was afraid of this friendship, afraid of the growing feelings for each other that they were both starting to show. But when he didn't take advantage of these feelings by trying to claim her as an object for his pleasure, she began to feel safe in his company. Whatever distrust harbored toward boys since high school days slowly passed, and five months after meeting him, she invited him to her room.

All that distinguished Ernest McQueen's classroom from other classrooms at Church was the bulletin board. Under the bright red letters reading "Souvenirs de Paris", Ernest had pinned his favorite photographs. There was one of the quay by the Seine where he fornicated at night with rough-looking strangers, the outdoor urinals of Pigalle where he exhibited himself to interested observers, the *Cinema de Montparnasse* where he saw the latest pornography from Sweden between sex orgies in the balcony, and the *Hotel du Minet* where he lived for two weeks as the wife of an Algerian hustler.

As he stood in front of the bulletin board in the silence of his empty classroom, he gazed at the pictures as though each told a story which connected logically to the next and ended abruptly at the *Hotel du Minet*. The story which unfolded for him wasn't a very pretty one. It was the story of a man whose insatiable lust drove him to search for "love" in Paris sewers. The "love" which he found there . . . the Great Dream of His Life . . . was another lover-turned-thief who, after conquering Ernest's lust by exhausting his body, ran off with his credit cards and travelers cheques. To protect himself from facing the reality of his affair with the Algerian, Ernest seldom thought about this familiar ending to his romances and remembered only the pleasure.

This flight from reality, piloted by his sex drive, was fueled during his childhood by his mother when she blatantly tried to change what nature had created as a boy into a girl. Then after she had transformed her unwanted child into a boy-girl misfit, domesticated to the point of complete helplessness, she relinquished her responsibility for her joke by enrolling him in the public schools.

His kindergarten teacher, amused by the little boy-girl creation, assumed her responsibility for the joke by forcing him to play with frustrated children who released their frustration by snatching his toys. Then when he ran to her in tears, begging for her assistance in reclaiming his toys, she would glibly lecture him on the importance of sharing. Afterwards, to help him recover from the shock of such "morality", she would dry his tears by reading him fantasy stories of evil witches and wolves and affectionate mice and pigs.

In this way with the teacher's assistance, he learned to

prefer fantasy to reality at an age when he needed reality for knowledge and guidance in growing. Sometimes at night, haunted by these fantasies, he would awake from a deep sleep and scream in terror because his sensitive mind couldn't separate the real from the unreal. But as he grew older, he learned to cope with these nightmares by learning to find pleasure in stories about mental and physical misfits who solved their problems by shrinking their conceptual awareness of life to the microscopic size of their sickness.

His teachers, impressed with his subsequent adjustment and sensitivity, used his "intellectual and moral growth" as a standard by which they measured other students. Many of the boys, resenting being asked to admire "a little fag", would express their resentment by viciously attacking him after school. Since his teachers offered no protection to him, he would have to escape his classmates after school by hiding from them in the cloakroom until they had left the playground for the day.

Once while hiding in the cloakroom, he overheard his teacher talk with a colleague about her sex life. Fascinated by the details of her promiscuity, Ernest decided one day, while the teacher was allowing the class "to release their inner feelings in play", to sneak in the cloakroom with a girl where he lifted her dress and began to examine her. Horrified at discovering them together, the teacher pulled him from the room by the ear and in front of his amused classmates threatened to castrate him if he ever approached another girl again. For the remainder of the year, she deepened his shame to the delight of his classmates by referring to it regularly during her talks on the importance of respecting girls.

By the time he was in high school, he was so fearful of censorship for his thoughts and behavior after years of humiliation and threats from both teachers and students that he protected himself from further character assault by becoming as inconspicuous as possible in class. To avoid the notice of boys who reacted hostilely to his effeminacy, he dressed and acted as much like them as possible and majored in French which only a few boys took. Despite his efforts, though, to escape notice, he still wasn't always able to avoid ridicule.

His gym teacher particularly found his attempts at behaving like a man amusing and would enjoy embarrassing him in front of the class by making fun of his "masculinity". Since he was at the age of sexual awareness (which he revealed by staring at aroused boys and men), several other teachers began to make fun of him and warn boys about him by telling them that they could always spot "one of those" by the way "it" eyed others. Embarrassed at discovering what some teachers were saying about him, he made up his mind to prove his manhood by dating a girl who was known throughout the school as "easy". "For laughs" she accepted, then crushed his advances by treating him as some inexperienced freak whom she found repulsive. After shattering his fragile ego, she thanked him for the opportunity to do her good deed and left him alone with his shame.

To recover his self-respect, he began to repress his sexual drive by concentrating on his studies. He would have been successful, if he didn't start having nocturnal emissions during sex dreams of boys. The combination of the dreams and ejaculations reinforced in his sensitive mind what he consciously tried to deny. Then one day while using the toilet at school, a teacher who had a reputation for being different knelt before Ernest and silently relieved him of his repression.

He accepted the change, which this and other encounters had begun, years later when a friend in college took him to the Hot Rocks Prison Bar and introduced him to men who had mastered sophisticated techniques for freeing guilt. Whatever thoughts he might have had about such perversity, whatever sexual curiosity he still might have had toward women were totally crushed during the lustful rape of his mind and body by men who had one thought only: completing the joke which his mother and teachers had started. Jubilant at finding himself among men whose conceptual awareness was no larger than an erect penis, Ernest pledged his life to helping others like himself by becoming a teacher: a missionary for the Gay Freedom Movement!

He was thinking about his dedication to teaching. . . of the many sexually frustrated boys at Church . . . when the school bell rang and his room began to fill with students. Abruptly his thoughts of his summer in Paris ended, and he turned away from the bulletin board as though someone had made a non-verbal request to him. His gaze moved past the squabbling teenagers, beyond the over-turned chairs and flying paper airplanes, to the door where a boy was standing, studying Ernest with a mixture of amusement and interest. Almost instantly Ernest felt an awakening which caused his body temperature to soar, his thoughts to constrict, his gaze to lower to the boy's pants, and he quickly strutted toward the boy and asked, stumbling excitedly over his words: "Hey, buddy. How would-cha like to make some easy money?"

Each morning during a ten-minute homeroom period Anne was expected to read the school bulletin to her students, particularly the thought for the day. Since her homeroom period was too short to discuss these thoughts, she concluded that the students weren't expected to understand them but instead to swallow them whole. To avoid filling her students with unchallenged absurdities, she would write the thought on the blackboard; she then would write a question next to it.

Such "profundities" as "Anything is possible if you wish hard enough" was followed by "Does that mean by wishing one can change the laws of nature?" "Sacrificing oneself for one's country is man's noblest act" was followed by "What if the country is run by a dictator who has no respect for his citizens' rights? Is sacrificing oneself for such a country *still* noble?" "Man chartering his own course is like a ship without a captain" was followed by "What about Alexander Graham Bell, Christopher Columbus, and

Frank Lloyd Wright? Did they have a captain?" "Man to be
true to his real nature must obey his instincts" was followed
by "Shouldn't the word reason replace instincts?"

Her second responsibility during the ten-minute
homeroom was to take attendance. This meant recording
the names of all the students absent on an attendance form
for the office, along with a count by sex of those present. If a
student missed school for three consecutive days, she had
to fill out an AO-1 report. This report, prepared in
triplicate, was to be given to the attendance officer who
would investigate the absences. Such concern for accurate
attendance records, though, didn't include classroom
attendance between homeroom in the morning and the
homeroom before dismissal at three. From first until
seventh periods, the responsibility of attendance was
turned over to the police who routinely collected and
returned to school students escaping the building in the
morning (usually after homeroom) and in the afternoon
(usually after lunch).

Most of these students, after being dumped back in
school, spent the remainder of the day, running the halls.
Anne believed the best way to attract them to class was to
make learning intellectually interesting. This, though, was
difficult to achieve. Most of her students didn't like her for
racial reasons and were always on the brink of open war.
She knew if she wanted to achieve anything with them she
would have to get them to think of her as a person, someone
they could respect and emulate. Before she could expect this
to happen, she first had to teach them to think independently. This she tried to do by putting questions on the board
which would force them to examine their prejudices
intelligently. Usually their replies were brief and illiterate.
Occasionally a student would probe for an answer with the
crude tools of his language and form a thought which,
though unpolished, was original and intelligent. Sometimes
unexpectedly she would even make a friend.

Such was the case today with one boy who, after
entering her room, studied her suspiciously with one eye,

while hiding the other eye behind a black and swollen lid.

"You a teacher?" he asked suddenly.

She noticed his frayed and patched clothes which, though too big for him, were still clean and well-ironed. "I sure am," she said warmly.

He tilted his head to one side and gazed at her with his un-blackened eye. "You don't look like a teacher."

She feigned surprise. "I don't?"

"No, you too pretty for a teacher."

"Why thank you."

"Tell me somethin'." He stepped closer, obviously encouraged by her friendliness. "How you get yer hair so light?"

"That's the color it grows."

With disbelieving look: "You shore?"

"Oh yes," Anne said, totally charmed. "Quite."

"My maw puts stuff on hers to make hers grow red."

"I'll bet she looks quite attractive."

"She looks all right." He then glanced about the room as though searching among the teenagers playfully entering and leaving for someone in particular. "Where's Mrs. Park?"

"She's no longer teaching here."

He lowered his gaze and for the first time sadness spread across his expression. With maternal interest, she noticed that his shirt collar was tucked in, and she was about to straighten it when he jumped back frightened by her unexpected movement. She dropped her hand to her side and said: "I just wanted to fix your collar."

He blushed, then bashfully stepped toward her. She then straightened his collar and patted it in place.

"Well, I gotta go now," he said after an awkward pause.

"Why?"

"There's a boy I don't wanna see."

"Is he the one who gave you the black eye?"

He looked startled. "How did-cha know?"

"I just guessed."

"You kinda smart."

"Not especially, just a good guesser," she said. "What's his name?"

"Who?"

"The boy who gave you the black eye."

"I don't know."

"Why did he hit you?"

" 'Cause I wouln't give 'em my lunch money."

"He sounds mean."

"He *shore* is!"

"Well, why don't you stay and point him out to me, and I'll have a little talk with him." The boy hesitated just long enough to communicate his fear of the tough. She wondered how many other teenagers like him were afraid to attend class for similar reasons. She didn't know his nor his classmates' potential, but she knew as long as any student felt unsafe in class, teachng here would be that much more difficult for her. "So how about it?" she coaxed. "Will you point him out to me?"

"Only if you gonna promise somethin'."

"What's that?"

"Don't-cha tell 'em I told-cha."

She crossed her heart, then raised her right hand. "I promise."

Many of the desks and chairs which a moment ago were arranged in parallel lines facing the front of the room were now being shoved aside. A group of students began to dance in the clearing to the music from a transistor radio which a boy held while talking to a friend. A few students, ignoring the noise and confusion, sat in their seats answering the questions on the board, as paper airplanes whisked past their noses and other students ran past their desks, occasionally knocking books and pencils to the floor.

As Anne was about to tell the dancers to sit down and the boy to shut off the radio, a boy entered the room. He was an exceptionally large boy, a bronze superman with a v-shaped torso that filled completely his tight-fitting, half-unbuttoned shirt. In repose his experssion looked hard and dangerous. She wasn't sure if this were a true reflection of his character or if it were an illusion created by his nose which was grotesquely twisted out of shape.

At first glance, because of his size and his expression, Anne thought he might be in his early twenties like her. But when she noticed his boyish features and mild acne on the forehead, she guessed his age to be about the same as his classmates. The similarity to them, though, was only in age. Unlike them, his movements were graceful and confident like someone who never doubted his importance or strength.

The students noticed the man-boy as soon as he entered. Heads sharply turned toward him and gazes followed him as if he were a viper too dangerous to approach. Their avoidance of him amused him and inflated his courage. One boy, sitting at a front-row desk reading, didn't notice the man-boy until a giant hand moved across his desk, pushing his book over the edge. Startled, the boy looked up at the man-boy, then jumped to his feet, overturning his chair, and backed away cautiously.

Amused, the man-boy pretended to lunge forward and by so doing frightened the boys so deeply that he shielded face with his arms and trembled. But when the man-boy just laughed and others in class joined him in laughing, the boy quickly grabbed his book from the floor and hurried from the room in shame. Anne was about to call the boy before he left and talk to him, but was delayed from doing this by the man-boy who (after sitting down and shoving the desk aside with his foot) began to massage his crotch as if masturbating.

"Hey, teach," he said in a voice as deep and masculine as he was big and strong. "Them sure is nice legs you got." He the removed his hand and exposed the outline of a huge serpent slithering down his leg.

She suddenly remembered the teacher whom she was replacing and the boy who nearly raped this teacher two weeks ago. Could this be the same boy? Was he the one responsible for those six teachers quitting?

Frightened, she stepped back, bumping into her desk. She then searched her desk top for some weapon to defend herself with. All she found was a small ruler.

"What's wrong, teach? Do I get you all hot the way I act?"

Anne didn't know whether to ignore him or to notify the office. Neither seemed possible now. The boy obviously couldn't be ignored and the intercom system (for some mysterious reason) never worked on call. Her only alternative, without leaving the room herself and possibly having the teenagers wreck it in her absence, was to send a note to the office. But as she scanned the confusion, she didn't know who could be trusted. She decided to try the girl nearby who was talking with a friend.

"I'd like you to take this note to the principal," she said, handing the girl the paper.

The girl quickly opened the folded paper to Anne's annoyance, then walked to the center of the room. "Hey, listen to this," she shouted to the class. "Can you send someone to Room 300," she read. "I'm having trouble with a boy. It's urgent. Thank you."

"Hey, teach. Why you wanna say that?" the man-boy said with laughter in his voice. "Don't-cha like for me to get you hot?"

Anne ignored him and requested the girl to return the note, but instead she gave it to the man-boy who placed it on his lap. "You wanna take it," he said to Anne. "Then take it!" And at the same time he made a suggestive movement with his hips and laughed afterwards when she blushed.

She nervouely grabbed her attendance book and sat down behind her desk, but rose when she felt something penetrate her skin. Almost matter-of-factly she brushed the tacks from her skirt and the chair and sat down again. As she glanced at the dancers twisting and shaking in what looked like painful acrobatic movements to the music she wondered how she could ever catch their attention long enough to take roll and identify the boy by name. The dancers all seemed to be in another world, safely out of her reach. In her nicest voice she asked the boy with the radio to shut it off. To her surprise, he agreed without excuses or protests. The hip-swinging dancers suddenly whirled around and stared at the boy.

"Hey, why did-cha turn off the sound," one girl said.

" 'Cause the teacher told me."

The girl glared at Anne, then walked from the room, muttering obscenities.

"Now the rest of you," Anne said, "why don't you sit down so we can start class." Most of them sat down without arranging their desks and chairs in any order. Some, though, dragged the desks and chairs to their original location, sat down and even opened their literature books. One girl, carrying a book, came to Anne's desk.

"Randolph," Anne said, reading the names in the attendance book. "Randolph Calhoun."

There was no response.

"He ain't here," someone shouted, when Anne called his name a second time.

After Anne marked an X next to his name, she heard someone shout: "I is too here." Annoyed by his delayed response, she erased the X a little too vigorously and made a hole in her attendance book. She was about to begin with the roll again when the girl standing next to her dropped her book on the desk. "What-cha mean by that first question on the board?"

Anne handed back the book. "Can't you see I'm taking attendance?"

The girl's expression shriveled into disappointment. "Ain't you gonna help me?"

Her question sounded like an echo of something Anne might've said once to her teachers when they had ignored her. Remembering her own disappointment, Anne set her pencil down and said patiently: "All I want you to do . . . after you read the section on Socrates' teaching methods . . . is to write a paragraph telling me how he would conduct a class at Church. What are some of the things he would ask you? Teach you?"

The girl shoved the book at her. "Find me the answer."

Anne handed the book back. "I want you to come up with your own."

"Is it on this page?" she said, pointing to the first page she opened.

The girl didn't seem to have any idea of what Anne said. Exasperated, Anne just looked at her, convinced that the girl was so accustomed to having teachers point to a page and say "copy it" that she never felt obligated to think for herself. After all, wasn't this Anne's experience? Wasn't this her university students' experience? She knew breaking this pattern. so carefully set by the schools, would be difficult. As she glanced at the man-boy, massaging himself, she suspected that it probably would be as difficult as trying to discourage him.

"Why don't you sit down," she said to the girl. "I'll help you later."

"Sheet," the girl said. "Some teach you is!"

The girl returned to her seat, dropped her book on her desk, then slumped into the chair and crossed her arms. When Anne hesitated before returning to the roll and looked at her, the girl stuck out her tongue at Anne, then sullenly stared out the window.

"Birdie," Anne said, returning to the roll. But her voice wasn't loud enough to be heard over the talking. "Birdie," she shouted. There was no response. She stood and leaned over her desk and shouted even louder. "*I want quiet!*"

No one paid attention to her.

The man-boy turned to the class and said: "Hey, don't-cha hear good. The teach wanna take the roll. So *shut up!*"

There was immediate silence.

"Birdie Smith," Anne continued.

"She's out in the hall," someone said. Anne put a check next to Birdie's name.

"Sinclair."

The skeleton-thin boy with the black eye sheepishly raised his hand. After completing the roll, she turned to the man-boy. "I don't believe your name's on the roll," she said pleasantly.

He flashed a large, all-white-teeth smile. "No Foolin'."

"Well, what is it?"

"Abraham Lincoln."

"That isn't getting us very far," she said. "How can I give you a grade in English if I don't know your name?"

"Maybe I rather haf somethin' else."

"Very well. Be difficult." She turned to the class. "Does anyone know his name?" There wasn't any response. "I asked you class: Does anyone know his name?" Several students looked amused. But no one volunteered a reply. She decided that it would be wiser to start the lesson rather than to waste more time trying to identify him. She could always ask someone for his name later, after he left. In the meantime, the best way to discourage him, she believed, was to get the class interested in the questions on the board, and maybe . . . if she were lucky . . . he would become bored and leave. If not, she could always seek help herself.

"On the board," she began, "I have written three questions."

"Sheet," several teenagers moaned.

"Let's dance," someone shouted.

Anne rose from her seat, walked in front of her desk, then said: "I think it's better if we did the work on the board." She was ready to explain the questions when one girl shouted: "Fuckin' honky!" It was said with such open defiance, such racial hate that Anne found herself stiffening. "There's no need to swear," she said as pleasantly as she could. "It's really for your own good."

"Who you kiddin'?" the girl said, even more defiantly. "You just wanna shut us up."

Anne had difficulty maintaining a pleasant attitude. It began to slip away when the man-boy, staring at her legs, said: "Wanna do somethin' for my good?"

Anne ignored the boy. Holding her head high with giraffe-like poise, she walked to her desk and sat down.

"Now as I was saying," she said to the class, "the three questions on the board . . ."

"Let's listen to the radio."

"Yeah," the class chimed. "We wanna listen to the radio."

"I'm sorry," Anne said firmly. "Not during class time."

"Who was Sock-ra-tease?" a girl who had colorful ribbons around her pigtails asked.

Anne looked at the girl, pleased by her interest. "Well, Socrates was a Greek philosopher."

"What's that?" Another girl asked with sweet, open curiosity.

Anne smiled. Once again today she felt like a teacher who was about to clarify some mystery. "That's a man who ponders . . . " Anne said, then corrected herself when she realized that the word ponder mightn't be understood. "That is, he thinks about things like: What is justice? What is virtue?" She then added significantly: "Important things like that."

The girl was all wide-eyed innocence. "My history teacher done told me Sock-ra-tease was a fag."

"Well, ah, yes, he did prefer men. But . . . "

"Did-cha know we got one of those Sock-ra-tease right here?" the girl with the colorful ribbons said.

"Boy, is that teach a Sock-ra-tease," a boy said, laughing.

Anne remembered the white French teacher whom she met in the lounge with Tom and wondered if he were the one they were talking about. Instead of probing, she dropped the subject and said: "Well, the Socrates I'm talking about was more concerned with important questions."

"What kinda questions?"

Anne sat on the edge of her chair, laced her fingers on the desk. "Let me give you an example." She paused, thought for a moment. "Suppose I ask you: What is beautiful? What would you answer?"

"Black is beautiful," one boy responded.

"Fine," she said, pleased with such a quick response.

"Now of all the kinds and types in the world which are most beautiful to you?"

"They *all* beautiful!" the boy snapped back.

"You mean even liars and cheats are beautiful to you too?" she asked, surprised.

"Hey, what-cha tryin' to do?" one girl asked, angered. "You tryin' to make us hate black?"

"Yeah," someone else said. "What-cha tryin' to do?"

She raised her hand to quiet the class. "You asked me what sort of philosopher Socrates was, and I am trying to tell you. Socrates was a philosopher who asked certain questions and challenged all answers to them."

"Now why he wanna do somethin' like that?" the angry girl asked.

"Because he never accepted any answer as true without tearing it apart and examining it." She rose, walked to the front of the desk. "You see, Socrates believed that *all* statements were subject to personal prejudice, and he wanted to expose this prejudice by asking probing questions." She was pleased to see that most of the teenagers were listening and the man-boy was growing bored. "Now let's try again. Suppose there was only white in the world. No other color." She looked at the girl who was angry with her. "How would you feel then?"

"Black is beautiful," she shouted back indignantly.

"Yeah," the class echoed. "Black is beautiful."

"All right," Anne said yielding to the pressure. "Why do you feel that way?"

" 'Cause it is, that's why," one girl said pugnaciously.

"But *why*?" Anne insisted.

" 'Cause Joy Franks say so 'n' she oughta know."

"Why?"

" 'Cause she a teacher."

"Do you believe everything a teacher tells you?"

"Hey, you tryin' to make us hate Miss Franks?"

"No, of course not. I was only trying to demonstrate the sort of discussion Socrates might have in his house with his friends."

"Well, I ain't interest'd in hearin' 'bout that fag."

She lowered her gaze, feeling defeated, and wondered how she would ever penetrate their programmed minds and make them think for themselves instead of gush war-chants. She lifted her gaze and was going to try another approach to her lesson when she saw that the man-boy was about to leave the room.

He paused, when he saw her look, and squeezed the huge bulge in his pants. "You wanna a little?" he said, mixing contempt and lust together in what appeared to be a smile. "I'll come back later 'n' give you all you want. Okay, teach?"

She began to tremble, and her trembling grew worse, after the man-boy left, when Sinclair whispered to her: "That's the one. That's the boy who's been takin' my money."

School Board Approves Audiovisual Program

School board members today narrowly agreed to implement next fall the audiovisual program at six Taylor District schools, after one board member who had been opposed to the program, unexpectedly voted for it.

President Richard Lathan, pleased with the voting results, said at a news conference that the decision to use Drexel Industries' audiovisual program to upgrade learning in the city's most deprived school district was an important victory for proponents of quality education. "In just one year," he told reporters, "I guarantee that the audiovisual program will reverse the embarrassing achievement record in these six schools by several grade levels and achieve in that one year what most teachers there can't achieve in three."

For the past five years, Drexel Industries has been growing rich selling this idea to other public school systems which, like the city's, have fallen below what some educators regard as "reasonable standards of achievement." According to the company's sales manual, reversing this poor performance in these schools can only be done by reaching each child on his level and moving him at his own speed to progressively more challenging materials through a series of tests which the child will take and grade himself without the supervision of biased teachers. Traditionalists, who disapprove of such testing and the program in general, quickly point out that children are more interested in grades than in knowledge, and that they will eagerly cheat to give themselves an acceptable score. The company executives ignore these charges by simply saying that "by correcting his own work, the child will learn immediately from his errors and gain a sense of accomplishment and confidence from his independent successes."

It is too early to predict whether the program will launch the six inner-city schools into the electronic learning age of tomorrow, as Lathan promises. It is probably more realistic to predict, as Acting School Superintendent Dr. Marshall Steele has often stated, that instead it will create only push-button freaks who, if lucky, will be able to add and subtract by rote.

Chapter 4

Birdie stared with a mixture of fear and anger at the pile of brick in front of a free-standing wall. For years the block-long chemical plant was just a brick fortress to her where employees entered, wearing plastic identification cards, and left coughing as if their lungs were allergic to fresh air. Then early last summer this all changed for her, and the plant became something quite evil when nearly a dozen black employees (including her father) became mysteriously ill after inhaling some lethal fumes from a leaking pressure-cooker-like vat inside.Although the community became rightly angered and accused the company of genocide and the company, to pacify the community and to protect its research, moved its laboratories to another city, no one in the community felt safe until a group of blacks finally destroyed the building during the summer riots.

Birdie suspected . . . as she stared at the ruins . . . that destroying the building wouldn't make the community safer. If what Joy Franks had once said were true and the company had discovered a gas deadly enough to exterminate the blacks, no black would ever be safe. Instead, the evil which motivated white scientists to create such a gas would always hover over her world as formlessly and invisibly as the poisonous gas had after seeping from the vat.

Several of her teachers made certain that she would always believe this by keeping alive racial fears without once permitting her to believe that maybe the leak was caused by employee carelessness or sabotage or even government regulations which made plant-operation changes impossible to implement. Her father reminded her of this fear whenever he tried to numb the pain of his illness with liquor. Usually she did what she had to do to cope and tried to forget by diverting her attention to less serious matters. This, though, didn't seem possible now. As much as she wanted to join her gang, standing nearby talking, and forget, she couldn't. The wall stood before her like a giant magnet, pulling her close to the center of her fears. In fury, she hurled a rock at the wall and watched it bounce off like a rubber ball to the ground.

"Hey, Birdie," one of her friends called unexpectedly.

Birdie turned toward her gang, eager to escape her solitude. "What-cha want?" she asked.

"Tell us the time you fight them two teachers."

"Again?"

"Yeah. Tell us again. Faith, she new and don't know 'bout it."

"All right. But this is the *last* time."

The girls gathered near Birdie. Although several of the six were taller than Birdie, none were as big. They looked like overgrown stalks next to her, sprouting skinny arms and legs. Birdie, on the other hand, was full-chested, voluptuous, more a woman in appearance than a 15-year-old tomboy. Her bush which added inches to her height, surrounded her head and covered her forehead, almost to the eyes, like a huge black hat.

Even though it was a cool September day, no one zipped her jacket. Each followed Birdie's lead of leaving it open, as she told them how she escaped from two male teachers by using karate.

"Karate?" Faith said. "You know karate?"

And three times for Faith's behalf Birdie demonstrated the deadly right-hand swing and the side kick which floored the two teachers. Each demonstration, though, seemed to be just a little more violent than the preceding.

On the third demonstration, she added the loud savage cry which sent the two white teachers running in fear to the principal.

"Gosh," Faith said, looking up at Birdie with large, glowing eyes. "You done that?"

Birdie had difficulty containing the pride. Her chest swelled to its limits, placing undue stress on her tight-fitting blouse. Whatever fear which had gnawed her passed. She felt suddenly free and in control like a bird in flight.

"There ain't nobody tough like our Birdie," one girl said. "Why she can lick anybody."

"Even Zelda?" Faith asked doubtfully.

"Oh, Zelda ain't shit," Birdie said.

"No, Birdie," Faith said. "You wrong. I seen her fight 'n' she mean."

"Zelda?" Birdie laughed. "She ain't mean. She only look mean 'cause of that pig-face of hers."

"Well, here she comes now. Why don't you show me how tough you is 'n' steal her one good."

"Hey, pig-face," Birdie said to Zelda who walked toward her listening to a transistor radio. "My friend here wanna see me steal you one."

Zelda, a diminutive girl, who appeared to have stopped growing at six, glanced at Birdie indifferently and continued to walk toward her, unperturbed. At first, Birdie was surprised. She had expected Zelda to behave differently . . . maybe cross the street or run . . . as so many other girls had done during similar confrontations with Birdie. When she didn't, Birdie did what she had to do to save face; she walked up to her, then knocked her off balance to the ground. The radio, which a moment earlier had screamed some popular song, stopped screaming as soon as it hit the concrete. As Zelda sat on the sidewalk, she gazed at the shattered radio, then at Birdie. Her look was angry and wild, and for a moment Birdie understood what Faith had meant when she said Zelda was mean. "You crazy nigger," Zelda said, jumping to her feet. "I gonna *kill* you."

Birdie laughed, undaunted by her threat or look, when

she saw that this slight-built girl barely reached her chin. "You 'n' who else?"

Zelda yanked something from her pocket which released a long, silvery blade when she extended her hand. "Me 'n' *this!*" And she walked cautiously toward Birdie.

Birdie stared so hard at the gleaming blade, which moved in a slow circle toward her, that her eyes ached from the concentration. She began to step backwards to Zelda's every step forward.

"What's wrong, Birdie," Zelda said savagely. "Scar'd?"

"Birdie ain't *never* scar'd!"

"Show me how tough you is then. Throw me like you done them teachers. Go on, Birdie. *Throw me!*"

Her girl friends withdrew quietly into the shadow of the brick wall and watched with excitement. Birdie could feel their excitement through her fear, and their excitement emphasized the urgency to subdue Zelda without losing face. But each time she was ready to try, she thought of what could happen if she failed, and she would then take larger steps backwards.

"Use that karate," Faith shouted. "Go 'head. Do that to Zelda."

"Yeah, Birdie," Zelda stepped closer, smiling strangely. "Use that karate!"

"Hey, look," someone shouted. "The cops!"

Birdie glanced toward the familiar red and white cruiser with relief. It was during that moment when she saw the cruiser accelerate past her, sending glass and twisted cans flying, that she felt the sharp pain of the knife sink into her. Grabbing her stomach, she fell to the sidewalk.

Her friends' faces swarmed low overhead, and their voices sounded strange and faraway. Everything began to melt and flow out of focus . . . everything, that is, except the disappointment in her friends' eyes.

No one visited her during those weeks convalescing at home. Her only companionship was her television. But as much as she once liked television, she could no longer enjoy it. Most of the shows were either too depressing to relax her or too absurd to amuse her. For this reason, at the most exciting moments in the show, her thoughts would drift inward, and she would painfully remember the disappointment in her friends' eyes. Occasionally to forget she would fill her bedroom with the loud, thought-dulling sounds of soul music. But instead of freeing her temporarily of her thoughts, the sad lyrics of the music would remind her of them and make her want to scream for help.

If only someone would visit her, she often thought. Maybe then it wouldn't be so bad. But no one came or called or even sent a card. Her father was her only relief from the loneliness. But he was usually drunk and would sit in a chair near the bed, staring vacantly at her through glassy eyes, a whiskey bottle in one hand, a half-filled glass in the other. Watching him waste away upset her. She preferred to remember him as he was, a robust and powerful man who could fight with one hand tied behind him. Since his illness, though, he was only a dim reminder of that man. All that remained of his once gorilla-like body and strength was a fragile skeleton rattling in clothes by far too big for him.

When he wasn't sitting there, staring vacantly, he would usually talk about the man he once was. At such times he would tell her about the white policeman he smashed in the face, the Jewish-owned store he looted, and the riots he started. He dwelled on the past with a morbid anger, repeating over and over again, that as hard as he fought the whites he still couldn't win.

"Them honkies got the cards stack'd 'gainst you," he said bitterly. "So I's awarnin' you, Birdie. You betta be careful 'cause if you ain't they really gonna get you good . . . 'n' if they don't them stupid girl friends will for sure."

Birdie's chest swelled, pressed tightly against her night dress, the fear of what the whites might do to her, building up within her. "Nobody gonna get Birdie. She gonna get well 'n' take care of herself. You wait. You see."

"Shit," he laughed. "You really think you somethin' blowing up yer chest like some tough boy. Well, let-me-tell-you-something Birdie Smith. You ain't nothin' in this white world, not even *shit!*"

"You see if Birdie ain't somethin'. She gonna show you. You wait 'n' see how she gonna show you."

He swallowed some whiskey, then wiped his mouth with the back of his hand. He was no longer listening to her. He began to slip away into a stupor. "You see how whitey gonna get you," he said to himself. "You just wait 'n' see."

She tried to convince herself that he was wrong, but she was unsuccessful. She remembered what Zelda had done to her, what the the scientists had done to him, and she suddenly felt like the mouse which she had once drowned in the bathtub, helpless and out of control.

Enroute to school a week later, Birdie stopped at the corner carry-out a block from Church Junior High School and had a hot dog and a Coke for breakfast and later at school, some laundry starch. Lunch would probably be over-cooked chicken and left-over coleslaw ... and whatever else the school dietician could ruin. Birdie wasn't in any hurry to head for lunch despite her hunger. Instead, she remained in the school toilet with the other class cutters and watched all the excitement around her.

Some of the girls fussed with their hair; others relieved themselves behind closed doors. But most of them smoked nervously a marijuana which was passed to everyone except Birdie. Birdie ignored the smokers by turning toward the girl next to her who lifted her skirt and said: "Look what I got! Ain't they pretty?" Birdie stared at the red nylon panties trimmed in black lace and watched the hands eagerly feel the nylon. One hand felt the bristly hairs the soft nylon covered.

"Where you get 'em?" one girl asked.

"Swift's."

"Bet they cost fifty cents."

"*They did not!*" the girl said indignantly. "They cost

five dollars."

"Shit."

"They do."

"Now where you get five dollars?"

"I stole 'em."

"Well, they nice," Birdie said, running her hand over the firm seat covered by the panties. "So nice I like to have a cock 'n' have it right in there."

The girl in the red nylon panties trimmed in black lace suddenly jumped back. Every eye in the toilet seemed to focus on Birdie.

"Hey, you betta not touch that, Birdie," one girl said. "That belongs to Rod."

"So?" Birdie said. " 'Sides, the only thing Rod got that I ain't got is a cock."

"He got more than that," someone said. " 'N' he gonna steal you in that mouth if he catch you touchin' her."

"Rod ain't so tough."

"He tougher than you."

"Nobody tough like Birdie."

"Shit! We know how tough you is."

Birdie nervously lowered her gaze and lighted a cigarette. When she looked up again, the girls had turned away and were talking madly about nothing.

The toilet didn't have adequate ventilation or windows, and the smoke and the smell made Birdie nauseous. Her discomfort was heightened by the strange tastes in her mouth and the furious sounds in her stomach. She now craved fresh air as deeply as she craved food, and without either soon, she would get sick. But instead of leaving the toilet, she dropped a lighted match into the disposal can with the same deliberation that she had dropped matches earlier in lockers, and she smiled with the same satisfaction when she saw the smoke puff out.

"Hey, why you done that, Birdie?" one girl asked. "You want that stupid-ass janitor to lock this toilet up too?"

"She done it 'cause she's mad that nobody think her tough no more," a voice from within the crowd answered.

Birdie turned to her right, then left in a frantic attempt to identify the speaker, but all she could identify was a lot of scoffing eyes. "You think I ain't tough, huh?" she said in what she thought was the direction of the voice. "Well, let me tell you!" And she could feel her chin jut out. "There ain't no body who can beat the shit from Birdie." And her head was swaying, and her pointed finger was moving. "Don't-cha never forget that!"

"Why Zelda stab you then?" the same voice said. "Tell us why . . . if you so tough?"

Birdie shoved aside some girls and marched past them to a small girl in the back. "You say that?"

"No, Birdie. Not me."

"Who then? Common. Who say that?"

"Oh, Birdie," one girl said, resting her hand on Birdie's shoulder. "We only psychin' you."

Birdie shook loose the girl's hand. "Nobody psych Birdie, *hear*?"

"Sure, Birdie," the girl said. "Now let's split 'fore someone blame us for the fire."

"Yeah, let's split," the girls echoed.

And Birdie for the first time found herself following the others from the toilet.

A few teenagers were walking the halls when the girls left the toilet. Several of these hall walkers glanced at the locked classroom doors and listened to the yelling inside, but without any apparent desire to enter. Having a place to walk their problems seemed enough to expect from school. So these few never paused long and soon continued on their way . . . pensive, sad, and easy prey for gangs.

Birdie watched them slip quietly down the hall and cast small shadows. Seeing them made her aware of her fate. But when she spotted the new white teacher leave the classroom, Birdie's mood swiftly brightened. The teacher, noticing Birdie come toward her, tried to unlock the classroom door and re-enter again, but in her haste she dropped the keys. A slow, almost sweet smile appeared on the teacher's face and quickly concealed, except for occasional flashes, her fear.

"Hello, dear," the teacher said.

"I ain't yer dear," Birdie said with both hands on her hips and loud enough for her gang to overhear.

"It's only a politeness, young lady. Nothing personal is meant by it."

"No white bitch honky call me dear. Hear?"

"Very well," and the teacher started to reach for the keys, but Birdie kicked them out of reach and stepped in front of the teacher. "May I pass please?" the teacher asked.

"You ain't goin' no where!"

"Yeah," the other girls joined in, as they swarmed the teacher. "You ain't goin' no where."

"But it's my lunch hour," the teacher said nervously. "And I want to eat."

Birdie eyed the teacher's purse which to protect the teacher clutched with both hands. "Gimme yer purse!"

"No!"

"I said: gimme it!"

And she grabbed for the purse, but the teacher jerked it away. Birdie then knocked the teacher backwards and snatched the purse after it fell to the floor. Before the teacher could reclaim it, Birdie was running down the hall with her girl friends following, laughing. But rising above the laughter was the teacher's scream: "Give me back my purse!"

"Man, that Miss Harte is sure mad," one girl said.

"Jesus, Birdie. You somethin' else," another laughed.

"Is Birdie tough?" Birdie asked. "Or is Birdie not tough?"

"You is tough, Birdie. Real tough."

There was nearly seven dollars in the purse. Five went into Birdie's bra, the remainder to her friends, and the purse in the general direction of the teacher. The only sounds in the halls now were those which the girls made as they ran to the exit. As Birdie headed for the stairs, she glanced at the teacher who was gathering the spilled contents of the purse. The teacher, pausing suddenly, glared at Birdie, in such an angry way that Birdie remembered her father's warning; even after Birdie left the others and was alone on the second-floor landing, she still remembered.

Birdie felt a compulsion to throw something, a book, a chair, *anything*, through the window by the stairs. Unable to find anything to throw, she tried to scream, but she couldn't force out any sounds. And for one passionate moment, she thought of plunging head-first through the window. But this thought passed with the banging of a first-floor locker.

She walked downstairs toward the noise.

Sinclair, dressed in old pants and a sleeveless shirt, was standing by his locker, looking at the badly burned jacket on the hook. It was one of the lockers she had earlier stuffed with toilet tissue and set afire. His school books and paper which had kindled the fire were almost in ashes.

"Why they done this?" he said, turning to Birdie. "Why they hate me 'n' done this?"

"Who hate you? Tell me so I can steal 'em one."

He stared at her with one eye while the other was hidden from view by a black heavy lid. "Someone do," he said. "'Wise they wouldn't beat me up 'n' take my money all the time."

"Who do that?"

"Some boy."

"Which boy? Tell Birdie which boy so she can take care of 'em."

"I don't know his name."

"You think he done this too?" she asked, feeling his gaze menacingly settle on her.

"No, he only want money." He looked at his jacket. "Boy, my mom sure gonna be mad when she hears 'bout this."

She reached into her bra and removed five dollars. "Maybe she don't need to hear." She held out the money. "Here."

"What's that for?" he asked, looking at her and not the money.

"For a new jacket. That's what for."

"Why you wanna give me money?"

"'Cause I like you."

"You sure?"

"Sure. Now take it."

He looked at the money uncertainly. He wanted it. She could tell by the way his hand anxiously opened and closed, but when he looked at her, into her, he shook his head stubbornly and by so doing freed himself of the desire to reach for it.

"Here," she said, stuffing the money into his hand. "Take it."

He opened his hand, and the money fell to the floor. Birdie stared after him, as he trudged away, the noises in her stomach coming regularly now. Without effort, without control almost, she screamed. Frightened by her scream, by the terror gushing from her soul, she ran to the exit, then out into the cool afternoon air.

Tom Slaughter wasn't listening to what Loretta Daniels said. All he retained of the conversation was that Loretta had just had an article accepted for publication. He remembered her saying something about the article being an outline for her doctoral dissertation on pragmatists like Carl Blanc, but he wasn't sure. She could've said that the article was a summary of the already-completed dissertation or for that matter was a possible subject for the dissertation. Knowing the facts weren't of concern to him. All Loretta expected from him (or anyone else) was for him to agree with her. This didn't require listening to do. So he sat in her all-gray-metal-furniture office looking bright and alert, while she lulled him into a mental trance with her golden voice and took him on an intellectual journey in which understanding ideas weren't nearly as important as agreeing with them. He would've remained in this mental trance until she had finished talking about pragmatism, if a girl in the hall hadn't unexpectedly awakened him from his slumber with a savage cry of terror. Startled, he sprang to his feet. His concern of what might have happened (or was happening) to the girl killed any further interest in playing the listening game with Loretta. But before he could put his concern into action, he was stopped by Loretta with a look which clearly said: "Sit down."

For a moment he stared at the wall, facing the hall, and then at Loretta who waited for him to obey her order. By her annoyed look, he knew he had no choice. It was either aiding the girl and sacrificing his future or listening to Loretta and protecting it. To Loretta's satisfaction, he did the sensible thing. As he sat down, he tried to convince himself that what had happened (if anything) to the girl wasn't important enough to deserve his attention. But he wasn't able to do this easily. Guilt had surfaced and made him hate himself for being so white. He wondered if being black . . . as Joy was black . . . would eliminate this guilt. Was leading his own race in their vengeful attack against the whites wiser than defending status quo? He doubted it. To him, it wasn't a question of being white or black; it was a question of being rich or poor. That was the choice, he told himself. The only *real* choice!

During his years in college struggling to become a famous basketball player, during his years teaching, while attending graduate school, he believed this and never allowed anyone to convince him differently. But as Loretta resumed talking, and as he listened to her talk, he suspected that his conclusions were superficial. There was an even more fundamental choice than this. This became disturbingly clear to him while he pondered what she was now saying.

When she said that the purpose of thinking was to create its own reality, he thought of the teachers who made lies sound like truth. When she said that pragmatic truth was what worked, he thought of the students who successfully cheated, stole, and fought to get what they wanted. When she said that autonomous man couldn't exist because men were fundamentally conformists, he thought of the bright, independent students at Church whom hateful teachers crushed into conformity with their wills. When she said that action should be compatible to one's feelings and not reality, he thought of those deranged students who lived in their world of make-believe. When she said that one needed to be flexible instead of rigid in his viewpoint, he thought of the eagerness with which some students experimented with drugs, perverted sex, crime. And when she said one must be absorbed by the nascent movement of our time and propagate the ideals and standards of this movement, he thought of the spread of anti-Americanism which had its philosophical roots in communism (pragmatism?).

After she finished, she awaited his verbal applause, but he hesitated (contrary to habit), too stunned by what he had begun to understand. "I sense you *disagree* with my thesis," she said in that lady-like voice which dared him to say yes.

Once again he was forced to make a decision. He tried to appear casual when he answered, but her wise look made it difficult. "Well, to be perfectly honest, Loretta. I don't fully understand some of your ideas, but those that I do make a great deal of sense to me."

"May I remind you, Tom. If you want to be principal here, I expect you to understand *all* my ideas and commit yourself to them *completely!*" She paused and looked at him with gray eyes which suddenly became as hard as steel. "Is that clear?"

"Yes, quite," he said without revealing any doubts.

"Good," she said, satisfied with his response. "Now the reason I wanted to see you today is because I have a special job for you."

"What's that?"

"We have a new teacher at Church, a Miss Anne Harte. It is my impression after talking with her that she *may* be a problem."

"In what way?"

"She has some very unorthodox ideas, and I want you to *motivate* her to see things *my* way. Of course, I'd like a report on her, so that I could have the usual details for my file. This way I can evaluate her progress."

He thought of Loretta's very private employee file, jammed with incriminating anecdotes which she used to compromise difficult employees. He wondered ... after agreeing to spy ... what information she had on him, what sledge hammer she would use if he should ever become difficult.

Like most business areas in the Taylor District, the buildings on Pranklin Street were either razed or severely damaged by the summer riots. Only a few of the original two-story buildings survived in recognizable condition. A corner drug store was one of them. Yet even that building had changed. Its large windows were boarded, then wall-papered with black-power posters, and its brick face was darkened by smoke. A Coca Cola sign hung lopsided over the entrance and squeaked as it swayed in the wind near where Anne waited for the bus.

A car with four teenage boys in it slowed down when it approached the drug store. One occupant, leering at Anne, rolled down the window and called to her. Ignoring him, she backed away from the curb and bumped into and almost knocked over a man with a half-moon scar on his cheek.

"You got some money," he asked before she could apologize.

The smell of liquor on his breath was strong and forced Anne to back away a few feet, nauseated. "I'm sorry," she said. "But I haven't any."

The man was finding it difficult to stand erect. He kept falling toward her, catching himself each time with a sudden step forward. "Don't-cha even got a quarter?" he asked.

Anne told him that she didn't have any money. A girl had taken her purse today and had left her only with enough change for bus fare. But the man who wanted money and not excuses didn't seem to believe her and suddenly became angry with her for withholding from him what he obviously believed was his to demand. Without revealing her growing fear of him, Anne repeated her explanation for not giving him money and studied him, as she spoke, for any gesture which might be violent. After muttering something to her in anger, he staggered toward the entranceway of the boarded drug store. Anne then hurried to the curb, relieved that the incident had ended without complications, and waited impatiently for the bus.

As she waited, watching three not-in-service buses pass, she wondered how much longer she would be able to avoid men like him. There were moments today when she felt as if she were center-stage with a spotlight and an orchestra to announce her presence to such men. The man-boy with the deformed nose and overly developed body was primarily responsible for this feeling. His determination to torment her with promises of a "good fuck" left her feeling uneasy because she never knew when he might try to consummate his lust. Since he was too big and powerful to fight off, her only hope was reporting him before anything happened. But this seemed impossible. There were too many students and outsiders in the school to point him out and separate him conclusively by description from the others.

To reduce certain unwanted attention, she dressed simply in loose-fitting clothes that concealed her figure. Anything which might attract attention from perfume to makeup was avoided or minimized. Yet it still didn't stop him from making obscene comments to her again today. His comments (and those from others as well) became an omen of what could follow, if she weren't careful.

She was thinking about this omen . . . about the man-boy . . . when she heard him shout across the street: "Hey, teach. Wanna fuck?"

Her blood rushed to her cheeks and made them suddenly burn. Several men who were passing stopped walking and stared at her, smiling. They seemed to be asking her with their smiles the same question. At first she considered hurrying into a nearby liquor store for safety, but she decided it would be wiser to talk to the man-boy than to run from him. She had to convince him by her attitude that he couldn't intimidate her. After she conclusively identified him, she could try other ways, if necessary, to discourage him. But when he crossed the street and stood in front of her, pressing his giant-size body against her, she knew by his look that talking to him would be a waste of time. He seemed to derive too much pleasure from trying to intimidate her to listen to anything she might say.

"How 'bout gimme a little teach," he said. "I make a good fuck."

"The answer is the same today, as it was yesterday, as it'll be tomorrow. No!"

"Shit, you don't fool me!" I bet-cha want it as bad as them white bitches I fuck at those fancy parties."

"Well, you're mistaken. So I'd appreciate it if you'd stop bothering me."

"What-cha gonna do if I don't?"

"I'll just have to call your dad then."

He laughed. "You mean at the pen?"

"Then I'll call your mother."

"How you gonna do that? She ain't never home."

She found it useless to continue this conversation, and she was ready to walk away when someone called her by name. Turning, she saw Tom Slaughter in a sports car. "Can I give you a lift?" he asked, extending his smiling face from the open window.

Smiling back, she said: "Of course."

As she bent over to enter the car, the man-boy grabbed her buttocks. She rose and swiftly turned to slap him. But before she could, he was strutting down the street, whistling. She settled in the plush-leather seat of the sports car. "Who is that boy?" she asked Tom who straddled the steering wheel, looking all arms and legs.

"That's Rod Ramwell."

"Then that is the same boy who tried to rape Mrs. Park?"

"So the story goes."

"You don't believe he tried, do you?"

Tom was looking out the window, slowly nudging the nose of the car into the heavy traffic. "I have my doubts knowing the teacher."

"Well, I don't . . . knowing the boy . . . and I told Mrs. Daniels this too. Do you know what she said?" Anne removed her head scarf and shook her blonde hair free. "She said I must have the wrong boy because Rod would never do anything like that. Imagine! That thug threatens the safety of *two* teachers, and she tries to deny it ever happened." She folded her scarf as if she were mad with it and not the principal. "I wonder what 'amusing' little remark she'd make if he did rape me."

"She'd be upset. Believe me."

"That I doubt."

Tom unexpectedly accelerated in front of a car, causing Anne to bounce against the seat from the sharp thrust forward. The driver whom Tom cut off braked his car to avoid a collision and began to honk his horn. Tom ignored the honking. "Don't you think you're being a little too hard on the principal?" he asked Anne. "After all, what can she do without any concrete evidence?"

"What can she do?" she said, her voice rising. "I'll tell you what she can do, Tom. She can spend some time in the halls instead of locked in her office with that attendance chart, then she'll have *all* the evidence she needs!"

"That's my job, Anne. Not hers."

"I don't care whose job it is. Something has to be done about that boy. He's dangerous and needs help, and when I talk to his mother . . . and I'm going to talk to her first thing tomorrow . . . I'm going to tell her a thing or two!"

"Well, let me know what happens. I may want to follow up on this."

Don't worry, Tom. You'll be the first to know."

Anne's apartment was an efficiency in a renovated town house. Against one of the apartment's walls which was stripped of the plaster to the brick was a wood-burning fireplace with shelves on either side of the fireplace lined with books of all types. Most of the furniture in the efficiency was purchased second-hand by Anne at the Salvation Army and was carefully selected to meet Anne's decorating needs. An old trunk, lacquered red, was used as her coffee table and storage container for bedding. A Hollywood bed, covered with a colorful spread and a half-dozen pillows, was her bed and sofa. For dining she had an old oak table and four oak chairs which she had stripped and stained herself. Most of the pictures, framed in silver metal, were advertisements of old movies based on books like *Les Miserables, Elmer Gantry* and other such classics. To fill space, she placed large, easy-to-care-for plants around the room.

Although she had lived in the apartment for over a month, she still paused by the door and smiled with pride at the sight of her first apartment. Today, though, with Tom by her side, she entered into the efficiency and hung their coats in the hall closet without pausing. She then poured some chilled white wine which they drank leisurely on the large floor pillows by the fireplace.

As they talked . . . or rather as Tom talked . . . she listened with boredom. Throughout the conversation, he kept making the point to her that success wasn't something earned, but rather something unearned, "a gift for playing ball with Mrs. Daniels." He summed this up and made it quite clear, after four or five examples, with: "It isn't how well you do the job, but how well you make Mrs. Daniels *think* you're doing it that counts." All this was made increasingly intolerable to Anne by his eagerness to boast afterwards about his "friendship" with "foxy white ladies" and his dedication to the American Dream. He didn't realize . . . perhaps because he was so misled by popular propaganda . . . that the Dream which he so desperately pursued by "playing ball with Mrs. Daniels" and befriending "foxy white ladies" wasn't the Great American Dream. That Dream which magnetically attracted immigrants to America's shores was the dream of freedom and opportunity for the hard-working and talented, limitless freedom and opportunity which socialist countries reserved only for gangsters corrupt enough to become "the big chiefs". A titled job, a flashy car, an apartment and other such symbols of "success" acquired through useful friendships would never give him this Dream, because the pride and self-respect which went along with doing a job well and honestly would always be denied him.

She wanted to tell him this, but decided against it. The illusions of success were all he seemed to want from life and right now, listening to him talk, all she wanted was to change the subject, which she adroitly did by turning the conversation to a movie she recently saw.

Like always she found herself complaining about the type of entertainment being offered to the American public: the violence, the perverted sex, the anti-heroes, and the human degeneration, masquerading as "art films". What particularly disturbed her was that no one seemed to object.

"Maybe that's because man is born evil," Tom said indifferently.

"You don't believe that?" she said, penetrating his indifference with shock.

"Then how do you explain all those people enjoying those flicks."

"The answer to that question can be found at Church . . . at all the Churches both public and private, from nursery to graduate school. That's where the corruption begins . . . not at birth, as you seem to think . . . but during childhood and adolescence and early adulthood through a ritual called 'education'. But it isn't education, Tom. It's head-shrinking. A perfectly normal head . . . or to be more precise, mind . . . is taken before it can form important concepts and gather life-saving knowledge, and it is reduced to the size of a flea through concept-shrinking educational activities. Then after twelve, sixteen, and even twenty years of such education . . . these shriveled and minuscule minds are released unfocused to society for the strongest voice and most powerful hand to lead. That, Tom, is why Hollywood gets away with releasing such trash on the public. That, Tom, is the only reason."

He tried to laugh off what she said, treat it as absurd. But he wasn't successful, because he knew ... and she knew he knew by the way he nervously shifted his weight on the pillow ... that she was right. His own experience (the black experience) had driven the truth through his Brooks Brothers' white armor and made his laughter sound like a confirmation instead of a denial.

"That's got to be the craziest thing I've ever heard," he said unconvincingly.

"Maybe you should read some books on pragmatism. You may feel differently then. You may learn ... contrary to Mrs. Daniels' teaching...that those respected educators spreading this philosophy are dangerous men. By preferring doing to thinking, social conformity to independence, pragmatic truth to Real Truth, they are economically and efficiently pushing society in exactly the direction they want. Which ... thanks to the media ... seems to be in the direction of rape, murder, and senseless wars!"

This time he didn't laugh. He just sat quietly on his pillow and looked inward. The only clue to what he was thinking ... to the struggle which he might have been waging with his conscience ... was revealed only by the perspiration forming on his brow.

Angry Parents Storm
School Board Meeting

Thirty-nine militant parents, representing mostly low-income school districts, yesterday stormed a board meeting and demanded for their districts a share of the $10 million federal grant, approved to be spent next fall on programs for Taylor District schools.

The parents, angered by the school system's favoritism to the Taylor District, revealed by their anger the growing sentiments among many low-income families that they weren't "poor enough" to qualify for decent public schools. Their complaints were directed, not only at the audiovisual programs, but also at the new buildings, special cultural events, and large staffing at many of the Taylor District schools. One irate parent from the affluent Forest Lane District, after claiming that no money has been spent in her school district in the past five years for maintenance, summed up the sentiments of these low-income parents by adding: "It's gotten to the point where only the Taylor District benefits from *my* tax dollars!"

ting the life of the unborn chil importance of language is en

Chapter 5

Betty Savage had spent 28 years of her 50 teaching bored high school students history without once knowing the joy of self-discovery. Her mother who thought of herself as a Modern White Parent made certain of this by crushing all Betty's individuality during childhood and turning her into a Little Lady (as recommended by the women's magazines) capable only of pleasing others. The few things Betty did that were an expression of her real needs and interests were done behind her mother's back. These unapproved activities were often as innocent as climbing a tree or making mud pies. Yet this didn't stop her mother when she learned of them from reprimanding Betty and placing her in a psychological strait jacket to discourage further "unlady-like" behavior.

By the time she enrolled in school, her mother had so successfully molded her by punishment and rewards into the popular image of the Perfect Little Lady that Betty had no distinction of her own. She could sit without moving, flatter adults with lies, listen to others without looking bored, walk with grace, and follow instructions without complaint. But what she couldn't do . . . wouldn't dare do . . . was make a decision for herself. It didn't matter whether it meant choosing between a cake or pie for desert, playing or reading, or going to a museum or a Walt Disney movie. There was always the possibility, ingrained in her through years of pre-school conditioning, that HER decision might be the WRONG decision.

Because of this conditioning, she adjusted without difficulty to school life. Her teachers made it easy by telling her when to sit and when to stand, when to go to the toilet and when to hold it. She learned to share her toys, memorize mind-dulling trivia, and even add and subtract. But any genuine curiosity for knowledge was quickly and effectively crushed through a routine so boring, so interrupted by juice breaks, gym breaks, and the like that she could never focus on anything long enough to understand it. Beneath Betty's cute-little-curtsy, yes-mam politeness was a frustrated little girl screaming for release from the duties of her life. By the time she graduated from college, the little girl was almost completely silenced by the boredom of doing what was expected of her, and though Betty had an inarticulate desire to become an actress someday, she yielded without resistance to her mother's wish to be a "respectable teacher."

From the start Betty adjusted well to teaching. The transition from following orders to giving orders was quick and painless for her. Her principal and supervisors had made certain of this by providing her with an inflexible plan for "educating" her American history students. Like an actress with a specific part to play, she was given very little room for improvisation or bursts of inspiration. Since she had always acted according to the script, she had learned to find security and even enjoyment in delivering memorized lines on cue, especially now that she could upstage students with her position of authority.

With the same "I'm-right-so-you-obey" attitude learned from her "educators", she told her students what to say and what to do, how to sit and how to stand. She broke the 50-minute class period into three 15-minute periods in which one was reserved for lectures, another for discussions, and a third for written work, and she allowed no alteration whatsoever to the routine. Like her teachers once, she prepared them intellectually for accepting further regimentation by telling them they were free and had certain inalienable rights (symbolically conveyed by the pictures on the wall of the Declaration of Independence and the Statue of Liberty) while she undermined the philosophical base of these rights and freedoms by indoctrinating them with dangerous concepts like "supremacy of the state" and "will of the people". Although she suspected that the individual could lose all rights in a sovereign state or a rational and just minority could be destroyed by the will of an irrational and barbaric majority, she never voiced these suspicions, afraid if she did, her superiors might accuse her of being un-American or worse, of being a communist.

To turn them into solid Americans, she had them read historians and thinkers (as her syllabus recommended) who regarded with contempt the free enterprise system which had made America wealthy and independent, and she defended any government controls which would forcefully redistribute wealth and weaken individual liberties. If such lessons advocating government controls of the economy contradicted the concept of freedom as conceived by America's Founding Fathers, she never said anything about it. Instead, she taught by her silence that there was no contradiction and tested her students mastery of this during discussions in which they would present their view on government. Those who gave strong defenses for Big Government received the best grades. Those, on the other hand, who tried to expose the contradiction of Big Government to Freedom by using totalitarian countries as examples, would be intimidated in front of the class with cries of horror and then inundated with extraneous and dull materials to paralyze their minds. In this way she was doing what her teachers had done to her (what educators had always been doing) she was making it impossible for them to understand issues abstractly.

This, her principal and supervisors had told her was good teaching, and she believed them (after years of being educated like this herself), despite the little voice inside her which sometimes expressed doubts. If a few students suffered from emotional problems, if a few turned to crime, if a few were incoherent thinkers, and if a few dropped out of school at sixteen to waste their lives on no-future jobs, she never permitted herself to become deeply concerned. Instead, she thought about her successes: the actor who portrayed degenerates in major movies, the senator who accepted bribes in manila envelopes, and the journalist who planted subtle racial slurs in his articles for magazines and newspapers. After all, this was what the Great American Conformity Factory expected her to do, and this she did to the best of her ability.

For her success at teaching, she was selected "Teacher of the Year" and was asked by *Classrooms,* the respected national education journal, to write an article detailing her methods for others to master.

Then everything changed suddenly. The old philosophy of teaching in which the teacher motivated the students through rewards and punishments was replaced by a new philosophy in which the students were free to learn whatever they chose with the teacher acting only as an observer. Many educators, believing this freedom would result in greater learning, discovered to their dismay (?) that students, after years of obeying authoritarian teachers, were more inclined to rebel than to study.

Betty like other traditionalists who doubted from the beginning the wisdom of this new philosophy couldn't cope with the change in the schools. Students no longer followed well-defined schedules, but were encouraged to "do their own thing" which in most cases meant setting fires, planning gang fights, attacking teachers, and even having intimate sexual encounters in the classroom. Whatever enjoyment she once derived from teaching was stifled by the violence and chaos which overnight spread throughout the schools. Frustrated by the impossible working conditions, she began to express openly what she only had expressed privately, that teenagers were barbarians who needed to be molded into socially useful citizens. If there were a villain for all this chaos and violence, and she was sure there was, it was those permissive educators advocating freedom (a concept which she had learned to blame for all the problems besetting America from drugs to crime). She believed this, even though occasionally she heard a little voice tell her that this was exactly what certain thinkers wanted her to think by "freeing" students without preparing teachers and students on the rational limits of liberty.

To minimize class problems, Betty let her students' mood (those prejudices and fears aroused by current news reports and movies) determine the direction of her lessons. No subject from race riots to environmental hazards was taboo. Whatever interested her students was openly discussed. If her lessons reinforced prejudices and fears learned through the media or environment, she didn't care. Her job, as far as the school system was concerned, was to keep the students calm and involved which she often succeeded in achieving by grading them on their adaptability to the new class routine rather than on any real understanding of the discussed subjects.

Although in this way she did reduce problems and left school with only a headache, she still would've quit and never returned to teaching again, if she weren't so close to retirement. Protected by tenure, she decided to retaliate against the system by organizing a strike among the teachers like herself who dreamed of bringing back the sane Good Old Days (or as it was popularly called, back-to-basics teaching). But before she could successfully bring off the strike and make front-page headlines with her story about the problems in the school, she was suddenly transferred to Church as punishment for her unprofessional behavior. Angered by her transfer to one of the worst schools in the city, Betty covertly began to plot revenge against the system.

She did this in two ways. One way was to tell students lies about certain teachers, especially the science teacher, Ralph Clearwater, whom she accused of overworking his students with difficult and irrelevant lessons which she claimed he was using to undermine his students' freedom. The other way was to spread discontent among teachers with discouraging stories about the school system. By filling her day in this manner, she was able to make an impossible situation bearable and at the same time help accelerate the collapse of the permissive era in education.

Ralph Clearwater believed that a student, pressured to listen to boring lectures or to do busy-work, wasn't learning, but instead was avoiding punishment by conforming to the teacher's wishes. Such pressure, though usually successful at getting thirty or forty students to work simultaneously together, did little to advance learning. Real learning, Ralph believed, occurred only after individually introducing students, when they were ready, to specific subjects of interest. Since all normal students (if they weren't "motivated" negatively to the point of discouragement) wanted to learn, his responsibility as a teacher was to see to it that they did learn by creating materials which stimulated their interest and at the same time broadened their knowledge.

With this end in mind, the young black teacher spent his entire summer preparing and organizing his science lessons in a way which would appeal to the interests of each student. In preparing his lessons, he was attentive to the importance of precepts to learning and used pictures, slides, film strips, as well as rock samples, plants, animals and even experiments as a base for building conceptual understanding of the world of science. Then, he carefully linked each lesson in a logical way which could encourage his students to move from one lesson to another. It didn't matter which lesson was selected by the student. All of them (whether on wind, rivers, animals, plants or any of the other many lessons available) were prepared like parts to a puzzle which needed other parts to complete a broad view of science.

A student, wanting to know about precipitation, for example, would learn among other things that the earth absorbed excesses in its rivers, then sent it to the sea, carrying with it tons of limestone. His curiosity about what the sea did with all this limestone would be satisfied upon learning about coral which, as it absorbed this limestone, slowly rose from the sea as an island. To understand what type of island it would become, what sort of animals, plants, even people would thrive on it, the student would have to have some knowledge about the island's geographical location and the climate. But just as important as that, he would have to know about the earth's position during its movement around the sun and the significance of this position to the temperatures on different areas of the earth. If the student wanted to deviate from this story and delve deeper into botany, geology, astronomy or other sciences, Ralph would encourage this by preparing supplementary material which would meet their individual needs, then after satisfying the student's curiosity, guide him back to the central theme of the lesson and lead him on to a general understanding of the world in which he lived.

Since he liked the workability of his teaching plan, he thought of ways of expanding it to include other high school subjects as well. He hoped by interesting teachers to integrate their subjects with his, just as he had integrated his individual lessons to his overview of science, that he could present to the students a cohesive picture of man and his world. The current practice of teaching subjects as entities in themselves like random details isolated from the whole was confusing to the students. To put all this random information together to form some larger concept would be a profoundly difficult and frustrating task for the student. The only way to simplify this task and accelerate the absorption of knowledge was for the teachers to organize it in some interesting way. Obsessed with achieving such a dream, Ralph talked to other teachers and tried to win their support of his learning experiment.

To his surprise, some of the teachers, especially Betty Savage, with whom he had discussed his idea were quite hostile to it. They told him bluntly, even if connecting subjects logically were possible (and they doubted it), his idea still wouldn't work because teenagers needed strong teachers to "motivate" them to study. Determined to disprove this, he set up his classroom as a miniature learning center for science. But before he gave his students the freedom to select their lessons, he first established certain rules. One of these rules, and the most important, was that no one (not even the teacher) could disturb a student while he was working without the student's permission. The second rule was that the student was free to work anywhere in the room he felt most comfortable. The third rule was that anyone who misbehaved was asked to leave the class. And the fourth was that each student had to return his materials where he found them upon completion of his work. During the first two weeks of his experiment, the majority of students showed no interest in his experiment. But by the third week many began to show interest in the subject without him pressuring them to work and out of boredom began to take the initiative to apply themselves, some even industriously.

Although he was delighted with this modest success, he knew he would never have any real success until he gained the cooperation of other teachers and linked his subjects to theirs. But this, none of them wanted to do, not even his few loyal admirers. Instead, they all tried to crush his dream with excuses (from student apathy to student behavior problems) and by so doing perpetuate what they claimed they wanted to end.

Disturbed by their attitude, he thought of his brother who, like the students at Church, violently rebelled against any form of authority. Unlike Ralph and a few other inner-city blacks, his brother wasn't rescued in elementary school by a scholarship for exceptional students and placed in a private school. Only a few chosen students were ever that lucky. The majority were left to survive as best they could in the public schools. Ralph knew he could've been like all the others, like his brother who turned to crime, if he too had remained in the public schools. Aware of the difference the right education made, he felt a responsibility to his race and to all those less fortunate than himself to share with them the education which he was fortunate enough to acquire. He was thinking about his brother's ten-year sentence for assault and robbery, thinking how different his life would have been if he had attended the type of school which Ralph dreamed about, when four boys raced into his room between classes and began to destroy his learning center. Ralph's first reaction upon seeing them was anger with himself for not locking the door. Unlike other teachers, he wanted students to enter and leave his classroom freely. But he stopped blaming himself and turned his anger outward just as a boy was putting a match to a stack of lessons.

As Ralph saw the papers leap into flames, he thought of the time and planning that went into preparing those assignments. He thought of all the work which would go into replacing that material, and the subsequent delay to his teaching. Furious, he hurried to the back of the room and smothered the fire with his jacket. But as soon as he put out the fire, the boy began to start another. Before he could set the papers on fire, Ralph slammed his fist into the boy's jaw, knocking him across the room. The other boys, frightened by Ralph's violence, ran from the room, while the boy on the floor, spitting out blood, cried: "Wait 'til I tell my maw. You just wait!"

Ralph stared at the boy and felt a mixture of guilt and anger, guilt for assaulting him, anger for the boy's indifference to property rights. Despite his guilt for hitting him (for using violence to check destructiveness) Ralph knew if the boy tried a third time to set fire to his learning center, he would not hesitate to hit him again. His violent side surfaced the moment his property rights were violated. "Get up," he said to the boy. "We're going to the office!"

Along one wall of the cafeteria was a serving counter. Four women shielded by glass stood in the designated locations behind the counter and passed from one to another styrofoam plates in assembly-line fashion for each to fill with the day's specialty. Dressed in white, their hair stringy and foreheads moist from the steam which rose from the food containers, these women with robot-like movements spooned the over-cooked, steam-dried food into plates without paying attention to what they were doing. Occasionally the food would miss the plate and fall back into the containers. Without realizing it, the woman responsible would pass the plate to the next person as though speed was more important than efficiency. On the glass counter by the cashier who alertly grabbed money from teenagers were rows of lunches, some without vegetables or potatoes or meat or pudding.

One boy, squeezing his nose, stared in horror at what he was expected to eat and grumbled to himself. Another teenager, after taking a mouthful of vegetables spat it out while others in protest hurled their plates against the wall. The five teachers on duty hurried about the room, reprimanding teenagers for discarding their food, but stopped when a fight broke out near the rear exit.

Anne who stood by the food counter watching could only see from her location in the cafeteria a circle of teenagers. A gym teacher, his cheeks puffed, his face red, was blowing his whistle as he stared at the circle. Unsuccessful at getting the teenagers' attention, he dived into the circle, then emerged a few moments later with two boys by the collar. The teenage spectators, protesting, reluctantly stepped aside as the gym teacher escorted the two boys to the rear exit.

"All right," the other teachers on duty shouted to the students. "In line."

Almost instantly a huge wave of bodies moved to the front of the cafeteria toward the serving counter, knocking aside chairs and tables enroute. Anne quickly paid for her milk when she saw them approach and stepped aside just as they reached the serving counter and spread the length of it. In no time the teenagers began to fill their arms with whatever they could grab from the freezers.

"Hey, put that back," the dietician shouted to a boy who removed a box of ice cream bars. But before she could stop him, he had run from the cafeteria. Others followed the boy's lead and generously grabbed whatever they could from the freezers, then raced from the cafeteria before anyone could stop them. In the confusion of noise and movement, Anne left the cafeteria, slipping but not falling on some sticky substance covering the floor, and headed to the teachers' lunchroom.

Betty Savage was sitting near the door, her glasses resting on the tip of her nose while she ate a salad from a plastic container and read a popular woman's magazine. Like always, she wore a tailored suit, white shirt and a bow tie, and had her gray-black hair pulled tightly into a bun behind her head. She looked up from her magazine, her gaze darting over the frame of the glasses, and smiled when Anne approached the table.

Anne placed her milk and brown bag on the table, then sat across from Betty. "That lunchroom is a mad house," Anne said, opening her bag. "I don't know how anyone can survive it."

"Well, now you know what happens when you free barbarians," Betty said. She then nipped at a celery stick like someone who had been told over and over again never to take big bites, and chewed the celery for what seemed to be an unnecessarily long time for such a small bite. After swallowing what her teeth didn't destroy, she blotted the corners of her mouth with the tip of her napkin.

Anne arranged the contents from her brown bag in the order in which she would eat her lunch. "Well, I can't blame those kids for their behavior," she said. "I would rebel too if I had to eat that food."

Betty didn't seem to hear her; she was staring at Anne's lunch in shock, nearly choking on a shred of lettuce which she was diligently chewing to death. "Do you eat all that?"

Anne glanced at the two roast beef sandwiches, slice of cheese, yogurt and apple, then laughed when she realized how huge her appetite was next to Betty's simple diet of celery and salad. "Isn't it awful?" Anne said. "I get so hungry by lunch time I could eat an elephant."

"But two sandwiches," she said, still in shock. "How can you ever keep that trim figure eating like that?"

"I guess I just stay trim breaking up fights all day."

Betty's pretty face twisted into agony as she watched Anne gluttonously eat half a sandwich. Anne stopped eating when she saw Betty stare. "Would you like a sandwich?" she asked. "I really have plenty."

Betty started to reach for one, then at the midway point slapped her own hand. "I can't!" she said like someone holding back tears. "My doctor absolutely forbids me!"

"If you change your mind . . . "

"Please, Anne. Don't tempt me." She gazed at the roast beef sandwich with its thick slice of tomato and generous spread of mayonnaise as though ready to snatch it from Anne's hand. "I'll hate you for the rest of my life if you force me to break my diet." With a painful grimace, she then ate her salad, chewing it quickly. She seemed too aware of Anne's food to concentrate on her chewing. "Are you still trying to reach Rod's mother?" she asked after finishing her lunch.

"Yes, in fact I sent her a telegram last night. But I don't think that's going to work any better than any of my phone calls or letters. That woman's never home!"

"Personally if I were you," she said after neatly folding her napkin and placing it into her tote bag. "I'd ignore Rod."

"I can't do that, not only for my own safety, but for the lesson in it to my other kids. If I let boys like Rod do as they want in class, I would teach my kids by his example that the world doesn't belong to the honest and decent, but to thugs like him."

"Doesn't it?"

"I hope not, Betty."

"Well, it does . . . believe me. What you see happening in the schools isn't accidental. I've been teaching too long to believe that. So take my advice. Stop trying to teach moral lessons. You'll only end up being fired like Ralph Clearwater."

"Then he was fired."

"Of course he was. After all, he did knock out the boy's three front teeth. Even in the Good Old Days, a teacher was never allowed that much license. So I urge you, if you can't ignore Rod, at least treat his behavior casually and joke with him about it. You'll be amazed how quickly he'll lose interest then."

"I don't see how being flippant and casual will do anything of the sort. If anything, it'll encourage him to be bolder."

"That's where you're wrong. I've learned from experience that it's only when I act moral and righteous that trouble begins. But the moment I let these little monsters know they can't shock me . . . the game is over!"

"That might work if it were all just a game of moral compromise to Rod. Then it wouldn't matter to him whether he achieved his end with words or action. But I don't think Rod thinks like that. Besides, even if he did, I still couldn't go along with the idea."

"I think you should give it a try. After all, your safety is at stake."

"There are some things more important than my safety, Betty."

"Are there?"

Her attitude surprised Anne. She had never expected Betty to feel this way. She had believed that beneath Betty's intolerance with school conditions was a woman of strong moral character. But now she knew differently. Anyone who suggested compromise on such an important principle couldn't be moral. She wondered how many other teachers at Church were like Betty.

"Tell me about the Clearwater incident," Anne said, changing the subject. "What ever did Mrs. Daniels do about the boy?"

"Nothing."

"Nothing?"

Betty poured a little fruit juice from her thermos bottle into a cup, then sipped enough to moisten her throat. "That's right, *nothing*! After all, Ralph did hit the boy, regardless of what that little barbarian did, and Mrs. Daniels would be committing professional suicide to try to justify it. There's always the chance, if she tried, that the boy's mother might protest, some civil-rights group might sue or worse some official downtown might disapprove. It's by far much wiser to treat the matter as she did—fire the teacher and exonerate the boy for starting the fire."

"But that's so unfair."

"You're quite right, but you must remember, we know what a monster the boy is. But others don't. To them it is a clear case of teacher brutality. And that, Anne, leads to the point of all this. Mrs. Daniels is an ambitious educator and ambitious educators don't create waves. That's why she never complained when principals from neighboring schools only transferred their worst kids here for our September opening. She knew reacting would only anger these principals and that would be terrible because one might be just lucky enough to know an important official downtown. Of course, you realize what that could mean. Mrs. Daniels could lose out on that glamorous job next fall. Well, you can bet she's not going to risk that—not for any reason."

"Is such transferring common?"

"Oh yes. It's been done for decades. Sometimes kids with serious adjustment problems will bounce from school to school all year."

"Why isn't this practice stopped. Surely downtown must realize how easily this can turn kids against the schools."

"The answer to that is very simple. Those officials downtown don't care what happens to the children. They've got a soft job downtown and as long as no one threatens it what do they care how principals solve their problems."

"No wonder the kids are so rebellious."

"So I ask you, Anne, do you still believe the world

belongs to the decent and honest?"

"Maybe it'd be more correct to ask, Betty, are the public schools run by the decent and honest?"

"Yes," Betty said, smiling, obviously pleased with Anne's conclusion. "Maybe that would be a better question."

Anne jumped, shrieking when a firecracker exploded behind her. Recovering, she turned. There was so much confusion in the hall that it was impossible to identify the culprit. The only person who looked suspicious was a girl nearby, poking her head from the restroom. Upon seeing Anne stare, the girl pulled her head into the restroom and closed the door. The cigarette smoke which had drifted lazily from the restroom into the hall was the only indication that the door had been open. Anne forgot the prank, like all the other annoying pranks she was exposed to daily, and hurried to class. She had learned during her first week here that trying to check serious problems left her no time for hit-and-run pranks. This disturbed her since she knew pranks were often tests to measure the limits of acceptable behavior. To check pranks only when they became serious would only teach teenagers right and wrong on a continuum of negative values. This, she certainly didn't want to do. But because of the amount of disorder at Church, she felt she had no choice. She wondered how long at this rate it would be before she became like Betty and ignored everything.

As Anne reached her classroom, an attractive and stylishly dressed black woman walked toward her. The woman was wearing a handsome blue dress and matching coat. A single strand of pearls were around her neck. On her fingers were several rings; one was a gold signet and the other was a two- or three-karat sapphire surrounded by diamond chips. Her curly black hair was luxuriously long and danced on her shoulders when she moved. From a distance, her face appeared soft and feminine, but at close range, hard and angry like someone who had fought for survival in a tough world and managed because of her toughness to survive well. With her was Rod Ramwell. His suede jacket was open, exposing his broad chest, partially hidden under a tailored sport shirt. Anne guessed by their physical likeness that the woman who was probably in her early thirties was Rod's mother.

Although the woman dressed with taste and chic, she spoke in the crude vernacular of the street and seemed to enjoy the shock-effect this had on Anne. Anne suddenly wished she hadn't sent the telegram. She had the feeling that trying to communicate with the woman would be as difficult as trying to communicate with Rod. This was made obvious when the hall walkers, curious about the woman, began to gather around her and, encouraged by Mrs. Ramwell, take her side against Anne.

To avoid a scene which she couldn't control Anne invited Rod and his mother into her classroom, then locked the door behind them to keep out the students. Mrs. Ramwell sat next to Anne's desk while Rod, after sitting in front of it, propped up his feet on the desk. He seemed amused by Anne's annoyance and to annoy her further, removed a cigarette from his pocket, then lighted it. Anne sat silently behind her desk, staring ahead at the clean souls of Rod's new shoes and repressed an urge to shove his feet off her papers and books.

"Why you wanna see me?" Mrs. Ramwell asked to the point.

Anne turned to the woman. "I wanted to see you, Mrs. Ramwell, because of Rod's behavior."

"Well, what 'bout it?"

"For one thing he is always making unnecessary statements to me."

"So?"

Anne nervously fingered the gold heart dangling from her neck chain, the gold heart which was a gift from Jeremiah Lee, and said patiently: "Well, to be perfectly honest, Mrs. Ramwell, I find his statements obscene."

"You ain't talkin' 'bout my Rod."

"I'm afraid I am, Mrs. Ramwell."

"How come nobody else say that?"

"I can't speak for others. But I am sure if they had expressed concern to you and showed the same interest in his behavior as I'm trying to show, he might not have gotten into trouble with Mrs. Park."

Mrs. Ramwell leaned forward and glared at Anne. "He got in trouble 'cause that bitch was puttin' lies on 'em."

"But Mrs. Ramwell . . . "

"In all the years he been in school nobody ever say things like that 'bout 'em. You's the only teacher he got who thinks he's trouble. You 'n' that bitch who say he tried rapin' 'er."

"You tell 'er ma," Rod said, amused.

" 'Sides, you got nobody to blame 'cept yerself for anything he do," she said viciously. "My boy told me how you is always teasin' 'em with yer sexy walk. My Rod told me everythin'."

Anne suddenly exploded. Her voice became razor sharp and for such a small woman in comparison to Mrs. Ramwell even sufficiently threatening to cause Mrs. Ramwell to look at Anne, startled. "Now just one moment," Anne said furiously. "He's the one who's the problem." And she pointed an angry finger at Rod. "Why he's grabbed me, exposed himself to me, made filthy comments and followed me around the school like a dog in heat. All without the slightest encouragement from me."

Rod threw his lighted cigarette to the floor and sprung to his feet. His massive head rushed over the desk toward Anne, forcing her to jerk backwards against the chair, startled. "Don't-cha put them lies on me," he said in a deadly voice.

Anne grabbed the armrests of her chair and squeezed them until she felt the sharp edges press hard against her palms. "Mrs. Ramwell," she said in a controlled, but firm voice. "If your son doesn't sit down, if he continues to be a problem, I'll . . . I'll . . . go to the police."

"If you go to the police . . ." Rod began in the same

deadly voice as before.

His mother shoved him back. "Hush, boy," she commanded. "I gonna handle this. So sit yer black ass down 'n' be good."

"I'm sure, Mrs. Ramwell," Anne said, releasing her hold of the armrests, "that his behavior now should give you some idea of what I go through in class."

"My boy ain't bad," she said. "He only act bad sometime when teachers like you put lies on 'em."

"If he's such a good boy," Anne said. "How do you explain his extorting money from his classmates?"

"What-cha talkin' 'bout?" she asked.

"I'm talking about how he beats up boys when they refuse to give him their lunch money."

"My son don't do things like that," she said indignantly. "Shore Rod ain't the best boy. Ever since his dad was sent up for stealin' medicine when my little boy was sick Rod been a little bad. What boy ain't gonna be a little bad after that? But that don't mean Rod gonna steal lunch money from kids. Not *my* Rod!" She then turned to Rod. "Ain't that right, son?"

"Shore is, ma."

"You see. Even my boy say you is wrong."

"Well, since you don't believe me," Anne said, rising. "Maybe you should speak to his other teachers and find out how they feel." She pushed her chair under the desk. "In the meantime, I'm going to talk to the counselor and see what he recommends."

Rod paused at the door before leaving and mumbled something which Anne couldn't hear. But she didn't need to hear it to know the meaning. His angry look said enough. She knew if she didn't act fast and decisively, he would release his anger with some act of violence.

Metal floor-to-ceiling shelves lined both sides of the room and gave the counselor's office the appearance of being a narrow passageway in the library stacks. At the end of the room in front of the window facing Anne, when she

entered, was a desk with a white man sitting behind it. The
man, whose head was bowed, looked as though he were
studying or reading something on his desk. On the floor in
front of his desk were four students; one boy and a girl were
lying together in a tight embrace while two boys were
rolling dice for money beside the couple.

Shocked by what she saw, Anne decided not to enter
the room, and called to the man from the doorway. When he
didn't respond, one dice player shook him. Startled, the man
looked up as if awakened from a deep sleep which left him
confused as to where he was. After quickly identifying his
surroundings, he glanced first at the students on the floor,
then at Anne.

"Could I see you outside?" Anne asked the man.

The man rose from his chair so quickly that he knocked
his knees against the desk. In the hall be began to gush a
lengthy apology for not noticing Anne. He told her about
how preoccupied he had been lately with the problems of
several teenagers. He told her about one boy who was
abandoned by his parents, of another who was arrested for
selling pills. He spoke convincingly about each case, too
convincingly, like a clever politician who knew exaclty
what to say to get a desired emotional response from his
constituents.

"Sometimes I wish I could do more," he brooded. "Be
more effective in my efforts to help these kids." He stopped
talking upon noticing that Anne wasn't overflowing with
sympathy. "Incidentally," he said, "I don't think you
introduced yourself."

"I'm Miss Harte, the new English teacher."

His human goodness stopped flowing. "Why you're
only a teacher," he said, surprised.

"Who did you think I was?"

"That's not important," he said curtly. "What do you
want?"

She hesitated. She doubted from what she saw in his
office and from what he just revealed about himself, that he
would be of any help to her. But when she remembered Rod,

and his potential threat to her safety, she decided to take a chance and said to the counselor: "I have a boy in my class whom I'd like you to see."

"Oh, that's quite impossible," he said, shaking his head. "I can't possibly consider taking on another student, not before next semester."

"But he's a serious problem."

"You don't understand, Miss Harte. I have more serious problems than I can handle." He told her again about the boy who was abandoned, and about the other boy who was arrested. He then added that he was already working until ten and eleven each night because of his tremendous overload of work. But now he spoke without making any effort to be convincing, like someone reading off meaningless numbers. "So you see, Miss Harte. I can't possibly take on another student. It's impossible, absolutely impossible."

"What about testing him then?" Anne asked. "At least by testing him we can identify the root of his problem."

"Oh, I can't do that. The school system doesn't allow us to give psychological tests anymore. It's against the student's human rights. So testing him is out of the question."

"What are you allowed to do?"

"Two things. One, I can counsel him and motivate him to sublimate his antisocial behavior. Or two, refer him to the Rose School where the staff is trained to work with extremely difficult cases. But unfortunately, the Rose School is overcrowded and has a two year waiting list. So what's left is counseling. But as I told you I won't be free until next semester. That means, of course, the burden of the problem for now rests with you."

"What if I can't cope with him? Then what?"

"That depends. Who is the boy?"

"Rod Ramwell."

"Oh, yes. He's the one Mrs. Park enticed with her provocative manner."

Anne glanced at him, annoyed with the ease with which

he placed the blame on the teacher. "That isn't what some teachers have said," she said coldly.

"Miss Harte," he said with the authority of one who knew everything. "I make it my business to *know* the facts, and Mrs. Park enticed Rod. I don't care *what* others have said."

"I might believe you if he weren't always making obscene gestures."

"Maybe you just misunderstand these gestures. After all, Rod is a very normal adolescent, and he is sometimes mischievous."

"There are some gestures that can't be misunderstood," Anne snapped back. "Furthermore, I would think if you took your job seriously you'd want to investigate my complaint. After all, I am the second teacher this month to complain about Rod's behavior."

"You forget one important fact, Miss Harte, which makes me hesitant. There are many attractive women at Church. Some are even beautiful. Isn't it strange that only two of them have complained about Rod, you and Mrs. Park?"

"If you're saying that I've encouraged him . . . "

"There is that possibility, you know."

"Mr. Little, I don't appreciate your insult."

The counselor looked at her with indifference. "I'm sorry I can't be of help to you at this time." He seemed satisfied with the conclusion he had reached about Anne. "Now you'll have to excuse me, Miss Harte. I have to return to my group."

"Oh, yes," she said furiously. "By all means. I wouldn't want to keep you from all your students."

"Miss Harte. Four students are more than I can handle in an hour. You must remember I'm trying to teach them to sublimate their negative behavior, and I need small groups in order to do this successfully."

"You forget, Mr. Little. I saw how you were teaching sublimation."

"You don't take my efforts very seriously," he said.

"How can I when you aren't concerned enough to want to see this boy. How can I when I look in on your group and see you at your desk asleep, while those four kids do precisely what they want to. It strikes me that sublimating their negative behavior to you is nothing more than reinforcing this behavior with indifference!"

"You obviously don't understand counseling, Miss Harte, and are daring to judge my work on the basis of some superficial knowledge you obviously learned in an introductory course in college." He then began to explain with condescension for her edification the problems of adolescents; the search for identity and the experimenting with different roles. His talk was a well-researched and erudite attempt to justify his indifference to Rod's behavior. Angered by his attitude, she walked away in the middle of his sentence and left his expensively learned thought dangling in the air behind her, as she hurried to Tom Slaughter's office.

Teachers Want Job Guarantee

Over 100 teachers on "sick" leave today marched in front of the Board of Education building downtown, carrying signs threatening to close down the schools if the school board implemented the audiovisual program next fall without first guaranteeing jobs to all currently employed teachers.

Many of these teachers, members of the local teachers' union, regard the decision to bring an audiovisual center to the city schools as the first step of a nation-wide trend to replace teachers with "push-button gadgets". School board president, Richard Lathan, expressed alarm this morning over the teachers' irrational fears and blamed it on his opponents who were using such fears to sabotage the program. "What the school board is trying to do," he said to reporters, "is modernize our teaching program, not rid the system of teachers. Drexel Industries doesn't have the staff, technology, or inclination to do that. In fact, it needs teachers, competent and efficient teachers, which it can train to use its teaching aids."
A Roosevelt High School teacher, after overhearing Lathan, shouted: "Then how come Boston lost 50 teachers after the program was implemented, L.A., 65; and Chicago, 72? Are you going to tell us *those* teachers weren't replaced by machines?"

Chapter 6

Birdie lowered her head almost to the level of the table and shoveled her lunch from the styrofoam plate into her mouth. Although no one in the cafeteria noticed her, she still sensed that everyone was as aware of her as she was of them. For this reason, she sat on the edge of her chair, cautiously eying the movement of bodies in and out of the room, ready to flee at the first sign of trouble.

Beside her were two boys. Between blasts of music from a radio, she overheard one tell his companion about the knifing outside the school this morning. He talked about the knifing as though it were the most exciting event in his life, more exciting than the movie he saw at a local theater in which "the bood pour'd outa this guy's guts all over the place." Nauseated by what she heard, Birdie shoved her food plate aside and tried to still her stomach with milk. But she stopped trying and left the cafeteria when she saw Zelda a few tables away stare at her.

In the hall she slipped past a crowd of teenagers, huddled near a water fountain with their hands over their ears, then hurried up the stairs. In her haste, she bumped into a girl on the landing. The girl was a black girl with white dots over her left temple who, unlike Birdie in her sweater and skirt, dressed like someone trying to conceal her femininity inside of a black leather jacket and levis.

"Watch where yer goin' nigger," the girl said, glaring at Birdie.

"My name ain't nigger," Birdie said indignantly. "My name's Birdie."

"Oh, yer name's Birdie," the girl mimicked. "Did-cha hear that?" she said to her three friends. "Her name's Birdie." The girl then made a sound like a bird for her friends' amusement.

Birdie braced herself for what would follow. Ever since she was knifed by Zelda, girls eagerly wanted to fight her. They seemed to believe, if they won, they could rise from obscurity to prominence among their classmates as quickly as Zelda had. In an effort to avoid a fight, Birdie continued up the stairs. But before she could get out of reach, the girl grabbed her sweater and pulled her back down.

Without hesitancy, Birdie turned and knocked the girl's hand away. For a moment, she became the old Birdie, the Birdie who had once terrorized the school with the aid of her gang. But when she saw three girls circle her, ready to fight, she lost her courage and tried to back away.

"Did-cha see that," the white-spotted black girl said to her friends. "The big teat tweet-tweet bird wanna play tough."

"Steal her, Casey," one girl said. "Steal the nigger bitch in the mouf."

"Did-cha hear that tweet-tweet bird," Casey said to Birdie. "My friends here wanna see me steal you one."

Birdie nervously looked for a way to escape. But the girls, sensing her intentions, tightened their circle and smiled when perspiration formed on Birdie's brow. Once again Birdie felt helpless, as helpless as she had felt yesterday when several girls jumped her and stole her money.

"What's wrong tweet-tweet bird?" Casey stepped close and brushed her flat chest against Birdie's protruding breasts. "Scar'd of Casey?"

"Birdie ain't scar'd of nobody!"

"That ain't what I hear. I hear you been runnin' scar'd ever since Zelda cut out yer guts."

"Well, you is wrong."

"Then show me yer stomach. Show me you still got yer guts."

Birdie backed away from Casey, but was halted by the wall. "I ain't gonna show you nothin'."

"Then I gonna look myself."

A chill passed through her when Casey reached for her sweater. It was humiliating enough to be knifed by a girl half her size. She wasn't going to humiliate herself again by letting Casey see her scar and maybe even laugh at her because of it. Before she could lift the sweater, Birdie shoved Casey backwards. She then knocked aside a girl blocking her and ran up the stairs.

"You betta stop," Casey said. "Or I gonna blow that head right off!"

Birdie froze in motion with one hand on the banister and one foot on the step. Something hard pressed against the back of her head. She didn't need to turn to know what it was. The cold, dangerous sound of Casey's voice identified it clearly.

"Okay nigger," Casey said. "Now turn around."

Birdie hesitated. She looked up the stairs in hope that a teacher would appear and rescue her. But no one was there. The first-floor hall was unusually quiet.

Casey pressed the object harder against Birdie. "I said turn!"

Birdie slowly turned to face Casey. A hand gun was pointing at her. Terrified, Birdie just stared at the barrel. "Now show me yer scar."

"But there ain't nothin' to show," Birdie said, swallowing painfully.

"You got three seconds," Casey said. "Three seconds, nigger!"

There was a wild look of excitement in Casey's eyes, the same wild look which Birdie remembered in Zelda's eyes when she came at Birdie with a knife. Birdie quickly lifted the sweater and exposed her humiliation.

"Gosh," one girl said, after bending over to look, her

buttocks higher than her head. "Look-it the size of that scar!"

"Didn't I tell you Zelda done a good job," Casey said.

"Wait 'till the others hear 'bout this," another girl said.

"I gotta better idea," Casey said. "I gonna make Birdie walk into that lunch room without 'er sweater so everybody can see for theirselves what Zelda done to her."

Birdie panicked at the thought of walking into the cafeteria, exposed. She knew, if she did, no one would ever let her forget the knifing, and she would be haunted by it for the rest of her life. There was only one thing to do now. She had to kick the gun from Casey's hand and run. But before she could try, she heard an explosion. At first she thought Casey had pulled the trigger; then she saw a white cloud of smoke drift from the basement toward the landing.

Casey put the gun into her jacket. "Jesus," she said, looking toward the smoke. "Someone blow'd up the school."

"Let's go see what they done?" one girl said, excited.

"Not me," Casey said. "I gonna get my black ass outa here."

As Casey ran to the exit, Birdie ran up the stairs two at a time. Someone was following her. Frightened, she jerked her head to the side to see who it was. When she saw two boys, her fears passed.

"You shore blow'd up that fountain good," one boy said.

"Yeah," the other answered. "But it took forever. That fuse musta got wet."

Birdie sat near the teachers' mailboxes in the main office and watched while Miss Halsted, dressed in colorful department store fashions, hummed a popular song and typed. Listening to her hum was almost as pleasant as listening to her sing again. The same effortless sweetness, the same golden richness that had thrilled Birdie and the congregation last Sunday at the Saviour Baptist Church now helped her forget her humiliating confrontation with Casey in the hall. Although only a thin wall separated the office from the hall, it could've easily been an ocean, separating two continents, one at war, another at peace. At times Birdie attributed this calm to Miss Halsted who by her presence encouraged the often quarrelsome aides to walk more quietly, address each other more courteously, and even hum happily. Other times Birdie attributed this calm to the office which by its magic powers could transform anyone entering into saints. Knowing which was true wasn't important to Birdie. As far as she was concerned just having a place like the office to visit was all that really mattered to her.

As she watched Miss Halsted, she was impressed with the ease and speed with which she typed. The keys seemed to click melodically to her touch and sing their own special song. What particularly impressed her was the pleasure which she derived from her work. Unlike the other aides, she didn't make lengthy phone calls or take sudden coffee breaks or even disappear from the office for suspiciously long periods of time. Instead, she sat most of the day in front of her typewriter, joyfully humming and typing as though this was the greatest pleasure in life.

Watching her, Birdie dreamed of the day when she could type like Miss Halsted and work in a similar office. Just knowing that such a happy and peaceful world existed made her eager to inhabit it. Several times in her excitement she had wanted to tell others about her dream, but always at the last minute she held back. She was afraid, if she told others, they would laugh at her as they had been laughed at for their ambitions. So Birdie did what she felt she had to do. Without telling anyone her reason, she enrolled in a typing class and practiced at home on an old typewriter she found in the alley. But when Miss Halsted leaned against the counter, dividing the office in two sections, and smiled at Birdie with her special smile which encouraged trust and affection, her fear of sharing her dream passed.

"Well, hell-ooo," Miss Halsted said in a voice of someone who sang rather than spoke words.

Birdie squirmed happily in the chair. "Hi, Miss Halsted," she said, following the black aide's lead and singing her greeting.

"How long have you been sitting there?"

Birdie walked to the counter. "Not too long."

"You know Mrs. Daniels is going to be mad if she sees you here again."

Birdie remembered the principal's anger the last time she saw her in the office. She anxiously searched Miss Halsted's pretty face for compassion. "You ain't gonna tell her . . . is you?"

"Tell her?" she said with musical sweetness. "Of course not, Birdie."

"Good," Birdie said with relief. She then removed some money from her bra. "Look-it what I got for you?"

"What's that for?"

"Them the two dollars them girls took yesterday."

"How *won*-der-ful! You got it back!"

"Oh, it ain't the same money. This here money my pa gave me."

Miss Halsted looked at her suspiciously in a way which made lying difficult. "Are you sure he *gave* it to you?" she asked without a lilt.

Birdie avoided her gaze. She couldn't tell Miss Halsted that she took the money from her dad after he fell asleep. So she crossed her fingers behind her back and nodded.

"You didn't have to pay me back."

"But I wanna give it back 'cause I felt bad when them girls took yer lunch money yesterday."

"Well, I have an idea," she said. "Why don't you buy us a barbecue chicken with it." She smiled as beautifully as she talked. "Would you like that?"

Birdie hesitated before answering. She thought of Casey, of all the girls like Casey. It might just be her misfortune to meet someone again enroute to the carry-out. She didn't want to chance that, not after her humiliation in the hall. "Well . . . I . . . " she stammered.

"Don't tell me those girls are *still* bothering you?"

Birdie nodded, too embarrassed to speak.

"In that case," she said, almost so delicately that the

words evaporated as quickly as they were sung, "you better not go to the store. I wouldn't want you to be robbed . . . and maybe even hurt." There was love in her voice. It made Birdie want to rush into her arms and just hold onto her tightly. But something stopped her, not just the counter which separated them, something within Birdie, a fear perhaps that she might be wrong about Miss Halsted and might be rejected. Birdie quickly handed her the money and returned to the chair. After sitting down again, she heard the door to Mrs. Daniels' private office crack open and saw Mrs. Daniels' head appear in the opening. Birdie quickly slouched in the chair in an effort to hide, lowering her head from view, just as the door flew open.

Mrs. Daniels marched toward Birdie, the heels of her orthopedic-like shoes clumping hard on the tiles. "Are you here *again*?" she asked angrily.

Birdie raised her head timidly and peeked at her. "I just sayin' hello to Miss Halsted."

"Miss Halsted is a very busy woman and she doesn't have time to visit with students. So go before I call your father."

"But I don't mean no harm, Mrs. Daniels. Honest."

She pointed her arm toward the door. "Go!" she commanded.

Birdie slipped past the teenagers in the hall. To avoid being noticed, she took the long way to the fourth-floor landing. At the landing, she sat against the wall with her legs spread as wide apart as her skirt allowed and lighted a cigarette. The cool fall air, seeping through a cracked window, chilled her. Staring ahead absently, she warmed herself with the daydream of someday leaving the school and working in an office surrounded with nice people like Miss Halsted. In the midst of her daydream, a voice exploded in her brain and shattered her tranquility. Startled, she looked into the sunlight rushing through the window ahead and saw Rod Ramwell. The light behind him softened the edges of his broad shoulders and massive head.

For a moment he looked like an angel with a broken nose, stepping toward her out of a heavenly beam of light. But when he stood in front of her, with his back to the light, she suddenly saw in his expression a mixture of amusement and contempt which, for reasons she couldn't explain, made him appear diabolic.

"What-cha doin' here?" he asked.

"None of yer business."

"Maybe it is. Maybe I hear things that make it my business."

She stared at him intently, certain that he knew already about the confrontation with Casey. "What-cha hear?" she asked nervously, putting out her cigarette on the cement floor and breaking it in half in the process.

"I hear yer waitin' for some hot boy to fuck you."

Relieved that he didn't know about her humiliation, she said contemptuously, "Well, you is wrong!"

"Rod ain't wrong." He sat next to her. "He knows girls." And he was looking at her in the same way she had seen him look at other girls, pretty girls like Mary Lou. "He know when girls need a little ."

A smile softened his hard expression, and he appeared uncharacteristically gentle. She almost doubted those stories about him being so tough. As his hand slipped over her leg, she was tempted to let it continue its journey. Instead, she shoved his hand away when she remembered all the girls he had made pregnant. "Don't-cha think of nothin' else?"

"Not when there's a snappy pussy 'round," he said, placing his hand on her leg again.

She closed her legs on his hand. "That one don't snap."

His hand forced her legs far enough apart so that he could move his fingers freely. "They all snap." And he tickled the flesh through a hole in her nylon panties. " 'Cause Rod he know how to make 'em snap."

"Well, that one ain't gonna snap." She pulled his hand out, then crossed her legs and stared ahead.

"Ain't-cha gonna give ole Rod a little?" he asked, amused.

"No!"

"Why?"

" 'Cause I don't wanna baby."

"Every girl wanna baby to take care of."

"Well, not Birdie."

"Then how come you act the way you do?"

With a sidelong look, she said: "What-cha talkin' 'bout?"

"Oooh," he said, smiling boyishly in a way which made her feel comfortable and attractive near him. "I seen the way you look at Mary Lou's baby yesterday."

"How I look at that baby?"

"You look just like you wanna baby somethin' crazy."

"You nuts."

"Rod he can tell them things. He know when a girl wanna baby. He know that for a fact."

He spoke so confidently that she looked at him curiously as though maybe he knew something she didn't. "Well, I *still* ain't gonna give you nothin'," she said, crossing her arms.

"Why not?" he said in a voice as gentle as his smile. "I make you a good baby."

"You ain't gonna make Birdie no baby . . . so just you forget it."

"I can't." And he lowered his gaze. "You too pretty to forget."

Unaccustomed to such flattery, she blushed. "Shit," she said self-consciously. "I ain't pretty."

"Now why Rod gonna tell you that if it ain't true?"

" 'Cause you wanna little ."

"Man," he said. "I can get that anywhere 'n' I don't even have to say nothin'."

"Then you ain't lying?" she asked, surprised. "You really think I's pretty?"

"Course you is!"

"Is I pretty like Yolanda?"

"Shit! Yolanda's ass too big."

"What 'bout Mary Lou?"

"She ain't got no teats."

"You think Birdie pretty than both them?"

"Sure."

She smiled, charmed. "You nuts!"

"You is pretty, Birdie Smith. And I bet-cha if you put yerself into some real slick clothes you gonna be the prettiest girl round."

She became uncomfortably aware of the clothes that she wore, of all her clothes that were either too old or too small for her. She had none of the new dresses or slacks or jackets which some of the other girls had. All her clothes were from the thrift shop, hand-me-downs on sale. "You really think Birdie be *that* pretty?"

"Oh yeah," he said, leaning toward her. "You be the prettiest?"

A wonderful excitement came over her as his hand once again made its slow journey up her leg, the sort of excitement which made her heart drum loudly and goose pimples run merrily about. In his arms she felt protected and secure. The fear which she knew when alone passed. She knew if she became his girl she would never have reason to be afraid again. Rod was the toughest and no one would ever dare mistreat *his* girl. Realizing this made her cling to him tighter, kiss him more passionately.

Sensations passed quickly through her, deeply felt sensations which made her squirm and sigh and breath heavily. But when he tried to enter her, pound recklessly at her wall of flesh which refused to open to him, she began to cry in pain.

"Stop, Rod. You hurtin' me. *Please* stop!"

But he wasn't listening to her . . . didn't seem to care about her . . . and he pounded faster and harder. She tried to shove him off her. But he was too strong, too determined. Helplessly flattened against the floor by his weight, she pleaded, even more urgently: "Please, Rod. You too big. You hurtin' Birdie."

"Fuck me, baby," he demanded. "Make that pussy snap. Common, Birdie. *Fuck* Rod!"

Then with one violent thrust which ripped apart flesh ... made her scream louder than she ever screamed before ... he tore into her and discharged himself as his body quivered out of control on top of her.

Schools To Get Center on Wheels

fe

School board members in an attempt to appease low-income parents, displeased with the distribution of the $10 million federal grant, and militant teachers, fearful of losing their jobs to automation, have approved a plan to hire four new teachers to man a mobile audiovisual center which will serve all city schools next fall.

The new plan, proclaimed by parents and teachers alike as "fair", will provide all students with exposure to audiovisual education and will guarantee jobs for currently employed teachers. Richard Lathan, school board president, though unhappy with the plan to service all the schools rather than a select few with the experimental program,

believes, nevertheless, that the program will work despite this attempt to weaken it by spreading it thin over the entire system. "Operational details haven't been finalized," Richard Lathan told reporters, "but after considerable discussion the board thinks the audiovisual program can be expanded without significantly reducing its effectiveness or increasing its costs."

Acting school superintendent Marshall Steele feels differently and refers to the mobile audiovisual center as a 10-minute-a-month lesson for each student in button-pushing. "What the schools need," Dr. Steele went on to say, "is a paid panel of students to evaluate school problems."

ommittee —

Chapter 7

Anne found it difficult to hold her students' interest in her lessons for an entire period. Some students would invariably grow bored and disrupt the class with embarrassing remarks about Anne's breasts, legs or ass. If she asked them to show more respect, they would tell her to get fucked. If she insisted, they would threaten her physically. If she ignored them and tried to work with others in the class, they would play a radio or phonograph. Angry, she would "lecture" them on how they were only hurting themselves with their indifference to school.

Almost immediately after she started to "lecture" them, they would stop what they were doing and listen. At such times she was certain she had made an impression. But the moment she stopped talking they would forget what she said and would again become disrespectful. Surprised, she wondered why her "lecturing" had no lasting effect on them. Although they all listened attentively, and in some cases with concern to what she had said, she noticed after her "lecture" they behaved as though they hadn't heard one word. Puzzled by this contradictory behavior, she decided to try an experiment, and for five minutes she screamed at them hysterically, overloading them with statements which made no sense. Instead of laughing at her, they once again listened thoughtfully and when she stopped, they again resumed with their disrespect. Again Anne grew angry. This time not with them, but with a system which had "created" them. Their years of schooling . . . instead of preparing them to listen thoughtfully . . . had taught them only to react to moods. Whatever potential these students might have was atrophied by intellectual neglect. All that remained was a sensitivity to moods which a teacher with the right tone of voice could use to his advantage.

Some students, on the other hand, grasped the purpose of her "lectures". But these were the students who did their work and didn't need to be "lectured". Seeing these students struggle with their lessons . . . while the others danced, fought and socialized...disturbed her and made her wonder how she would ever tame the others. She knew if she couldn't think of a way it wouldn't be long before her good students would become discouraged and would stop trying, and her life at Church would become, as it was for so many other teachers, just a job for a pay check. The only thing preventing her from being like them was the memories of her successes. She knew, if she could succeed at teaching once, she could again. Yet there were times when she was certain it was impossible at Church.

Perhaps the most discouraging obstacle to teaching . . . the one which seemed to be at the root of all the disorder . . . was the vast ability range of students in each class. In several classes, this ability range stretched from first to eighth grade levels. For this reason, assigning unit work which would interest the majority was impossible. The only solution was to create lessons that would challenge each of her 170 students on his level. In order to do this with so many students, she would have to prepare and mark daily about 100 different lessons. With the right books and materials, this would be no real difficulty. But this wasn't the case at least at Church. The few sets of books and materials available to her were almost totally useless. Instead of presenting a survey of the subject honestly and simply, the materials and books wasted hundreds of pages on veiled racism, clever ambiguities, pompous intellec-tualizing, and all the other gimmicks so commonly employed by educators intent on sterilizing the mind. To make matters even more difficult for her, even if she had the needed materials and books, she still didn't think she could teach successfully. For she had no way of determining the students exact level of preparedness. Achievement tests, once used for this purpose, weren't considered valid according to several influential officials because they were loaded with ambiguities which made the tests confusing to inner-city students. Since no one had created tests which these influential officials could approve, all such testing stopped and test grades were removed from the permanent records.

Also removed from the records was any information which might help a teacher determine a student's ability level. All a teacher was allowed to enter on the permanent record was the final course grade. Tom Slaughter justified this policy by telling Anne that some teachers once used the permanent records to write evaluations which would prejudice other teachers against the students. But when Anne told him that evaluations were needed to simplify her job of preparing work for the students, he merely replied that grades were all she needed to know. Anything else would be prejudicial and unreliable, then quickly left before she could destroy his argument with reason.

Mrs. Daniels did her part to deepen the problem by advising teachers never to fail more than 10 percent of the class. If a teacher disobeyed her, she warned she would be compelled to write up a negative teaching report on him. Three such reports, she added, was reason enough to be fired. Her argument in defense of her position was that failing more than 10 percent indicated to her that a student wasn't learning because a teacher *wasn't* teaching. A few teachers, to make themselves look good, began to earn a reputation for giving undeserved grades to students. Other teachers, feeling guilty about such dishonesty, would have special "reviews" before each test in which the answers were fed mechanically into the heads of the students. In this way, these teachers were able to convince themselves by having their students gush out answers learned by rote that they too were good teachers. But when one teacher, suspicious of the value of this practice, repeated the exam a week later to test retention, she confirmed what most teachers refused to face: real learning wasn't crammed into heads during drills, but was an intellectual accumulation of structured knowledge.

For most teachers, promoting or failing students wasn't of primary concern. Instead, they were mostly concerned about the gangs of students terrorizing the halls and classrooms. For Anne, these nomadic gangs of terrorists were a major problem. Their attacks, often planned with uncanny timing, usually occurred when she had the class involved in a project or discussion. At such times, they would burst into her room and multiplying rapidly would spread disorder. Before she could stop them, they would vanish, leaving behind a plundered and vandalized classroom. Sometimes she would be lucky enough to halt them at the door before they had a chance to enter. Even sometimes another teacher passing in the hall would overhear the noise and assist Anne at clearing the troublemakers from the room. But usually most teachers were as helpless as Anne at preventing such destruction and avoided intervening out of fear for their own safety. This left Anne alone to end disorder in whatever way she could. The results were often discouraging.

One girl . . . during such a raid on her class . . . for no reason flung a book at Anne. Infuriated, Anne grabbed the girl by the arm to lead her from the room. Before Anne could, several other class raiders stopped Anne at the door. One six-foot girl, claiming to be the book-thrower's cousin pointed a knife at Anne and promised to cut her throat if she didn't free her cousin. Fortunately Tom Slaughter, during one of his routine visits to her class, interceded. He told the six-footer not to bring such a weapon to school again and the book-thrower to report to her regular class. After he settled the teenagers in Anne's room, he told Anne that it was against school policy for teachers to touch students. He said if she were unhappy with someone's conduct she should notify him.

After that incident, Anne made an effort to notify Tom each time she had a serious problem. Unfortunately, since Church was a large school, she wasn't always able to find him. When she did, by the time they both arrived at her classroom the troublemakers would be gone. Sometimes, though, they would both return in time to catch the teenagers in action. At such times, instead of counseling them (Anne learned later), Tom would busy the troublemakers with errands. Consequently, any threat to send disobedient teenagers to him didn't discourage misbehaving, but instead encouraged it. When Anne complained of this to Tom and stressed the need for some type of punishment, he defended his position by quoting Mrs. Daniels who vehemently opposed punishment because "it would turn the school into a battlefield with barbed wire and armed policemen to hold back angry students from attacking teachers." Anne who disagreed with this told him that if the schools ever became such a battlefield it would be because students were given the freedom to steal, abuse, slander, and riot, and go unpunished.

Since Tom was often reluctant to cooperate with Anne on important issues out of fear of upsetting Mrs. Daniels, Anne decided to turn to parents for help. Most parents of recalcitrant students, Anne quickly learned, fell into three categories: those who believed it was Anne's responsibility to keep the teenagers out of trouble, those who promised cooperation without ever fulfilling their promise, and those like Rod Ramwell's mother who blamed Anne for their teenager's behavior. In almost every case the results were the same. The teenagers would return to school after she contacted their homes just as belligerently as before, convinced now, though, that Anne was as impotent at controlling them as other adults, and to prove this point to Anne, they began to make it impossible for her to teach even occasionally.

Determined to break this cycle, Anne prepared a list of misbehaving students (as Tom Slaughter had recommended) and wrote in detail what each had done in class that day (identifying both the good and bad things). Then as soon as school was out, she would call parents and give them a full report. She continued doing this for nearly a week, even though she saw no improvement in behavior, but stopped when one parent whom Anne was calling daily about his misbehaving daughter came to school and whipped his daughter shamelessly in front of the class while Anne vainly tried to stop him.

She realized after that incident that the only way she could bring order in the classroom would be alone. In an effort to keep out students not registered in her classes, Anne would screen the teenagers at the door each period before admitting them to class and would charm those who tried to enter, but didn't belong in her room to go to their scheduled class. If someone looked unfamiliar and claimed to be a member of the class, she would insist that he get a note of admission from the office. Afterwards, she would lock her door . . . like most of the other teachers at Church . . . and in this way by reducing the flow of disruptive students in and out of the class end many of her problems.

With her classroom problems reduced, Anne was able to try teaching again. One of the first things she discovered was that many of her students had little interest in reading. She blamed this on all the unimaginative "Run, Jane, Run" types of books which they were forced to read in primary school. Whatever interest her students might have once had toward reading was carefully killed by the repetitious words in such books, mechanically arranged to bore them. She knew if she wanted to hook her students on reading she would have to supply them with books which didn't insult their intelligence.

In an effort to stimulate their interest again, she collected old paperbacks and magazines and left them on a table for the students to take. Most of the paperbacks were purchased by her at the Salvation Army for only 15 cents and sometimes during once-a-week specials for only 10 cents. The magazines, on the other hand, were discards which she found in the incinerator room of her apartment building. In order to interest a large mix of students, she selected her publications carefully. There were some on cooking, auto mechanics, history, science, decorating, beauty secrets, and anything else which teenagers might enjoy. She believed by having materials for a wide variety of interests she would then have something in the pile suitable for each student to enlarge his knowledge and at the same time to strengthen his grasp of the written language. But instead of reading the publications, some students used them as weapons to swat others, while a few tore out pages to make airplanes, while still others transformed innocent pictures into graphic sex scenes. After working with the students individually, she discovered that this was because many couldn't read well. Those who could didn't fully comprehend what they read.

Anne, who believed this was caused by the primitive teaching methods of painfully and mechanically making students memorize new words, tried to solve their reading handicap by preparing lessons in the phonic method which introduced students to new words by training them to identify the basic sounds for letters or combinations of letters and by teaching them suffixes, prefixes and common root formations in order to discover the meaning of new words. Such an approach to reading, she believed, was easier and more sensible than trying to memorize all the words in the English language. By teaching reading like this, she hoped to change her students' attitude toward the printed word and encourage them to work productively on their own at expanding their reading and speaking vocabulary. Watching her students shape new words on their lips while independently doing their work was often all the reward Anne needed to justify the many hours spent, thinking up appropriate lessons.

To identify the precise ability level of her other students, she prepared a lengthy test which started easy and became progressively harder. After mimeographing the test, she passed it out to all her students and instructed them to answer as many questions as they could. With the test results before her, she then prepared suitable lessons for her students and arranged these lessons by skills in one of the seven learning centers which she had created. Each student was free to select the center of his choice and progress within the center from easy to difficult work as well as from one center to another at his own pace. To minimize her work, she wrote the lessons in such a way so that each student could see his own mistakes and correct them himself. This left her free to work individually with those who needed help as well as time to prepare more lessons which focused on their most important deficiencies.

Some students who previsouly had shown no interest in school began to change and concentrate on their assignments. They liked working independently and didn't need grades or praise or other types of popular rewards to keep them interested in their lessons. For them, just being able to learn what they felt was necessary in order to live independent and useful lives was sufficient motivation. Those years of being tortured with trivia or with primitive teaching methods could temporarily be forgotten. Slowly, that little fire which once burned bright within each began to blaze again, and they now *wanted* to learn. Without any coaxing from Anne, they would report each period to their respective centers and would work quietly, moaning with disappointment if the period ended before they had a chance to finish their lessons.

For almost two weeks everything went well. But on the third week, after the report of her success spread throughout the school, a gang of students barged into her room between classes and destroyed her centers. Inconsolable, Anne brought up her concerns at a faculty meeting about the gangs of troublemakers in the hall. Mrs. Daniels assured her . . . and other concerned teachers . . . that she would do whatever was necessary to end the disorder. After several days elapsed without anything being done,

Anne again raised the question. This time Mrs. Daniels reluctantly agreed to schedule hall checks in order to round up the troublemakers. The first day of these hall checks the teachers worked hard and rounded up nearly 75 students. When Mrs. Daniels saw all the teenagers she was forced to punish, she became visibly upset and turned to the teachers for suggestions on what to do. Most teachers recommended suspension. But Mrs. Daniels quickly dismissed this by reminding them of the complicated procedure. According to her, she not only would have to meet with each of the 75 to-be-suspended students and their parents, but would also have to prepare reams of reports on each student for downtown administrators to study before receiving approval to suspend him. Such action, she warned, would involve weeks of work for only a few days maximum of reprieve from the teenagers. So the question remained: What was to be done about the troublemakers?

To make a show of concern, Mrs. Daniels had an assembly and urged the teenagers to behave and return to class. But her talk had no effect on them. Finally in what seemed to be a desperate reaction to teacher pressure, Mrs. Daniels arranged another assembly and invited a local black leader to talk to the students. But instead of calming the students and encouraging them to apply themselves to their studies, the black leader made them angry by telling them provocative stories of student repression in the school which, he claimed, opponents of the student panel wanted to perpetuate. For the remainder of the day, the police stood on guard in the halls to bring an end to the rioting which the black leader set off with his inflammatory "talk" on student power.

Loretta Daniels believed that her once-a-week, after-school faculty meetings were the ideal time to "educate" teachers. Teachers were usually too exhausted after a long day of taming angry students to think about what she said to them. For this reason, she was able to pour her philosophy painlessly into their vulnerable minds by persuasively repeating each week the key ideas which she wanted them to retain. Although some teachers brazenly slept or daydreamed through the faculty meetings, the majority, on the other hand, left their minds wide open for her to assault. Her success, though modest in the beginning, was made possible by the efforts of other educators who had prepared them intellectually for her philosophy. All she had to do was bring to the surface all the nonsense they were taught in school by planting key ideas in their minds which would synthesize everything into one compact point of view on education. This she did without any real effort. For within a month they were all beginning to sound alike. Phrases like "Children learn not by thinking, but by doing" or "Children need to be stimulated to act as members of a unit" or "Schools must be child-centered, not subject-centered" burst from their lips spontaneously. They began to believe . . . as she wanted them to believe . . . that the best way to achieve the ideal school environment was to establish a student panel in all the schools. She would have probably succeeded at winning their support . . . had them screaming downtown for students to rule them . . . if Anne Harte hadn't interfered.

The new English teacher from the beginning began to reveal the most disturbing determination to alert teachers to the fundamental errors in Loretta's philosophy with questions like: What would happen if a student panel made up of non-thinkers *did* run the schools, *did* make policies, and *did* select the curriculum? How could decent, thinking individuals protect themselves then from the capriciousness of mindless thugs, educated to obey their instincts and achieve their objectives by force? Would America (the most powerful and freest country in the world) be any different from other totalitarian countries in history, if she allowed "intellectuals" to turn students into non-thinking conformists who could be ruled by violence and force by a thinking elite?

Some teachers found her questions interesting, while others shocking. Yet they all listened and pondered what

Anne said in a way which made them impossible for Loretta to fool with the "innocence" of her ideas, the magic of her voice. Disturbed by Anne's growing influence, Mrs. Daniels wanted to fire Anne immediately. But she couldn't without a good case against her. Tom's report which she now had on file was useless because he provided her with none of those incriminating anecdotes needed to embarrass the teacher professionally. Instead, it was a carefully worded appraisal of the teacher which served only one purpose: It wasted paper!

Determined to get rid of the teacher, Mrs. Daniels did the next logical thing: She called Kenneth Ward to school!

A timid-looking supervisor whom several teachers had scared from school with stories about the students' violent behavior appeared unexpectedly in Anne's classroom. After he left, Anne composed a letter to the head of the English department with carbons to the supervisor, the principal, the union president, and the acting superintendent of schools.

> Today I received Mr. Kenneth Ward's evaluation of my teaching (the letter read). Although I'm not surprised by the content, I am surprised that he considers it fair.
>
> It isn't my habit to have my students spend the period doing janitorial work, as Mr. Ward stated in his evaluation. But today during second period I had no choice. Between classes my classroom was vandalized and I needed the students' assistance to clean the mess. Furthermore, second period, when he visited my classroom, wasn't a scheduled class period for me, but was instead my planning period. The students who were helping me had voluntarily given up their gym class (with the permission of their gym teacher) so that I could have an attractive room for

my next class.

I feel, if Mr. Ward was a professional, he would've understood this when I told him, and he would've returned during my class period. I also feel, if Mr. Ward was a professional, he would've visited me sooner. After all, I've been teaching at Church Junior High School for over three weeks.

What particularly annoys me (and frightens me if anyone in the department takes such evaluations seriously) is that he has checked personality, personal appearance and the like non-applicable. I would like to think that a fair evaluation covers everything and not just the negative.

Next to control and influence over the students, he rated me unsatisfactory. I assume that was because the students talked while cleaning the room. I think Mr. Ward should observe what the students are doing in the hall all day. Maybe then he would understand better what unsatisfactory control really is!

Finally, if Mr. Ward felt his observations were fair, then I would think, as a professional, he would want to discuss them with me. Instead, he hurried from the room without even saying goodby after his 10-minute visit as though he had other motives for his unprofessional evaluation.

I think it's time someone evaluates the supervisors before they start evaluating teachers, don't you?

Lathan Asks Board To Fire Steele

School board president, Richard Lathan, angered by Dr. Marshall Steele's continuous criticism of the audiovisual program, has today asked board members to fire the acting superintendent charging him with misconduct which range in seriousness from attacking the audiovisual program at PTA meetings to circulating inflammatory student-power bulletins in high schools.

In a 10-page report to the school board, which summarizes Dr. Steele's 15 years in the public schools, Lathan refers to Dr. Steele as "a dangerous madman who, if not fired, will seriously cripple public education in his scheme to become superintendent of schools." Lathan documents his accusations by charging Dr. Steele of inciting a riot, while principal at Roosevelt High School five years ago, in order to turn students against the faculty who then opposed his proposed bill of student rights. "Imagine," Lathan told reporters, "he was responsible for nearly a quarter of a million dollars in damage to Roosevelt High and instead of being fired . . . as he should've been . . . he was quickly removed from the school and promoted to assistant superintendent."

Lathan blames this on tenure, which by giving job protection to incompetent teachers and administrators increases the chances for ambitious educators to use unethical and dangerous schemes to gain advancement. "Last week's rioting at Church and nine other junior and senior highs is a perfect example of this," he went on to say. "I am convinced, after researching Dr. Steele's background, that the disturbances were carefully planned by him in order to demonstrate the 'popularity' of his student-panel proposal which he is trying to use as an issue to pressure the school board into electing him superintendent."

Dr. Steele, temporarily replacing Superintendent Fritz Spender, fired last spring for cashing the paychecks of fictitious school employees, regards the charges against him as contrivances, desperately created to turn public opinion against him. "Lathan is behaving," he went on to say, "like someone who's afraid, if he doesn't quickly fire me, I may discover something embarrassing about him and Drexel Industries."

Chapter 8

Anne tried to insert her key all the way into the lock, but couldn't get it in far enough to turn it. Annoyed, she banged it with her English book, then removed the key and watched the lead, stuffed into the keyhole, fall out, pulverized.

If she hadn't seen the teenagers break pencil points in the keyholes, she would have never solved the problem so easily and would've called the engineer. With all the repair work the engineer had throughout the school, it would take weeks . . . as it had with her broken classroom windows . . . before he could replace the lock. In the meantime, she would have been unable to keep out intruders. Relieved that this wasn't the case, she opened the classroom door, then locked it after entering.

Since the destruction of her learning centers, Anne learned something new each day about the troublemakers in the hall which made their rebellion more understandable. Several days ago it was the two boys who were severely burned in a fire started by an arsonist. Yesterday it was the girl who was drugged and raped by her older brother. And today it was the boy who was shot by his mother's boyfriend for refusing to go to the store for a pack of cigarettes. The tragedies of which she was becoming aware seemed endless, unrelieved. Saddened by them, she wondered how she could ever help them learn and realize their dreams. So many forces worked against her, turning them bitter and angry. Maybe if enough other teachers were trying to teach, her job would be easier.

But instead of teaching skills useful to students in a highly technological society, they did exactly what the school system expected them to do: They shamelessly turned their students into non-thinking, inarticulate sub-humans who in their frustration to survive would either rebel and turn to crime or beg the government for support and free education. The schools benefited from this because their failure to educate would guarantee them federal grants. The teachers benefited because they would always be guaranteed work. The federal government benefited because it could always justify taxing the working public for the various programs for the non-working public. The one major flaw Anne saw in this was: What would happen to the economy when there weren't enough producers to support the growing non-working consumers? How would the government avoid mass starvation then?

One parent summed up her frustration with the teaching practice in the public schools by telling Anne about her son who . . . when in second grade . . . couldn't even read the label on a can of beans. Upset, the mother saw his teacher and requested that her boy remain in the second grade another year. But the teacher refused to demote him, because she was convinced that any boy like him who displayed such a mature understanding of how the welfare system worked would eventually learn to read on his own. In the third grade, when he still made no progress in reading, the mother again saw his teacher and this time asked her if she would give him special reading lessons. The teacher said she didn't have time, but not to worry. Any boy with his precocious understanding of the advantages of affirmative action employment for minorities could probably read better than anyone in the class. Finally in the fourth grade, still concerned about his illiteracy, she asked the principal to assign him to a special reading class. The principal refused, warning her that a boy with his sensitivity would suffer undue psychological stress if placed in a remedial class.

"My boy is now 12," the woman complained to Anne.

"And he still don't know how to read. Why he can't even get on the right bus 'cause he don't know what the sign say. I keep tryin' to tell him to talk to his teachers . . . maybe one of 'em will offer to teach 'em. But he just don't pay me no mind. I just don't know what's gonna happen to that boy. Sometimes he really worries me."

After that talk with his mother, Anne found it impossible to reprimand him for the turmoil he caused in class. How could she blame him for being rebellious when all he was taught during his seven years of school was a lot of facts from which he could make no inductions, a lot of memorized words which made no real sense to him? She knew by his willingness to swallow all these ideas whole that he once had a dream. But how long could his dream of maybe someday becoming a teacher or doctor or lawyer remain alive when he was reminded daily by his inability to get on the right bus that he'd be lucky to learn enough to enter . . . let alone finish . . . college.

Whatever dream he might have had by now was probably reduced to a dim hope that maybe someday he might still be able to fulfill himself, that maybe someday a miracle might happen and he might learn something. It was because of this dream . . . or what was left of it . . . that Anne's experiment with her learning center had been a success. She gave her students a chance to believe in their dreams again by providing them with a blueprint for learning, and they showed their appreciation by working hard. But that was all over now. The destruction of the centers had abruptly ended their dreams and once again had driven them into hiding. How long these dreams would remain alive before dying from neglect was uncertain. After all, these teenagers were young, and, for this reason, could endure just so much disappointment before giving up completely. For all she knew, many of them might have reached their limit and might have abandoned their dreams for good.

She knew that as long as this Great American Tragedy continued she would be spending most of her teaching time trying to rekindle that dream. Yet she never remained pessimistic for long. If she could achieve her dream of being a teacher, after a wasteful public school education, so could some of her students. But what about the vast majority? There were by far too many who . . . unlike her . . . were totally stunted by their education. One non-reader in her class, spent the entire period in his macabre world where he drew strange pictures of people being mutilated by fighter planes, tanks or laser beam guns. Another slow learner who wore leg braces and transported himself about school on crutches was forced into serious withdrawal by teenagers who continuously abused him. Since she was already overwhelmed by the emotional problems of many less seriously disturbed students, she turned to Tom for help with her more critical cases. But when Anne suggested placing these students in special education classes, away from the cruelties of others, where they could work out their problems and develop their potential, he said the schools had no money for such classes. It was all being spent "extravagantly" by a racist society in middle-class public schools. Anne quickly reminded him that because of busing there were no middle-class public schools in the city. According to newspaper reports, the majority of working-class parents had enrolled their children in private schools to escape the chaos of busing, leaving the city schools to be filled by mostly inner-city students. He then made some remark which she didn't hear and walked away after expressing regrets at being unable to help her with her problem.

Like some teachers at Church, Anne was convinced, after the learning center experiment, that the only solution to minimizing the problems caused by idleness was to provide the students with work which challenged each on his level. Since she didn't want to do this by creating another learning center for vandals to destroy, she decided the best solution was to obtain good published materials which her students could carry with them. This way if a gang vandalized her room, they would be unable to destroy their work because their work would be with her students who could be almost anywhere at that moment. But more important than this, her students would benefit from this because they wouldn't be obligated to complete their work within the 50-minute-class period. Instead, they could work as long as necessary (wherever they chose) and learn as much as they were able to absorb. Since the assignments would reach each student on his level and would be self-grading, they would see their errors as soon as they had made them and thus progress from one level to another at their own speed.

Unfortunately, there was one catch to this solution: How was she going to pay for the materials? The Board of Education, which had no budget for "luxuries", preferred to spend what it did have of the taxpayers' money on new schools and expensive programs instead of on necessities. Since good materials were costly, running nearly $7 per student, and only a small number of her 170 students had such money to spare, she would have to raise the nearly $1,000 difference herself, if she wanted to teach here successfully.

She was thinking of ways of doing this when the bell rang. Like always when the new period began her attention turned swiftly to the students, rushing into the room. In order to busy those willing to work, she quickly passed out mimeographed work which some students turned into airplanes or balls and flung across the room, as she stood by the door charming troublemakers into reporting to their scheduled classes. Several girls, determined to get attention, began to ask Anne intimate questions about her sex life. One girl said she had a bet with a friend that Mr. Slaughter was fucking her in his office. The other said that Miss Harte didn't like men and was giving her pussy to Mrs. Daniels. Who was right? they asked Anne. Anne concealed her disgust and told them that nice girls didn't ask such questions. But when they laughed at her and began to tell her in detail what they claimed to have seen her do, Anne quickly shut the door and locked them from class.

Most of the boys who arrived for class sat in the back, talking. Several played cards. A few girls were giggling over a picture they were studying. Anne asked the girls to put the picture away and the others to stop talking. But none acknowledged her request. Each period it was the same struggle to get their attention. Discouraged by her failure, she told those few waiting for class to begin to read each of the five paragraphs which she had mimeographed and on the back of the paper summarize in their own words the main idea.

"Do what you can," she said in conclusion. "For those of you who find the assignment too difficult I have a similar one on my desk that may be easier."

"What-cha say?" one boy in the back shouted.

Anne raised her voice so that it could be heard over the talking and repeated her instructions.

"What paragraph?" the boy asked.

"The ones on that paper on your desk."

The boy lifted the paper and showed Anne both sides. "There ain't nothin' on it," he said, amused.

"Then please come up here and take another paper."

"Bring it to me. I's too tired to walk."

"Well, when you get your strength back, please take another sheet from my desk."

The girl with the picture asked Anne, after putting the picture away, for an explanation of the assignment. Again Anne repeated the instructions. This time her voice revealed traces of annoyance. If only she didn't need to repeat everything; if only they would listen.

Instead of allowing herself to be discouraged by this type of thinking, she once again focused her attention on her immediate goal. When she was sure that everyone willing to work understood the assignment, she asked for the homework. Some students looked at her as if to say: What homework? The majority were too busy talking to hear her. A few handed her wrinkled and stained papers. As Anne was about to walk around the class, individually encouraging the other students to start on their assignment, a girl came to her and pointed to a word for Anne to pronounce. The girl was quickly followed by a boy who looked puzzled and said that he didn't understand what he was expected to do. Again Anne repeated the instructions, carefully with examples.

"What-cha mean . . . main idea?" he asked.

In the middle of her explanation, the fire alarm rang.

All the students were in the hall, when Mrs. Daniels announced over the intercom that it was a false alarm. Only a few of her better students returned to class; the others used the balance of the period to run wild through the halls, amusing themselves breaking windows and starting fights. Anne looked at the over-turned chairs and desks in the classroom, the trampled mimeograph work with bright black footprints on them, and she slumped into her chair, saddened.

After lunch, Anne again wondered how she could raise money for materials. This time an idea came to her when she saw a boy upon entering her room stuff himself greedily with a cupcake, then walk past her with the swollen cheeks of a chipmunk. Anne noticed others who just returned from lunch were also still eating. As soon as the teenagers settled in their seats, she asked a girl, playing a radio, to shut it off.

"Oh, man," the girl with the radio moaned. "I can't now. It's helpin' my de-jest-gin!"

"Well, I have something to tell you which will really help your digestion."

Dottie shut off the radio, then said: "Okay, but it betta be good."

When Anne had the attention of the entire class, she talked briefly to them about the learning center and how much they seemed to have benefited from it. "Of course," she said. "You all know how disappointed I was when it was destroyed, perhaps as disappointed as some of you. But I believe if we all had our own books we wouldn't need to worry about that happening again."

A card player in the back of the room put down his cards. "Tell me somethin' teach," he began. "How we gonna get the money for them books? Rob a bank or somethin'?"

"Yeah," another student said. "How we gonna pay for 'em?"

"We can have a bake sale," Anne said.

Lydia licked her lips in mock hunger. "You mean you wanna have us make cookies 'n' cakes?"

Anne nodded.

"Hey, that's a *good* idea! We can make all kinds of money that way."

"Well, you ain't gonna get me to cook," one boy said. "I ain't no sissy."

"If you don't want to bake," Anne told him, "you can always prepare the advertisements."

"The what?"

"The advertisements."

"What's that?"

"That's the posters and bulletins we will need to let everyone know about our bake sale."

"I wanna collect the money," the card player said slyly.

"Shit, you steal us blind," a girl said. "All you good for is fightin'."

The card player smiled. "You know somethin', nigger. You's right." And he made a fist, then punched the palm of his other hand with it. "I can make meatballs for you."

The girl laughed. "Get him!"

"Before we get all carried away," Anne said to the class, "how many want to raise money for books this way?"

Hands shot up like flag poles. Several students raised two hands and placed one near their neighbor so that it looked as if he were raising his hand also.

"Good," Anne said, pleased. "Now all we need are the recipes and ingredients, and we are all ready to begin our little business."

"I gonna bring the sugar," Dottie said. "We got all kinds at home."

"And I gonna bring the butter," Lydia said.

Anne raised her hand to silence the class as others also shouted promises. "Before I can take pledges I'll first need to know what we're going to bake. Otherwise I won't know what we'll need."

"Hey, let's make chocolate chip cookies," Dottie said.

"I hate chocolate chips," Lydia said. "Let's make fudge."

Dottie glared at Lydia and said saucily: "Well, I don't like fudge!"

"That's 'cause you *look* like fudge!

"That's better than havin' frog eyes like you."

Lydia jumped to her feet, knocking over her chair. "Who you call frog eyes?" she said angrily to Dottie.

"Girls," Anne said. "Let's cut out this nonsense and be serious."

Lydia turned to Anne, almost in tears. "Well, then you tell that bitch not to call me frog eyes."

"Please girls . . . both of you . . . let's end this name calling. We'll never get anything done if you're going to fight."

"Hey, how 'bout us makin' everythin'?" Michael said. "Cookies 'n' cakes 'n' fudge 'n' . . . " He stopped and looked dreamy as he licked his lips.

"I don't know about everything, Michael," Anne said. "But we can try different things and see what sells best, and then make just those foods."

The card player looked at her approvingly. "You know," he said, smiling. "You ain't so dumb for a honky."

Tom Slaughter liked her plans for a bake sale and arranged for her to use the kitchen in the teachers' lunchroom. It was understood that by third period the room would be clean and available for the teachers. Lunch was the only break many teachers had from the students since the 50-minute-planning period, promised to teachers in their contract, was often spent on hall or cafeteria duty or any other duties the principal could think of to make a teacher's day longer.

To be certain the teenagers finished by third period, Anne started the baking at nine each morning. Since she didn't want her bake sale to be a "life experience" lesson of limited teaching value, she decided to use the sale as an opportunity to undermine the welfare philosophy taught in the schools by educating her students to think intelligently about the moral and social-economic advantages of a free enterprise system. Before commencing on their project, she told them that liberty depended on one fundamental principle: An individual *must* have the freedom to make what he wants and the right to own what he makes! How long he stayed in business, creating pies, shoes, cars or whatever depended on the product's value to the public over different or competing products. In the case of their bake sale, how successful it was would be determined by how many students preferred their food to their competitor's food. Because each consumer was allowed a *free* choice in a *free* market, capitalism . . . she stressed repeatedly . . . was the most democratic and moral system known to man.

To get them started on their venture, she instructed them to select recipes which would be easy and inexpensive to try, and for them to price their food low enough to attract business and high enough to make a profit. During their lunch hour, when the teachers' lounge was being used, she invited local businessmen to class to talk to her students, and she encouraged her students to visit stores after school to inquire about how businesses were run. When she didn't have a speaker at lunchtime, she had them think about such things as: What were the ways in which a free country protected the public from corrupt businessmen? What should be the rational limits on man's right to make and sell whatever he chose? What were the employee's or employer's moral responsibility to each other? How many different businesses could one successful business support? What were the advantages of a successful business to the employee and employer? And what were the qualities which an employer looked for in his employees?

In an effort to involve as many students as possible in the bake sale, she asked each student to select a job which they most wanted to do. Some chose to keep financial records, others to prepare advertisements, and still others to bake or clean up. Through division of labor, she taught them how specializing in a task of high interest could lead to efficiency and success, thus enabling an employer to spend his increased profits on expansion and hiring. For homework, she asked them to write papers on what could happen to their liberty if the government taxed the profits of their business to support expensive and impractical programs, if the government forced them to obey regulations on hiring, baking, pricing, safety standards which increased operating costs and decreased profits, or if the government ran a business like theirs and forbade them to compete with it.

Many of her students showed considerable interest in their project. Her lessons on the free enterprise system, which gave them the moral and intellectual background they craved, were beginning to change their attitude toward work. For the first time since her learning center experiment, they now wanted to learn as much as they could and become as efficient as possible at it, because now they understood (as they never understood before) that through work well-done today they were contributing to a better and more moral world for all tomorrow.

As the students worked at their given tasks, busily removing cakes and cookies from the oven or dropping doughnuts into the sizzling vegetable oil, they revealed none of the hostility or indifference to her that once was apparent in class. When she cautioned them about opening the oven door too often or standing too close to the hot burners, they listened, then obeyed. When she showed them how to spread icing to give it those soft-waves which made cakes look so delicious in bakeries, they watched her, then followed her instructions exactly. When their assembly-line creation turned out well (as it so often did), they would dance and scream for joy. But when it didn't because of some mistake in judgement, they would groan with disappointment, and Anne would have to coax them after explaining the cause of their error to be a little more careful the next time.

Like the bakers, the dishwashers also showed interest in their work. Instead of regarding dishwashing as demeaning, they thought of it positively, as an opportunity to do what they most liked to do: run their fingers through the bowls and lick them free of frosting or dough. Even the students working on the advertisements were enjoying their task. Trying to make letters as neat as a printer's and trying to draw pictures of doughnuts and cakes as life-like as a photograph seemed to be the sort of challenge they needed to keep them motivated. Although someone occasionally would finger a cake and steal some cookies, most of them (determined to see how much money they could make for books) would avoid doing that.

Within no time, the kitchen's cold and sterile look, which white walls and floors and steel appliances gave it, vanished. The agreeable aroma of cakes, cookies and doughnuts mingling with the cheerful voices of students working productively transformed the room into a warm and cozy kitchen. For Anne the sight of them working brought back pleasant memories of her childhood, baking cookies and cakes which her mother served to friends like delicacies from a Great European Chef's Kitchen. As Anne recalled these memories, she felt a very special love for her mother, for the gentle way she guided her to independence. This same special love, which Anne had for her mother, was now being offered to Anne by her students. It was evident in the way they talked to her, smiled at her, and even just watched her. Their entire being glowed and radiated a happiness which conveyed: thank you for this happy moment in our lives, thank you for showing us the way to self-confidence and independence!

Word traveled throughout the school fast, and soon outsiders began to appear at the kitchen door. At first, Anne was worried that they might disrupt the baking. But her fear quickly passed. Some of her tougher boys guarding the door were sufficiently persuasive in attitude to discourage the uninvited from entering. In the cafeteria during the bake sale, these same boys would maintain order by seeing to it that everyone formed a single file and waited patiently to be served. Occasionally Anne would have to discourage the boys from becoming too eager at maintaining order. But this was only necessary in the beginning before she told the boys to explain the rules to the others which they had to obey to be served.

Since the treats tasted as delicious as they looked, her students sold everything by the middle of the first lunch period. For them, this success gave them what each needed: the ego satisfaction of achieving! It confirmed to them (to everyone involved in the sale) that work well-done was its own reward. In order to be sure they had enough for the second lunch period, many of her students wanted to bake after lunch and leave what they made in the refrigerator for the next day. A few students objected, worried that someone might steal everything. But Anne quickly ended their worrying when she promised to lock the kitchen door herself each night and thus reduce the chances of theft.

The teachers were quick to congratulate Anne on the success of the bake sale. Some said that they didn't even mind cafeteria duty now. The teenagers were calmer, and there was less theft. Even Tom complimented her and used it as an opportunity to make a point, more, it seemed, to convince himself rather than her, about how much the teenagers benefited from "doing" rather than from "thinking".

Although Anne appreciated the staff's approval (with the exception of Tom's comment), it didn't please her nearly as much as the $150 profit she had made to date. If the bake sale continued to be so profitable, she would have enough money in several weeks to order many of the materials she needed. On the fourth day, while Anne was alone reviewing some recipes the students gave her, someone knocked at her classroom door. Usually she ignored the knocking because she expected it to be a mischievous hall-walker eager to enter and vandalize her classroom for amusement. But this time the knocking was unlike anything she had ever heard before. It was hard and urgent, and made the door tremble. Concerned, she hurried to the door, cracked it open, then peeked out. A man as black as she was white, seething like a volcano erupting, stared at her through the crack. She noticed immediately, as though deliberately searching for it, a bulge under his jacket by his left hip which she assumed was a gun. Since she had heard many stories about adults coming to school and attacking teachers for no apparent reason, she quickly concluded that, if she didn't slam the door shut immediately, she would be shot. But before she could, he placed his mighty hands on the door and shoved with the full force of his two hundred and twenty pounds, knocking Anne backwards into the room.

Her hands were still spinning, her feet still racing backwards in an effort to regain her balance when he entered the room and stood by the entrance like a huge black wall. "You Miss Harte," he said like a hired gunman verifying his victim's name before shooting.

After she stopped all motion and was able to stand erect again, she paused long enough before answering his question to consider lying. But years of telling the truth had become such a habit that it was impossible, even under the present circumstances, to lie. "That's right," she said bravely. "I'm Miss Harte!"

"What's this I hear 'bout you teachin' my Dottie to hustle."

"Your Dottie?"

"Dottie Jones, my little girl."

"I think there's been some mistake, Mr. Jones. I'm not teaching Dottie to hustle."

"That ain't what I hear. I hear you is makin' my Dottie hustle cakes in the lunchroom. That's what I hear."

"You're quite mistaken, Mr. Jones. I'm not making Dottie do anything she doesn't want to do. In fact, I've made this quite clear from the beginning to all my students. After all, it is the only way to teach my students an understanding of how business works, the basic *moral* principle behind a free enterprise system. Compulsion of any sort would only negate this principle. Now, as far as hustling, well, Mr. Jones, I certainly don't think selling a product like cakes and cookies to students who want to buy them as hustling. Although I believe . . . as I'm sure you do too . . . that a bake sale is usually a wasteful learning exercise, I am doing my best to make it profitable both educationally and economically for all of us. And just as soon as we raise enough money for materials for all my students, I plan to end the bake sale and resume with the class work. So you see, Mr. Jones, I am interested in teaching your daughter. It is my dream to give her . . . and all my students . . . the best education I can."

"Look-it-here, Miss Harte. You save all that bull shit for them other parents 'cause I know better. You say you is teachin' moral principles. Well, let me ask you this: What kinda moral principles is you teachin' that teaches my Dottie to steal sugar from home?"

"But she told me that she got the sugar with permission. In fact, I paid Dottie for the sugar yesterday with the money from the sale, and told her to give it to you. Didn't she do that?"

"She ain't done nothin' of the sort."

"In that case I better talk to Dottie and find out what she did with the money."

"That ain't what I want you to do. What I want you to do is stop teachin' Dottie to hustle 'cause if you don't I gonna call the superintendent 'n' really raise some hell."

"You can be sure, Mr. Jones, that Dottie will have nothing to do with the bake sale anymore. That's a promise."

"Just to be sure I gonna see the principal 'n' tell 'er a thing or two."

After he left, Anne thought about what Mr. Jones said and became sympathetic to his concerns. From his viewpoint, he had good reason to question her professional integrity. After all, she too would be concerned if she had a daughter stealing sugar from home for a bake sale at school.

As they both knew, many evil teachers taught in the system and derived pleasure from wasting young minds with corrupting activities. Wasn't it possible that she could have been one of those teachers, that her bake sale could have been one of those corrupting activities?

But that wasn't the case. She and all her students knew this. Yet why didn't Dottie defend her? Why did she lie to Anne about the sugar and to her father about the money? Was it really too late for these teenagers? Were they already too corrupted to be reformed?

Later that afternoon, Anne received a note from Tom requesting her to see him. Although there wasn't anything in the note to suggest it, she knew it had to do with Mr. Jones' visit.

Like Mrs. Daniels' office, Tom's was all gray-metal cabinets and furniture. But instead of Mrs. Daniels' impressive arrangement of pictures and awards to reduce the tedium of the institution-like furnishings, he had just a bulletin board with notes pinned to it, some on top of others in confusion. A bookcase was placed beneath the bulletin board with several basketball trophies holding up the rows of books. Most of the heavy furniture was against one wall, giving the room a lopsided appearance. After Anne entered, she mentally shifted the furniture around until everything found its proper place, then thought of all the hours needed to file the stacks of paper, which stood like white mountains on the desk and chairs, in the cabinets partially blocking the window.

"One of these days," he said to Anne, picking up a pile from the edge of the desk, "I'm going to make a big bonfire outside and burn all these papers." He then opened a file cabinet and dropped the papers inside.

"What are they?" she asked curiously.

"Job memos, policy changes, stuff like that," he said, as he closed the cabinet drawer. "But the only problem is that most of the jobs in these bulletins have already been filled before being publicly announced, and the changes in policy are so continuous that what is a policy this week won't be next week. So the bulletins and memos are superfluous. Sometimes I am convinced that all this information is sent out just to keep everyone busy." He then sat on the edge of the desk, very much like an athlete ready to spring into action at the call of his name and dribble a basketball across the court. But instead of wearing shorts and a t-shirt, he was wearing an attractive sports jacket and rep tie, and looked like a handsome, light-skin playboy dressed for a luncheon at a walnut-paneled athletic club.

He seemed to forget his reason for wanting to see her and began to study her as if she were something rare and exotic. Annoyed by his silence, uncomfortable by his staring, she shifted her weight to one leg and said impatiently: "Tom, I've got a lot to do before three. Why don't you tell me the reason for the note so I can get back to class."

He lowered his gaze to the checkerboard black-and-white tile floor. "Mr. Jones saw me this afternoon."

"I thought he was going to see Mrs. Daniels."

"She was at a conference downtown."

"I suppose he was angry."

"Quite."

"Did you quiet him?"

"I did . . . eventually. But in order to do this I had to . . ." He paused, unable to finish what he wanted to say.

"Well?" she asked impatiently.

"I had to promise to cancel the bake sale," he said softly.

"Did I hear you correctly?" she said, startled. "You promised to cancel my bake sale!"

"I'm sorry, Anne." He was looking at her again with his striking green eyes which were now begging her to understand. "I had no choice. He was very upset and would've gone to the superintendent if I didn't calm him."

"But Tom. What about the kids? Their materials?"

"I realize it was a big decision. But I can't have the kids stealing from home just so you can have a bake sale."

"But I borrowed the sugar with permission, and even returned the money for it. No one stole anything. Ask Dottie, if you don't believe. Ask my class! Mrs. Jones knows this. Dottie told me so a half-hour ago. Yet he lied. He deliberately lied to make me look bad."

"That's a little hard to believe," he said skeptically.

"Why should it be? Welfare cheats like Mr. Jones lie all the time. Lying is just another way to get something for nothing. He doesn't really care what goes on in the schools. He couldn't care less what I taught his daughter, just as long as it *isn't* the truth! This he can't allow, especially if it means his daughter will start learning what a despicable man he is. So he lied to you and me. He had to lie in order to get even with me for teaching his daughter that it was immoral for an able man like him to live on welfare. Dottie told me this. She told me everything they said to each other."

"That still doesn't change matters, Anne. Mr. Jones was upset, and I had to quiet him. I can't have any parent getting all excited because of one teacher. Downtown would be furious."

Images of Mrs. Daniels came to mind. Anne could almost hear the elegantly dressed educator with the orthopedic shoes say the very same thing. Angered, Anne said to the educator in a Brooks Brothers' disguise: "You mean to tell me . . . even if a teacher is right and the parent is wrong . . . the parent gets his way. It doesn't even matter if the students are learning and enjoying learning, the teacher still must obey? Well, what happens to my students? What happens to the books and materials they need for school? Doesn't that matter either?"

"Have you thought of possibly mimeographing your work like all the other teachers here are doing?"

"My," she said sarcastically. "You certainly believe in being fair, don't you?"

She then left his office. She had learned quickly that trying to reason with Tom was futile. An ambitious man like him was too busy trying to look good to his bosses to be concerned about being fair and rational.

Now because of his ambition she could no longer continue her bake sale. She remembered how much her students had enjoyed their little business, the pride they took in its success, and she knew they would be deeply disappointed. What could she say to them to soften this disappointment? Should she tell them the truth? Should she tell them that this was what could happen when the free market was regulated by bureaucrats and other such crooks?

No, she told herself. She mustn't say anything yet. She didn't want to discourage them needlessly. She had to talk to Mrs. Daniels and try to persuade her to override Tom's decision. That was the next step, the logical step. After that . . . well, after that, she could always tell them the truth.

Documents Reveal Lathan Accepted $10,000 Bribe

WASHINGTON (JDI) . . . A high federal government official today received from an undisclosed source documents which prove that school board president Richard Lathan last week was given $10 thousand by Drexel Industries for his part in persuading board members to approve the audiovisual program.

The documents, according to a federal government source, identify Lathan as well as twenty other board members in school systems throughout the country as recipients of a total of $200 thousand in bribes from Drex-el Industries. "If this is true," the official said to reporters, "and I have little doubts from the information available, this means that Drexel Industries has used payoffs to get an unfair competitive advantage in their bids for a lucrative share of the monies from federal grants to public schools."

The news broke during a hearing to fire Acting Superintendent Dr. Marshall Steele for what Lathan had once called his "Machia-vellian" practices. Lathan and Drexel Industries' executives were unavailable for comment.

Chapter 9

Rod Ramwell knew very little about his father except that he was a convicted bank robber, an inevitable fate, according to his mother, for all blacks who had dreams of a more prosperous life for themselves than welfare. Although as a child Rod had heard other blacks make similar remarks, he never gave consideration to these remarks. His mother who made a nice living "modeling" protected him from this harsh reality during his pre-school years with fascinating stories about faraway places. These faraway places were especially real for him during his childhood whenever he sniffed his mother's perfume. One fragrance would take him to China, another to Arabia, and still another to France. His favorite was a sweet-smelling flowery perfume which his mother often bathed herself in. Almost immediately upon smelling its exotic scent he would be transported on gossamer-like wings to a tropical paradise. Sometimes to forget his loneliness while she was at work he would open a bottle and extravagantly spray the perfume around the room. Within seconds, instead of pushing a toy jeep through an imaginary jungle, he would actually believe he was in his jeep driving along a narrow, unpaved jungle road in search of a lost civilization while colorful birds sang to him and strange-looking flowers greeted him with their welcoming scent.

Sometimes the magic spell of the perfume wore off before she could return home, and he would find himself exactly where he always was, on the white carpeting, staring at the red-velvet upholstery of the furniture and at the large lamps, disguised as fountains and Grecian goddesses, and in his loneliness, he would sometimes wander to the window and gaze outside. Once while looking into the alley below . . . into the strange world outside which his mother had forbidden him to visit alone . . . he was stunned by the sight of a man beating another man with a metal pipe until he gushed blood like a punctured garden hose. When his mother returned home from work, Rod was still standing by the window staring in horror at the body.

For months after that, dressed in flannel pajamas of little animals, he would insist on cuddling next to his mother in bed and would fall asleep in the fading scent of her perfume. If he awoke during the night and she was gone, he would panic. Frightened by the darkness, by the memory of that murder, he would jump from bed and search the apartment for her. Not finding her, he would cry himself to sleep on the living room floor and would awake the next morning beside her in bed, her absence during the night as unreal as a bad dream.

During his pre-school days, many men visited his mother, and, as she instructed Rod, he called them all "uncle". Since they always brought gifts for him, he looked forward to their visits. Sometimes his "uncles" would take him to the ball park or to the movies. Occasionally they would show him playing cards of women, chained to beds being sexually abused by rough-looking men. Once after returning home early from a movie, he saw an "uncle" standing nude over his mother, firmly holding her head against his hips, while he had intercourse in her mouth. In his child-mind, Rod confused what he saw with what he had seen in the alley and on those playing cards except instead of whips and pipes the weapon was a penis. To stop this "assault"Rod began to beat the man with his little-boy fists until he was whisked by his mother into another room where she began to comfort him against her warm, exposed breasts by telling him the facts of life.

His view of reality expanded when his mother enrolled him in school. Her many stories about what a wonderful place school was had deceptively left him with the impression that school was an adventure like climbing Mount Everest or shooting the rapids in a canoe, all of which he had done countless times in his imagination. But instead of finding high adventure in school, he found boredom. There was the boredom of learning to sit quietly with his back straight and his hands folded on the desk when he yearned to read and write. There was the boredom of listening to the teacher tell stories about "The Three Little Pigs" and "Little Red Riding Hood" when he was starved for stories about faraway places like China and Africa. There was the boredom of playing with toys when he was restless to capture some of his impressions of school on paper with crayons. And there was the boredom of memorizing nonsense songs when he preferred just to listen to the teacher play the piano.

At the end of the first semester, commands like "Sit down!",'Shut up!',"Stop fussing!" had become so commonplace that they often whirled about his head like an invisible wall, rebuffing knowledge. If he permitted himself to be sensitive to the special needs of the little soul inside him and he dared to try to read instead of play games or count instead of learn nonsense songs, the teacher would swoop down on him and reprimand him, making him feel stupid and foolish for attempting to be intellectually curious in the first grade. Yet despite these unhappy experiences, there were times when the lessons did interest him, and he followed the instructions exactly, thrilled by the challenge and adventure of discovering something new and useful. But these lessons would always be boldly interrupted by the teacher at the most thoughtful and important moment for him with an "Okay, little men and women, it's time now for games." If he ignored her, as he sometimes did when engrossed in his work, she would snatch his paper and would send him to the corner of the room where he would stand by himself as an example to the class of the Little Boy Who Didn't Follow Instructions!

By mid-morning or mid-afternoon he would be so exhausted from doing nothing that he would fall asleep. But these brief escapes from the regimented boredom of school were always ended by the teacher who pulled him awake by the ear and made him feel guilty with her scolding for daring to be bored in school.

After a year of this, he stopped trying completely and began to live for three o'clock (for that magic time when the big hand was on the twelve and the little hand was on the three), and he could run from school free!

For him, for many children like him, being free meant watching television after school in which boredom was the three-minute commercials between fast-paced stories, blatantly conditioning him to appreciate crime and violence. At school, especially during recess, these stories became the foundation of his learning, the source of all his wisdom. Like his classmates, he enjoyed sharing this learning and wisdom by retelling in detail of cars and planes exploding, hurling broken bodies into the air, and of honest workers, caricatured as ugly and stupid, being stripped of their dignity and earnings by dishonest parasites. Sometimes enroute to and from school he would watch teenagers set fire to vagrants sleeping in the alley or masked men with guns intimidating store owners before filling their pockets with money from cash registers, and he would enjoy these sights in real life as thoroughly as he had enjoyed them on television.

Despite his pleasure of observing life, his observations weren't enough to satisfy him. He needed a more direct contact with life, and he found the opportunity for this at school. The same imagination which once helped him discover lost civilizations or climb Mount Everest was now used to plot mischief against the teacher. At first his plotting was purely imaginary and only done when the teacher barbarously crushed him for not following the lesson or for asking too many "unnecessary" questions. But he soon tired of just thinking up pranks, and he began to satisfy his growing need for vengeance and action by setting traps for the teacher.

One of his first, and for that reason, most amusing, was tying a window plant to the teacher's chair so that when she pulled her chair in after sitting down, the plant would crash to the floor. After that he bravely amused the class and angered the teacher with new pranks each day. Sometimes he would giggle all the way home and most of the early evening, when he remembered the teacher's expression at slipping her foot into her spare shoes which she kept at school, and her toes made contact with the raw egg, or when she opened her lunch and saw all the ants he rounded up in the playground building a home in her sandwich. His favorite prank . . . one which resulted in him being suspended from school for a week . . . was hiding a black snake in the teacher's drawer. The teacher was so frightened by the sight of the snake slithering out of the drawer when she opened it that she could only stutter and point before she sank to the floor, unconscious.

In no time he earned a reputation for being a "problem". Teachers would often talk about him as though he were someone evil, someone to punish. None of them seemed to examine the repressive conditions at school as possibly the reason for his behavior. They didn't have time for such clear thinking. They were too busy devising punishment and finding excuses for expelling him. Since he liked being expelled . . . enjoyed the freedom it gave him to do what he wanted . . . he would happily provide them with the excuses they needed to send him home. Then, in the fourth grade he had a teacher who was unwilling to expel him, who instead derived sadistic pleasure from keeping him after school, writing: "I will do what the teacher tells me" until his fingers ached and he couldn't move the pencil. When he was bold enough to try to escape these after-school classes, she would grab him by the arm and twist it, smiling sweetly. "You're going to do what I say, aren't you, Rodney?" To make certain he agreed, she would give his arm a painful twist and hold the pressure until he cried: "Yes mam!"

Determined to avoid this bullying teacher, he stayed home from school for a month without telling his mother and returned to school only after an attendance officer scared his mother and him with threats that he would be taken from her and placed in a reform school if he didn't return to school immediately. For two weeks after that, he obediently did what the teacher asked, convinced if he didn't that she had the power to put him away for life. The fear of being separated like his father from the familiar (his mother and the security of their home) and of being turned over to the unfamiliar (a prison with bars and angry guards) made him docile and willing to endure the unendurable. But by the third week, he stopped trying to cooperate, because no matter how hard he tried he still was unable to please. His teacher in her search for faults (his inability to sit straight enough and answer her questions fast enough) would viciously insult him with her booming voice, until he felt angry enough to kill.

Instead of killing her, he persuaded his classmates to rebel. Since he was bigger and stronger than most of them, he found them easy to persuade. But it wasn't just his physical superiority which was responsible for his success. Many of them . . . like Rod . . . were angry and frustrated for similar reasons, and were quite responsive to Rod's persuasion to free themselves of her control over them.

On cue from Rod, they would fling books at the teacher, set fire to the bulletin board or wastebasket, and knock plants off the window sill. In anger the teacher called homes, kept them after school, forced them to write nonsense sentences, and viciously humiliated them with her sharp-tongue reproaches. But such efforts as these to control them only fed their discontent. To protect herself, the teacher began to turn the class against Rod by telling the students whenever she deprived them of gym or recess or kept them after school, that she was punishing them because of Rod, of what he was making nice boys and girls like them do. In this way, and by generously rewarding them with extra long recesses when they were good, she was able to weaken Rod's power. The climax came one day when she decided to entertain the class with seamy stories about "those diseased street-walkers on Pranklin." One boy, interrupting the teacher, pointed at Rod and said, grinning: "Hey, teach. You's talkin' 'bout *his* ma!"

Hurt and embittered at having his mother brought up in conversation like that, Rod leaped on the boy while his teacher shoved chairs and desks aside to give them room to fight. Before Rod's fists could decisively connect with the boy's body, the boy delivered a powerful blow which painfully reshaped Rod's nose. As Rod sat on the floor, blood rushing down his mouth and chin, the teacher smiled and said almost too pleasantly: "Next time, Rodney, be more careful who you fight." The sight of her smiling, looking so pleased as though she wanted exactly this to happen to him, angered him so deeply that he attacked her, swinging furiously at her face and chest, until the principal, summoned by the children's excitement, pulled him away from the startled teacher.

As the teacher tried to explain to the principal what had happened, Rod and his classmates shouted her down and accused her of hitting Rod first and breaking his nose. Parents learning of the incident from their children protested the teacher's brutality and in this way forced the principal to transfer the teacher to another school to bring peace to the community. Stories about the fight, which spread throughout the school, convinced teachers to regard Rod as a terror-to-be-avoided. Eager to enjoy the new freedom this reputation gave him, Rod organized a gang which soon developed a talent for extorting money from students and which in the sixth grade "persuaded" several girls to sell themselves to their classmates. Although some teachers knew about his activities, none did anything about it because they found it more practical to teach nonsense rather than morality.

In junior high school, though, he met a teacher (a very

attractive teacher named Mrs. Park) who wasn't indifferent
to his behavior, and one day, while reprimanding him for
his obscene gestures in class, he decided to teach her a
lesson and give her just what he believed she needed. But
before he could do anything more than rip her blouse, she
escaped.

Because of insufficient evidence, Mrs. Park's charges of
attempted rape were dropped. Rod made certain of this by
requesting classmates to swear that she had tried to seduce
him. Angered by the principal's willingness to believe Rod
and his friends, Mrs. Park quit, accusing Mrs. Daniels of
encouraging delinquency, and was replaced a week later by
Anne Harte.

Rod was standing on Pranklin Street thinking about
Anne, when he saw her across the street, waiting for a bus.
The wind was playing games with her skirt. One moment it
would wrap the skirt around her, the next moment inflate it,
and now beat it against her so that it clung to her thighs like
a pair of tight pants. The sight of her shapely body,
silhouetted in cloth, stimulated his imagination, and in his
haste to make contact with her, he was almost hit by a car
while hurrying across the busy street. When he finally
reached the spot where she was standing, she was gone and
was moving to the rear of the bus which was driving away.

A few moments later a station wagon stopped at the
corner. His mother, after lowering the window, called to
him. Behind the wheel was a graying blond-haired white
man named A. Theodore Livingston III who at 35 had
squandered an inheritance on women and gambling and
now at 38 earned his living making "arrangements" for his
wealthy friends.

His mother . . . one of the most popular "arrangements"
. . . was sitting in the front seat with her feet tucked
underneath her skirt. She looked feminine and expensive,
nothing like the tough prostitutes in short pants and leather
boots on Pranklin Street, and was smiling happily as
though she had just been named Miss Black U.S.A. She
seemed a little high. Maybe from too many pills and too

much alcohol. Maybe from not enough sleep and too much hash. He didn't know. He didn't care. Seeing her with her white pimp made him angry.

"Where you been all week," Rod asked abruptly.

"New York."

"Why the fuck you wanna go there for?"

" 'Cause Theo gone 'n' fix'd me up for a big blast. Honest, honey. You shoulda seen all them fine folks there. All of them famous 'n' rich 'n' givin' money'way just like it was popcorn."

Rod thought of that party, of all those white men lining up for their turn with his mother, their turn for something black and different. He felt a tightness in his throat as though something was lodged there. When he suddenly swallowed, it was painful, almost as painful as it had been that day several years ago upon learning that Theo had taken her off the streets in order to groom her for her introduction to White Society. Rod now wanted to reach through the open window and grab Theo's snow-white throat and squeeze it until it turned as purplish-blue as his v-neck sweater. Instead, Rod stepped back from the car.

He knew there would always be men in her life. She had made that clear long before she met Theo. Good paying jobs were scarce for black women with no education. So she did what she could do best, and they ate and lived well. He understood this, even as a child. Yet he still hated her for always leaving him for other men.

"Hey, what's wrong with you?" she asked Rod. "Cat get-cha tongue?"

"Nothin' wrong," he said softly. "But I wish you tell me where yer goin' sometimes."

"Hey, don't-cha tell me you is turnin' into one of those mama boys," she laughed drunkenly.

He glared at her furiously, stunned into silence by her remark.

"He's right, Ida," the white man said. "We should've told him. It isn't fair to leave the boy for a week without telling him what you're planning."

Her brown eyes sent out hot flames from under her painted eyelids. "Don't-cha start tellin' me what I should say to my boy," she said savagely to the startled white man.

"Easy, Ida," he said, obviously not wanting to get involved in a family quarrel. "I like the boy. In fact, I'd even like him to work for me someday. Now there isn't any harm in being nice to him, is there?"

"You be nice to 'em," she said. "But don't-cha get no ideas of gettin' my boy in yer racket. I can take care of 'em myself." She turned to Rod. "Ain't that right, honey?"

Rod didn't say anything. He thought of all the men she would have to bed to earn that money. He remembered her coming home occasionally with mysterious illnesses which required many visits to the clinic, and he became ashamed of himself for accepting her money. But what could he do? How could he stop her? They needed money to live, needed it for all those expensive dresses and perfumes and jewels she liked.

"Rod," she said impatiently. "I's talkin' to you. Now is you gonna talk to me or is you not?"

"What-cha wanna hear me say? Hello stranger. Nice seein' you 'gain."

"Okay, okay! Next time I gonna leave a note or somethin'. Now hop in here nice 'n' gentleman-like 'n' Theo will drive us home in style." She was smiling sweetly, as sweetly as the prostitutes on the street when they approached him. He had once loved that smile, even trusted it. But not anymore. Now he knew what that smile meant. It was just a smile to lure him close before springing loose the trap that made him feel the pleasure of loving her and the pain of losing her again. He stepped back, bumping into a lamppost.

She opened the car door. "Well, get yerself inside," she said.

"I wanna walk."

"Walk," she said, startled. "Why?"

" 'Cause I wanna."

Her smile disappeared without any trace of ever

existing. She was alert, sober, eying him as she might a stranger of whom she wasn't sure. Then she lowered her gaze, fidgeted with the small beaded purse on her lap as though she had seen something in his expression to make her feel sad and contrite.

"What's wrong, honey?" she said gently. "Don't-cha like yer ma no more?"

His heart skipped a beat and thumped against his chest. She was reaching out to him. He wanted to embrace her, hold her tight as he had so often as a child. But he couldn't. He just stood there, hardening like cement, and waited for them to drive away.

"Say somethin'. At least say yer glad to see yer ma. Common, Rod. Please?"

But instead he looked away. He couldn't face the emotion which she was trying to extract from him. Disappointed, she closed the door and said to Theodore: "Can't even be nice to the boy no more. It still don't do no good." They drove off, leaving him behind.

As he continued along the street, he saw a woman in black hot pants and a white sweater, leaning against the entrance to an abandoned store. Although she had a young, trim body, her face which was scarred and heavily painted to conceal the scars was a face of someone middle-aged. She was eating French fries.

"Wanna date, honey?" the woman said, smiling.

He went to her and took her last French fry. "You think you can take what I got?"

She looked at the bulge in his tight trousers. "There ain't nothin' you got that I can't take."

He grabbed her by the arm and pulled her into the abandoned store. "Well, let's get on with it then."

"Not in here we ain't!"

"Why not?" And he pointed to an old mattress by the entrance. "We got a nice bed. What more you want?"

"Well, that ain't for me. I ain't no two-bit whore. You wanna a little, then let's go to a hotel."

He yanked her close, then held her head firmly in place

by the neck. "But I wanna have my pussy here."

She tried to break away, but he merely tightened his hold. "Okay," she said, no longer resisting. "But let's see that green stuff."

He threw her down on the mattress. "I got somethin' better for you," he said. "I got me nine inches!"

She rolled to the end of the mattress, sprang to her feet, then removed a knife from her boot. Pointing the knife at him, she said savagely: "If you come close, I gonna cut that pretty face of yers *real* good!" She cautiously moved toward him to the door. "So you just stay nice 'n' still while I go on my way."

But before she could pass Rod and reach the door, he blocked the door, then kicked the knife from her hand, sending it flying arc-like to the floor. Angered, the woman charged him, her nails turning into claws, ready to strip the skin from his face. With one hard punch in the face, he sent her head first to the mattress unconscious, blood oozing from her mouth. He then ripped her pants off and brutally entered her. As he pounded hard and furiously, he thought of his mother in New York, of all the men in her life. He exploded with a violent tremor which lasted long after his ejaculation. Afterwards, he tore open her sweater, removed the money from inside her bra, then spat on the still-unconscious prostitute and left.

Birdie became unexpectedly sensitive to odors, especially familiar odors like tobacco and liquor. To prevent vomiting, she would leave the windows open at home and would empty the garbage or spray the bathroom and kitchen whenever she smelled anything even faintly disagreeable. Sometimes just the thought of eating, particularly fried foods, swimming around in grease, would nauseate her. Foods like toast and crackers and liquids like juices and ginger ale, on the other hand, didn't, and for this reason, became her main source of nourishment. At first she blamed her squeamishness on something she had eaten the night before, but stopped when by the second week she started to vomit as soon as she lifted her head from the pillow.

Although she usually felt better by noon, she never was able to eat much without becoming bloated and full. Since she noticed no change by the third week (and was even losing weight and demanding more sleep), she decided to see a doctor. But like many inner-city teenagers, she procrastinated because of her exaggerated fear of doctors, inculcated in her at school by visually disturbing "educational" films which, instead of teaching her ways to avoid diseases, scared her with horror stories of what these diseases could do to the body.

She was emptying her stomach of a whip-cream-like liquid on the school steps, splattering her shoes and legs in the process, when she finally decided to go to the school infirmary that morning. The decision was partly made for her by Anne Harte who was descending the steps while Birdie was vomiting. With the English teacher to guide her, Birdie went to the infirmary, very much like a frightened patient being wheeled into an operating room.

Rod's heartbeat quickened at seeing Anne. Her blue skirt which gently outlined her body moved easily like a slow peal of a bell when she walked. As he followed her to the office, he couldn't keep his eyes off her body, off her skirt which moved back and forth hypnotically. The sight of this movement brought to mind images, violently exciting images of other women. He thought of these other women, of how he would like for them to have been Anne, when he stepped and slipped on a banana peel in the hall, just as Anne disappeared into the office.

Ernest McQueen was standing near the office, dressed as usual in his tight levis and a t-shirt with a cluster of keys hooked to his black-leather, silver-studded belt. At first glance he looked masculine like a member of a motorcycle gang. But the illusion, created by clothes, vanished upon seeing Rod recover his poise and stand erect again. Almost instantly, the French teacher's mouth opened wide enough to swallow a cucumber, and he stared with fascination at Rod's crotch. Startled, Rod lowered his gaze to see what he saw and smiled at seeing his penis which had come alive for Anne boldly press against his trousers as though trying to break through the material. Amused by the teacher's interest, Rod lifted his gaze just as the teacher—with exaggerated manliness—approached. Rod was about to tease Ernestina (as the boys called him) about his little gold earring . . . his insignia in his right ear advertising his masochism . . . when Ernestina, obviously encouraged by Rod's amusement, said unexpectedly: "Five dollars for your thoughts."

"Not enough," Rod said smiling. He then squeezed the bulge and watched the teacher's expression twist into a caricature of lust.

"Ten bucks," the teacher said, obscenely licking his lips.

Rod removed his hand and made the bulge throb. "You ain't even gonna get a lick for that."

Rod walked to the stairs, then turned toward the teacher who was standing in the same spot where Rod had left him. With a mischievous smile, Rod stroked the bulge in his pants, slowly, sensually, as though masturbating.

The teacher trembled. "Twenty-five," he shouted. "That's my last offer."

Rod laughed, then ascended the stairs.

The students, clustered together by the toilet, chattering, suddenly separated into two groups. Rod strutted through the separation like a giant oak flanked on both sides by seedlings. One boy, not seeing Rod, stepped in front of him. Without warning, Rod knocked him aside and sent him flying off-balance to the floor.

Birdie who was standing by the locker watching, cringed when she saw the boy stretched out on the floor. For a moment, it was like seeing herself on the sidewalk after Zelda had knifed her. Ever since her knifing, she found herself turning inward, withdrawing, at the first sign of violence. Once again she became uneasy and fearful, a feeling she had almost forgotten since she started seeing Rod.

"What's wrong with you?" Rod asked Birdie

She didn't reply. She was still thinking of the knifing, of all the unnecessary violence and hate which she knew so well, and she began to ask herself questions too profound for her to answer. Why? Why did everyone hate and hurt each other? Couldn't they love one another just a little?

"Ain't you gonna talk?" he asked, interrupting her thoughts.

"I's thinkin'."

"Well, don't. It makes you look ugly."

"Thanks!"

He smiled and his toughness softened. She preferred him when he smiled because his broken nose seemed to straighten and he didn't look so mean. He was staring at her now, obviously impressed with the way she was dressed. Her clothes no longer clung to her body, emphasizing it with bold, vulgar lines, but instead gently concealed her figure, giving her a mature, feminine and quietly sexy look. Holding her head a little too high to be comfortable, she smiled at Rod, delighted by the effect her new attractiveness had on him.

"Where you learn to dress like that?"

"From Miss Harte."

"Why Miss Harte wanna dress you up so nice?"

" 'Cause she a nice woman."

"Is that who you been seein' lately?"

"Maybe."

"What-cha mean . . . maybe?"

"Just what I say."

He cocked his massive head to one side and looked at her, amused. "Ain't you gonna tell Rod where you been hidin'?"

"No!"

She then worked the combination to her locker. Before she could open it, he turned her around and pressed her against the locker. He then stroked her long, slender neck with his fingers, gently, exquisitely. Her body responded immediately to his touch, to the wonderful sensations which centered in her neck and generated to other parts of her body like tiny, marvelous electric shocks. He smiled, pleased by her responsiveness, and he pressed his hips against her, forcing her to feel and enjoy feeling his readiness.

"How 'bout bein' nice to Rod," he said. "You ain't been nice to Rod for a long time." And his voice was smooth, without any suggestion of roughness. It was the same smooth voice which had broken down her resistance many times before, the same smooth voice which had made her want love. She had wanted to believe in him and had been ready to, until he had unexpectedly tried to force her to sell herself to the boys at school several weeks ago. "So how 'bout it, Birdie? How 'bout a little ?"

"No."

"Why?"

" 'Cause I ain't interest'd."

He then nibbled her ear. The marvelous sensations which shot through her were magnified beyond endurance by the pressure of his body against her body. "Tell Rod you wanna a little ," he whispered. "Common, Birdie. Tell Rod."

She wanted to yield to him. She was ready, as ready for him as he was for her. She was about to tell him this, scream it, when in his excitement he squeezed her breasts too hard. The pain was sharp, almost as sharp as Zelda's knife, and it cut through her pleasure swiftly. She jerked away from him and banged against the locker which protested by filling the hall with a metallic scream. She then turned to open her locker.

"Common, Birdie," he said as he playfully rubbed his hips against her. "Rod needs a little ."

She knew as long as she submitted to him she would never have to worry about being bothered by the girls. But now . . . still feeling the pain in her breasts . . . she believed submitting was by far worse than anything she would ever face alone. Determined to free herself of her psychological dependency on him, she reared her hips and knocked him off balance, then hung her jacket in the locker.

"Hey, why you so mean to Rod," he said, startled. "Didcha forget already how good he fucks you."

"Sheet," she said, remembering how rough he was, how quickly he left her afterwards. "What's so good 'bout the way you fuck?"

She removed her books from the locker, then pressed them proudly against her breasts. With cool alertness, she studied Rod for his reaction and became annoyed when he laughed. She remembered how the other teenagers had laughed at her yesterday. It was the first time since she started seeing Rod that anyone had dared. She didn't need to be told why they or now Rod did. She once believed, as many inner-city blacks still believe, to want to be educated and smart was foolish. No one ever hired a smart black. But that type of thinking all ended after she had met Miss Halsted. It had all ended because she now had a dream, a beautiful and wonderful dream.

"What-cha gonna do with them books," he said, still laughing. "Starta fire?"

"I gonna read 'em," she said coldly. "That's what!"

"Shit, who you kiddin'?" he said. "You can't read."

His amusement shattered her pride, made her determined to salvage the remains. "Wanna bet?"

"Yeah!"

She opened a book to the first page. But when she saw all the unrecognizable words, she hesitated.

"See. I told-cha can't read."

She angrily jerked her head up. "Well just you wait."

"Well, read!" he taunted her.

She then looked at the picture. Pretending to read, she made up a story to suit the picture. He listened, impressed. Afterwards, she slammed the book shut. Pleased by his surprise, she said smugly: "There. You see. Birdie *can* read. She ain't dumb like you."

"Rod ain't so dumb," he said sensitively.

"Why don't-cha read if you so smart?"

" 'Cause that's for punks."

"You just sayin' that 'cause you stupid."

He looked at her, puzzled. "Why you wanna be smart all-of-a-sudden?"

" 'Cause I wanna get a good job."

"Now what kinda job you gonna get? Be maid for them white folks?"

"Not Birdie. Birdie gonna work in a nice office like Miss Halsted 'n' support her baby good."

"What baby?" he asked, surprised.

"The baby I gonna have."

"You pregneck?"

"I is."

"Whose baby you pregneck with?"

"Now whose do you suppose?"

"My baby?"

She nodded.

"You ain't jivin' me," he asked suspiciously, "is you?"

"No, it's true. I know for a fact 'cause the doctor told me so." And she proudly rubbed her stomach.

"Hey, let me feel too." He reached under her sweater and touched her stomach. "I don't feel nothin'."

"That's 'cause it's too soon."

"There's one way to know for sure."

"How's that?"

"I gonna put my hand right up that pussy 'n' feel till I touch it."

"No you ain't," she said, pushing his hand away. "You ain't never gonna come near my baby."

"Why not?"

" 'Cause my baby ain't gonna be like you."

He seemed to enlarge before her into a giant, too big for confinement in such a small hall. "That's what you think," he said in a voice as powerful as his build. "He gonna be just like Rod 'cause Rod done made 'em."

"Well, Birdie gonna raise 'em 'n' he ain't gonna be nothin' like you."

"Shit," he said. "What sort of man is my baby gonna be with a drunken pa like yers 'n' a bitch like you to raise 'em?"

"You wait," she said. "You see."

"Shit, I see a lot. I see you whorin' round Pranklin to support yerself while yer baby wonders where you is. That's what I see."

"Birdie smart. She ain't gonna hustle niggers for money. No sir. Not Birdie. She gonna get a good job 'n' bring up her baby right."

"Yeah, well I know diff'rent 'n' if Birdie got some brains she gonna get abortioned."

Horrified, she shielded her stomach with her books. "Nobody gonna kill my baby," she said. "He's mine 'n' nobody never gonna take him 'way from me."

She backed away from him as she spoke, eying him suspiciously, as though she expected him any moment to hit her in the stomach; then after moving out of his reach, she turned from him and ran down the hall to her English class.

Lathan Resigns Position
Pending Outcome of Trial

Richard Lathan has today resigned his position on the school board pending the outcome of his trial next month in which he will attempt to prove his innocence of accepting a $10 thousand bribe from Drexel Industries for influencing school board members to spend monies from a federal grant on an audiovisual program.

During an interview with reporters, Lathan vehemently denied the authenticity of the documents, presented several weeks ago to a high government official in Washington, and claimed that the information in them were "pernicious lies" conceived by his enemies to destroy him and Drexel Industries. "My enemies are worried," he told reporters, breaking his two-week silence on the corruption charges, "that if the audiovisual program is successful, schools will no longer need those multi-million-dollar federal grants for frivolous education programs any more. This, of course, as we all know, would upset many administrators, especially Dr. Steele, because it could mean an end to their jobs or their pet programs."

Dr. Marshall Steele, who had always been critical of Lathan, today refused to challenge Lathan's statements. "The poor man is upset about his predicament," Dr. Steele told reporters. "Therefore, I don't think it would be fair to condemn him for anything he might say about me or my colleagues at this time."

Chapter 10

Like most women, Anne attracted her share of men. A friendly smile, a polite hello, or a glance which lasted a second too long was all they often needed from her to approach her and gallantly offer their service or friendship. Since most men regarded her as an object to conquer solely for their immediate pleasure, she often discouraged them the moment their interest became primal. She had no intention of repeating her experience in high school by becoming another victim of some unprincipled thug. As far as she was concerned, she needed more from a relationship than just physical love. She needed a man committed to the same values as she, a clear-thinking man of integrity with great and humane goals. Such men, unfortunately, were scarce. They weren't always on the streets, in the grocery store, or on the bus looking for someone to take home and bed, for sex in itself wasn't any more important to them than it was for her. If she sometimes smiled at a stranger or stared a little longer than usual, it was only because she sensed by his attitude a quality which she admired and which set him apart from the masses.

Such was the case with Tom Slaughter. Like many men interested in her, Tom was attractive and athletic-looking, with a casual manliness in dress and style which encouraged women to try to change him. In this respect, Anne wasn't any different from the other women in his life, and she responded to him with the same immediate desire. But unlike most of his other women, her interest in him ran deeper than the superficial, to the very core of his being which he guarded with the same skill he once guarded his basketball from his opponents. She sensed the reason for his self-protection was because of an inner conflict of values which he sometimes revealed with a painful grimace when certain key issues were discussed. At such times he would become silent and would drift out of reach into his own private world of thought, making it difficult for her to communicate with him. She knew as long as he guarded himself from her she would never be able to work successfully with him at Church, and her job at teaching would become even more difficult. But just as important as that, she knew, if she didn't free the man . . . the giant whom she believed was locked inside him . . . she might not meet the man she dreamed about, the man who could energize her life by scaling mountains with her.

Determined to free the man, she dated him during her first weeks at Church and enjoyed dating him as well. Eating delicious and exotic foods under a crystal chandelier with heavy silverware or watching a gifted performer demonstrate his talent perfected by years of dedication to his art made her temporarily forget in his presence their differences. At such times, in this attractive setting, she would convince herself that he wasn't as she had often suspected, interested in her as some status symbol like his expensive sports car and clothes; instead, he took her to these places to please her and to reward himself in a relaxing setting for completing a hard day of honest work. At least, this was what she wanted to believe when they were out together. But when they were alone in the privacy of her apartment, she would think differently the moment he refused to talk about the performance or their dinner, and began to talk instead about the many white faces he recognized or the pleasure he got from being warmly greeted by certain headwaiters or ushers.

She knew it wasn't easy for him being black, growing up rejected in a superficial and cruel white world; his sad green eyes made prominent by his light skin, often confirmed this. But instead of objecting to this superficiality and cruelty, he accepted it and eagerly sought to be a part of it. His dedication to the illusions of the Great American White Dream made her soon realize how impossible a friendship with him was.

Sometimes in desperation she would wait for those vulnerable moments, usually after serving him his favorite candlelight dinner at home, to break through his superficiality. At such times she would talk about students like Rod, and how important it was that they were properly reeducated to respect others' rights and taught some skills useful to them in the highly technological world which they would soon face. But instead of being persuaded by her argument to assist her, he remained loyal to his dream, promised to him by Mrs. Daniels, and he tenaciously played his administrator's game by shifting the responsibility of students like Rod to her and of defending his administrator's point of view with arguments which were intended to make her feel guilty for any failure at reaching them. His commitment to this game, which probably protected him from any guilt for his own indifference, angered her and she was about to end their friendship by telling him this when one evening his attitude changed and he began to reminisce about his struggles to escape the slums. His reminiscence, for the first time, revealed an understanding of himself which was absent in the past. He talked differently about those "foxy white ladies" he had once dated, not as white symbols to impress others with, but as ruthless and sexually depraved white bitches out to use him in bed. While he talked about the models and Mrs. Daniels' policies and everything else that bothered him, he emerged from his Brooks Brothers' white camouflage as he began to reveal the soul of a man too honest to play the game anymore.

Impressed by what she hoped was the emergence of the Renaissance man, she told him that maybe together they could reach some lofty heights. Maybe at Church they could do something which would really correct the racial injustice so that the next generation wouldn't suffer as he had. He smiled softly, nodding, and reached for her hand. But this gesture of friendship, this attempt at establishing a union, was done with such calculated timing that she responded to it with suspicion, as though what he had just said was all a line to prepare her for seduction. After quietly withdrawing her hand from his, she promised him with her smile and by her attitude that if he were sincere that they could easily enjoy a long and wonderful friendship. Although he was apparently annoyed, he tried to conceal his annoyance with politeness.

That evening after he left, she went to bed confident that she would soon learn whether Tom was a scoundrel or a Renaissance man. His future actions and decisions at school, she was sure, would clearly identify him.

Rod Ramwell had suddenly changed his tactics with Anne. Instead of openly soliciting her as before, he would follow her, waiting in the background, it seemed, for that moment when she would be psychologically ready for him to approach. Sometimes he would step out of a crowd and stare at her, smiling in his bold and lustful way, as though she were a nude in a magazine centerfold, a sex symbol to be coveted and used. At such times, he would hold that look just long enough to intimidate her and make her tremble. Afterwards, he would disappear in the crowd like an apparition, leaving behind no trace of ever existing except the raw memory of his lust. Othertimes, during the confusion of a student fight in the classroom, someone would unlock the door, and he would enter and stand by the door, watching with amusement while she vainly tried to bring order. Then, like a sergeant screaming orders to recruits, he would command the teenagers to sit down. After they were all sitting and waiting for class to resume, he would stare at Anne for several moments, again in that same lustful way, then leave, whistling.

At night she would remember that look and would have

reoccurring nightmares in which a huge bird with penetrating, evil eyes would slowly circle overhead, then unexpectedly descend, its legs extending from its feathered body like out-stretched arms. Just as she was about to reach the safety of her apartment house, its huge hook-shaped talons would sink into her shoulder blades and lift her high into the sky, then release her over a mountain peak which pierced the sky like an enormous spear.

She would always awake at this point perspiring and trembling, and would cling to the pillow for comfort.

Since there were meals to prepare, dishes to wash, desks at school to clean of obscenities, lessons to prepare and bulletin boards to redecorate, she never thought about the dream for long during her waking hours. She would have probably continued busying herself with her job without Rod or her dream having any significant effect on her if, one day while alone taping posters to the wall, Rod hadn't entered her unlocked classroom. Frightened by the sight of him, by the hard and dangerous look in his eyes, she jumped down from the chair she was standing on and stepped behind it, hiding her legs, at which he was staring, from view.

"What do you want?" she asked nervously.

"I wanna talk to you."

"I'm busy."

He strutted toward her, stripping her of clothes with his look and making her feel nude and vulnerable. "But I wanna talk to you."

She lifted the chair off the floor a few inches, but dropped it when she realized it was too heavy to use as a weapon, and frantically looked for something else. But all she saw nearby was some tape.

"Stay away from me," she warned him, as the distance between them shrunk. "If you don't, I'll . . . "

He shoved the chair aside, then stepped in front of her. "You what?"

His awesome size, his passion (thinly concealed by a smile) left her feeling powerless. "I'll . . . I'll go to the police," she said weakly.

"Why you wanna do that." His smile broadened and made the crooked line of his broken nose seem suddenly straight. "Rod wanna be yer friend 'n' make them bad kids obey you."

She stepped backwards, but was halted by the wall. "I don't need your help, thank you."

He extended his arms and pressed his palms against the wall, trapping her between his arms. He then moved closer, touching her just enough so that she could feel the hardness of his muscular body against her. "Maybe he know different. Maybe he know how crazy you been for help."

She tried to slip under his arm, but he lowered it and forced her upright again. "Let me go, Rod," she said. "You're making me angry."

"Rod don't wanna make you angry, teach," and his voice was soft and gentle, deceptively charming. "He only wanna make you happy."

"Then leave!"

"Now you know that ain't how Rod wanna make you happy. He wanna give you all nine inches of his dick 'n' he ain't gonna leave 'til he do. That's how Rod wanna make you happy."

Once again she tried to escape. But his extended arms were like steel which she couldn't budge. She was about to scream, but before she could, he smothered her lips with his.

Trapped in his arms, she experienced the same terrifying helplessness which she knew during her rape in high school, accomplished now, not by drugs as then, but by Rod's almost super-human strength. She suddenly hated men, men like Rod who felt they could take her at will as though they had been divinely endowed with this right.

She released this hate when his arms began to crush her body like a vise and his mouth began to devour her lips like a vacuum pump, and she slammed her heel on his toes as violently as he claimed her, then shoved him away. As he grabbed his foot and hopped around, swearing, she ran to the desk and grabbed a pair of scissors. The scissors were of long, gleaming steel, the expensive type used by tailors or seamstresses, and in her hand, as dangerous a weapon as a butcher's knife.

He was saying something to her, as he limped toward her. But she didn't hear him. She only heard her heart thump as it sent blood rushing angrily through her, and a voice in her brain scream: "Kill him, Anne. Kill the bastard!"

"Get out," she said in a low, savage voice when he approached her. "Get out and don't ever come back again!"

"But teach," he said, not taking his eyes off the scissors. "If you ain't nice to Rod, he gonna talk with them kids some more. Now you don't wanna have Rod tell them to make more trouble for you, do you?"

"So you're behind all that destruction in my room?"

He grinned boyishly, proud of himself, of his power to cause her so much grief. "Them kids listen good to Rod, don't they?" He stepped toward her cautiously. "Now why don't you give Rod a little pussy? Then he see that everythin' go nice 'n' smooth for you."

She tightened her hold on the scissors and waited for him to take another step closer, so that she could swiftly plunge the scissors into his hard flesh. "Come closer," she thought. "Come just a little closer, you bastard!" And when he took another cautious step forward, her hand holding the scissors sprang toward him, toward his groin. But he arched his body and jumped away in time. "Hey, is you crazy?" he asked, startled.

"Get out," she said. "Get out before I *kill* you." And for a moment after saying it she was as shocked at saying it as he was at hearing her say it.

"Okay, teach," he said, backing toward the door. "But I's awarnin' you. Them kids is gonna be meaner than hornets for not bein' nice to Rod. You wait. You see!"

After he left, she was still holding the scissors as before, fiercely, ready to attack. But now as she held it, she was conscious of her intent, of the dangerous anger rushing through her to her hand, to her tight grip on the scissors.

Frightened by the powerful emotion which had briefly consumed her, she let the scissors slip from her hand to the floor and backed away, both, it seemed, at once without lifting her gaze from her hand.

That night she had the same nightmare; only this time she didn't awake until after she was impaled on the spear-like mountain peak.

Tom Slaughter saw Anne walk toward him. But when she avoided his gaze and started to walk past him without even saying hello, he stopped her by extending his arm like a patrol boy halting traffic. Instantly she glanced up at him, annoyed, as though he degraded her and the entire human race by existing, and by so doing she made him feel angry and guilty and . . . looking into her blue eyes . . . weak. But then that was how he always felt near her. Her well-timed remarks or her sharp, disapproving glance cut through everything he lived for, dreamed of, and made his ambition seem ugly and dangerous. He never met a woman like her who could cause so much personal upheaval with such swift, on-target disapproval. Sometimes he found himself pulled in one direction by his ambitions and in another direction by her. Why couldn't she be happy with him as he was? Why did she have to be like Joy and always find fault with him? But more important . . . and this was the question which most disturbed him lately . . . why did he still want her, knowing what she was, what she did to him?

But as he looked at her, at her womanly body quietly silhouetted by her clothes, the answer to that question seemed too obvious. He dropped his arm, took a long side step and stood in front of her. "Aren't you even going to say hello?" he asked, shielding her in his shadow from the harsh hall lights.

She ignored his question as though the answer to it was too obvious to verbalize, and said, more as a command than as a request: "May I pass please?"

"For Christ's sake," he said, angered. "Will you stop all

this shit and tell me why in hell's name you've been avoiding me?"

She was ready to reply. He could see the sharp edge of her remark form on her lips, ready to spring loose on target, when a student passed. "Tom, I don't want to talk about it," she said, holding back what she wanted to say. "Let's just forget it. Okay?"

"All right," he said, agreeing eagerly. "It's a deal. We'll go out for dinner tonight and smoke a peace pipe."

"I'm sorry, Tom. I don't want to see you again."

Although this was evident by her attitude, it still struck him hard, hearing it. Any moment he expected her to say that she was kidding. But when she didn't and the meaning of her words had sunk in, he felt his expression grow heavy and sad. "So it's going to be that cut and dried," he said.

"Now may I pass, please."

He didn't move. He couldn't move . . . not if it meant losing her. Somehow he had to persuade her. But what could he say? That she was right? That he was a fool, being brainwashed and used by the establishment against his own race? Was this what she wanted to hear? If it were, he wouldn't say it, not as long as it meant he would have to sacrifice his future for her. Why couldn't she understand how important a job downtown was to him? Why couldn't she accept the good with the bad, and give him a little support?

She tried to walk around him. But he merely stepped in front of her again. She tired a second and a third time. Each time the towering administrator blocked her movement with the same ease he had once blocked basketball players from making a basket.

"Tom," she said angrily. "I'm in a hurry. Will you *please* let me pass?"

"Not until we finish talking."

"There's nothing to talk about. You already know how I feel about you and your loyalties to Mrs. Daniels."

"I suppose you'll be happy if I forget my ambitions and

remain in the ghetto like just another nigger on welfare with whom you can play angel of mercy."

"That isn't what I want of you, Tom, and you know it. Your ambition has nothing to do with our differences. It's just the way you go about furthering your dreams . . . the principles you abandon . . . just so you can guarantee yourself a job downtown someday."

"Now I have no principles."

"What else can I think when you protect boys like Rod? Do you honestly believe that transferring him to Mr. Gates' English class will stop him from bothering me? Well, Tom, if you do, you're naive!"

"What would you prefer me to do? Pulverize him with my will?"

"That isn't what I prefer. What I prefer is for you to counsel him. If you respect me that's the least you can do."

"I've done all I can. That's why I transferred him."

"I should've known better than to turn to you. How could you counsel a sex deviant when you need counseling yourself."

He looked at her stunned. Her remark plunged to the core, tearing through protective defenses, and she exposed him to what he was, to what he *knew* he was: a black con man cleverly trying to rape his white women! "My," he said bitterly. "You white folks really love to cut us up, don't-cha?"

"Now will you excuse me."

She walked past him, but he reached out with his long arm and pulled her close. He squeezed her arm tightly, partly out of need to hold onto her, partly out of anger for hurting him. But when she complained of the pain, he released his hold and said gently: "How about it, Anne. Let's smoke that peace pipe. Okay?"

She looked away, refused to be persuaded. "I'm sorry, Tom," she said. "It's too late." She then shifted her body weight. "Now will you excuse me. I must go."

He stepped aside and watched her walk away into the harsh light of the empty hall. After she left the building, he felt an urgency to run after her and promise her anything. Yet he couldn't budge. Her price was too high.

And now it was over. Did Tom really believe that it could have been any other way? She was so white, so very white! How could she ever understand him? His ambition?

And yet . . .

And yet there were moments in which a look, a smile or a word would bring them close. It was never like that with the others. There was always a wall. But not with Anne. With her he could actually feel the closeness sometimes.

Then the wall went up, and it was over. Couldn't it have been different, just a *little* different?

School Board Exonerates
Dr. Steele of Misconduct

School board members today exonerated Dr. Marshall Steele of misconduct after unanimously agreeing that Richard Lathan's report, charging the acting superintendent of being a "dangerous and ambitious madman," was obviously contrived in retaliation for Dr. Steele's opposition to the audiovisual program.

"In view of the evidence against Lathan and Drexel Industries," one board member told reporters, "it is impossible to give credence to his charges against Dr. Steele. In fact, most of us feel that Dr. Steele by having opposed the program from the beginning has revealed an exceptional courage and intelligence which we hope in some meaningful way to reward."

Dr. Steele told reporters that he was pleased to learn of the school board's decision and expressed hope that its members would have time to consider seriously his suggestions for a student panel.

Good News

Chapter 11

Anne Harte knew that before she would ever submit to Rod Ramwell she would have to believe that the world did belong to thugs like him, and her only hope for survival anywhere would be to seek protection from the strongest and most ruthless and live out her life under his dictatorship. Even then she would probably still rebel against enslavement to some Neanderthal mind. For years she had fought to live free of such tyranny. She wasn't going to change easily and submit. Somehow she had to stop Rod from demanding from her what she felt no man had the right to demand.

After school she went to a nearby police station and spoke to the white sergeant who listened to her story about Rod and his friends with interest. Occasionally as she summarized her nearly three months at Church, he would interrupt her and ask her to elaborate on some of the embarrassing things Rod had said and done. At first she provided this information reluctantly with a blush. But when she realized how much pleasure he was obviously deriving from her embarrassment, she just stopped talking and stared at him, startled.

He shifted his long, phallic-looking cigar to the side of his mouth and leaned back in his chair with the masculine conceit of one who was aware and proud of his own beauty. He then looked at her, not as a policeman interested in Law and Order, but as a man interested in bedding her. Anne closed her unbuttoned jacket and concealed her legs from view under the chair. Her only thought as she sat near him, observing this six-foot-four-inch, two-hundred-and-forty-pound Servant of the People was that she was wasting her time talking to him.

"This Rod Ramwell sounds like quite a problem," he said. "But unfortunately, from what you tell me, there isn't much I can do about him. After all, pretty women like you are harassed everyday by guys on the make. Who can prove who's responsible? Still, there is something I can try. It's a little unconventional, but it may work."

"How unconventional?" she asked, suddenly suspicious of any assistance he might offer.

He flicked his cigar ashes into an empty coffee can, then leaned toward her. "What I had in mind was this," he said in the casual voice of a man, certain of his appeal to women, "I could come around school occasionally . . . you know, in uniform . . . and say hello. Maybe even take you out to lunch now and then. Once the word got out that you were seeing a cop those boys would stop bothering you just like that," and he snapped his fingers for emphasis. "Of course, it would be strictly a favor. Naturally I wouldn't expect anything in return, unless, of course, you insisted." And he smiled slyly, as handsome men accustomed to seducing women of their choice often smiled when sugar-coating their sales pitch.

She rose gracefully, then said: "Apparently you don't take my concerns very seriously. You believe that I'd be quite willing to 'offer' myself to you rather than Rod, because you think of yourself as bigger, stronger and handsomer than the boy. Unfortunately for you, you are wrong for two reasons, Sergeant Connally. One, I refuse to be coerced into submission by any man, and, two, I regard any man who tries exactly what he is: a *thug!*"

She then marched angrily back to school, three blocks away, and entered the principal's office. Before addressing Mrs. Daniels, she paused long enough to recall her conversation with the principal about the bake sale. She remembered how quickly Mrs. Daniels had defended Tom's decision to end the sale and blame Anne for "turning a student against her father." No thought was given at the time to right or wrong. All Mrs. Daniels was concerned about was censoring Anne for teaching a girl values which contradicted the values of her morally corrupt father.

Could any principal who behaved like this be sympathetic to Anne's problem with Rod? She doubted it. In fact, as she stood in front of the elegantly dressed principal, Anne was certain the principal would shift the blame for Rod's behavior to Anne by cleverly twisting the facts to make her appear as some evil teacher. Anne was prepared for this, as prepared as she had been unprepared for the sergeant's attitude, and she was ready to protect herself in whatever way necessary. But to her surprise, Mrs. Daniels wasn't her usual self, that cultured educator who stifled with a charming smile and an attitude of authority any resistance to her point of view. Instead, she listened to Anne as a sympathetic colleague, committed to helping others. This new Mrs. Daniels emerged unexpectedly when Anne told her how Rod was using his friends to pressure her to submit to him. The Cultured Leader of Church responded immediately with what seemed to be sincere concern, leaving Anne with the positive impression that her problems with Rod were over, for good!

But whatever positive impression she might have had during her talk with Mrs. Daniels passed with time. Despite Mrs. Daniels' promise to talk to Rod, Anne saw no change in Rod's behavior. She wondered if Mrs. Daniels spoke to Rod or if, instead, she just forgot to. Several times she wanted to talk to the principal again, but she procrastinated to give Mrs. Daniels just a little more time.

Since she was unable to teach even occasionally during her regular class periods because of all the disorder and was spending most of her class time repairing the damage the students did to her room, she decided for the benefit of her better students to schedule voluntary classes twice a day during her lunch and free period. From the start, she liked these classes, even though they left her no time for herself during the school day, because the students revealed a sincere interest in learning. Their dedication to ideas filled her with energy and courage to remain at Church, and it sent her home at night eager to prepare lengthy lessons which would broaden their knowledge. She began to think of these students as the next generation of doctors, writers and scholars who would someday re-shape the world, wipe out ignorance and tyranny. For these precious few, she knew she'd never give up teaching. Yet despite her thrill of exploring ideas with them, she could never fully relax and enjoy her two classes quite as much as she had wished.

Invariably in the middle of a lesson, she would remember that predatory bird in her nightmare and any moment expect its talons to sink into her flesh and carry her away from class. Usually the memory of the nightmare would return in the disguise of Mrs. Daniels whose voice would unexpectedly enter her classroom through the intercom system.

"Attention *all* teachers," the principal would say, sounding more like a raucous bird than a prominent and cultured educator. "In ten minutes there will be a hall check. *Repeating:* in ten minutes there will be a hall check."

With a flip of the office intercom lever and a few impersonal words into the microphone, Mrs. Daniels swiftly would interrupt Anne's class, and in the process agitate unrest throughout the school. A moment ago the noise outside was tolerable, almost unnoticeable, but that all quickly changed when gangs of students began to stampede through the halls, kicking doors and shouting obscenities as they sought hiding. Earthquake-like tremors shook the building causing Anne's class to quiver with excitement. Whatever enthusiasm her students might have shared toward her lesson, disappeared. She wondered if she would be able to set off again, at least this period, those marvelous little explosions in her students' heads which she had so easily set off before the announcement.

Not even these students, her best students, had a

chance, she thought, discouraged. How could they in all this turmoil?

Anne was about to give up trying to teach for the period and eat her sandwich which was still in her brown bag on her desk when one of the eleven students present spoke. "Man, them niggers sure is tearin' up the school," a girl with bright red pigtails said. Then she added with large, innocent brown eyes: "Don't nobody care?"

"Maybe not, Sally. Maybe that's exactly what some educators want them to do. That's why they frustrate them so deeply so they *will* riot!"

"Now why would they wanna do that?"

Anne fingered the gold heart, chained to her neck, with the picture inside of Jeremiah Lee. "Because there are people in this world who are insane and evil, and not much different than those men we talked about yesterday."

"You mean Hitler 'n' Mussolini 'n' all?"

"That's right, Sally. Like them, these 'intellectuals' also want power, and they hope by causing rioting in the schools to get it."

"How's that gonna give 'em power, Miss Harte?"

"Think about it for a moment, Sally. Suppose this rioting got worse? What could happen then?"

A hand rose straight up, then moved from side to side like a windshield wiper. "Yes, Randolph."

"I know what's gonna happen. Somebody is gonna call the cops. *That's* what's gonna happen."

"But suppose the police couldn't end the rioting, and there was raping and even killing. How would your parents . . . the community, even the nation . . . feel about it then?"

"They'd be mad as hell."

"Okay," she said to her students. "They'd be mad, and justifiably. What then?"

"They gonna demand the schools get tough."

"Exactly," she said. "Now how will the schools get tough? What sort of leader will be appointed, what sort of ideas spread, and most important, what freedoms and rights will you lose as individuals?"

"Attention *all* teachers," the principal said over the intercom, as Anne's students began to respond to Anne's questions. "There will *now* be a hall check. All teachers are expected to go into the halls immediately!"

Anne glared at the intercom. For the third time today, her classes were interrupted by hall checks. Angered by this, she marched to the door, then pulled it open so hard that it knocked against the blackboard and bounced back hitting her.

"Oooh," one girl said. "Is Miss Harte mad. I never seen 'er that mad . . . never!"

As Anne stepped from the room, she was unexpectedly knocked off balance back into the room against the door by a rush of teenagers entering. When she recovered her balance, she saw Rod standing before her. Teenagers poured into the room, moving around him, and began to destory bulletin-board displays and overturn chairs.

"Hey, teach," Rod said, winking. "Them sure is nice legs you got."

Mrs. Daniels was working at her desk on her atten-dance chart, extending a green line, when Anne entered and slammed the door behind her. Startled, Mrs. Daniels dropped the pen she was holding and looked up. She then removed her glasses, chained to her neck, and let them bounce against her chest. "*Miss Harte!*" she said, shaping key words into a lady-like fist. "I would appreciate it if..."

Anne stepped in front of Mrs. Daniels' desk and leaned over it, placing her hands flat on the attendance chart to the principal's horror. "Mrs. Daniels," she interrupted, "don't you think it's time you do something about those rampaging delinquents?"

Mrs. Daniels eyed her dangerously with cold, gray eyes. "In case you haven't noticed, young lady," she said, "I *am* doing something. I'm having hall checks as you suggested some time ago."

Anne stood erect after removing her hands from Mrs.

Daniels' desk and noticed Mrs. Daniels stare at Anne's fingerprints on the immaculate attendance chart. "Funny," Anne said, and the anger in her voice matched the coldness in Mrs. Daniels' eyes, "I get the impression that you are only trying to make a show of doing something."

The makeup of Mrs. Daniels' well-cared-for face cracked as her flesh creased into a grimace. "How dare you make such a statement!"

"Then stop announcing the hall checks ten minutes in advance so the kids can hide. All this is doing is discouraging teachers from wanting to end this silly game of hide-and-seek with the kids." She then added, as though it were her main point: "Or is that what you want to do? Discourage teachers from teaching? Encourage students to destroy?"

"Miss Harte! You've been in the public schools long enough to know our policy."

"Which one? You have so many."

"I'm talking about the one regarding suspension!"

"What makes you think anyone has to be suspended? Why not keep them after school instead and re-educate them? Or would teaching students to respect others' rights and property be too much to ask from you?"

"Did I understand you right?" she said, horrified by Anne's suggestion. "Did you say I should re-educate them?"

"We should, Mrs. Daniels...all of us!"

"Miss Harte, most of us work very hard from nine to three. Don't you think working us overtime, doing what good teachers should be doing in their classes daily is asking a bit too much?"

"Some problems here, Mrs. Daniels, can't be solved by teachers alone. They need support from you and other administrators."

"Judging from your complaints lately I get the impression that you aren't happy here."

"You're right, Mrs. Daniels. But that's because you allow kids like Rod Ramwell to wander free, molesting me at will."

"After my talk with Rod the other day, I am *thoroughly* convinced that *you're* responsible for your problems with Rod."

"No, Mrs. Daniels . . . it's you . . . your administration . . . by willing an atmosphere of chaos which allows him the luxury to do whatever he likes, unchecked."

"*Miss Harte!* You're making it very difficult for me to be *patient* with you."

"If you don't do something about Rod, if you continue to permit his friends to bother me, I will really do something to make you lose your patience."

"Well, *thank you* for the warning," she said, trying to smile as charmingly as she had in all the pictures of herself framed on the wall. "Now you'll have to excuse me. I have *work* to do."

Student Panel Approved
By Board of Education

Board members today have approved Dr. Marshall Steele's proposal to form a salaried student panel made up of two representatives from each city school. The monies from the $10 million federal grant to the public schools, reserved for innovative programs, will be used to pay each student on the panel $50 a month as an incentive to cooperate with principals to resolve school issues.

During a newspaper inter-view this morning, Dr. Steele referred to the decision to implement immediately the student panel as a bold, wise step toward eliminating the terror in the schools. "I am proud to be part of a school system which has the wisdom to try this innovative idea," he told reporters. "I know as a result of this decision we will see in the next few weeks major changes in attitude among students toward their schools and toward learning."

The millions of dollars rai
Pl————d '—— '---' ‐broug
unmoved by pr' life object
furdi

Chapter 12

Ernest McQueen was always prepared for unexpected romances. He believed, if he weren't, he might not remain as popular as he was, and his most memorable romance, which to this day he still daydreamed about, would never have been consummated in the park toilet with the two uniformed policemen.

During his entire "gay" life, he had never met anyone . . . especially two policemen . . . who could "rape" him from front and rear so savagely. His pleasure was unlike anything he had ever experienced before, and it didn't diminish significantly afterwards when he was handcuffed nude to the urinals. In fact, he rather enjoyed this final act of sadism because he had the opportunity to share the details of his romance, while his body was still warm to its memory, with the "gay" Baptist minister who discovered him.

Because of the unusual nature of this encounter, his subsequent romances with strangers . . . though sometimes interesting . . . seemed tame and ordinary, and lacked the tense excitement he knew and loved with the policemen. There was a sameness to his sex, an "Okay fag, bend over!" attitude with only a few really exciting moments for relief. But all this changed for him when he discovered while teaching how willing his male students were to try anything for a little money. His special classes at Church in the storage room with precocious boys whom he eagerly freed of sexual inhibitions proved surprisingly satisfying. This was particularly the case when the counselor discovered him and two boys together. Seeing the counselor stare at them in shock caused Ernest to unexpectedly ejaculate as he acknowledged for the first time the probable consequence of his corruption: being imprisoned for statutory rape with horny, sadistic convicts!

Mrs. Daniels was late for the faculty meeting again. Several teachers were irritated. One remarked jokingly that the principal was afraid to leave her locked office until the students departed for home. Tired, Anne paid little attention to the conversation and sat near the library stacks and kicked off her shoes. She was pleased that Mrs. Daniels was late. Her tardiness gave her a chance to relax and to forget her encounter with Rod today.

She looked about the library as if for the first time. As many times as she had been here, it still amazed her to see neatly stacked books and attractive bulletin boards, walls free of graffiti, and desks and chairs unmarked by knives or magic markers. If she hadn't heard the conversation nearby of discontented teachers, she would believe she was somewhere else . . . not at Church . . . but at some other school untouched by vandalism.

Seeing this order made Anne angry. While many teachers screamed and fought their way through six hours of disorder, the librarian spent her day alone in her office reading books and listening to classical music on the FM radio. Despite teacher complaints, students seldom were admitted into the locked library except occasionally in small groups, chaperoned by their teachers. Anne was convinced that Mrs. Daniels preferred this. Keeping an attractive library was one way of maintaining an illusion of Church.

Look around you, Mrs. Daniels could say during her weekly faculty meetings in the library. See how well-kept everything is. Surely you teachers are mistaken about your complaints. Of course we have *problems* at Church. Doesn't every junior high school our size? But vandalism and gang fights . . . *really* now! At *Church*?

It was easy to agree with the principal in the relaxing setting of the library. Who had the energy after six hours in the classroom to disagree? It was much simpler to pretend that the six hours in the classroom were a dream and the 45-minute faculty meeting was reality. But today some of the teachers weren't placid. They were restless and talkative, angry and ready. Anne closed her eyes, too tired to hold them open, and listened to the conversation nearby.

"It's been three weeks," one teacher was saying. "And my broken windows still haven't been repaired."

"Well, at least your heating unit works. That's more than I can say about mine. Ever since those damn kids jammed paper and pencils into it my room's been a deep freeze. To this day I'll never understand why that heating unit wasn't placed out of reach. Doesn't that architect know anything about kids?"

"You think that's bad," another said. "Why I have ten live jets in my science lab with no central controls. Just the other day some joker turned on all the jets, then . . . as the gas escaped . . . removed some matches!"

"What do you expect in a school system like ours?" another teacher said. "Rational planning? Well, if you do, you're naive. According to a friend downtown, the Board of Education is spending millions to build seven new schools like Church and in order to fill them with students, they will be closing usable old schools. What makes this so outrageous is no one has set aside any money for buying books or basic supplies. I guess all those Great Thinkers downtown want are pretty new schools for kids to destroy."

The door flew open and a teacher ran into the library. After recovering from what obviously had been an exhausting race through the halls, she shouted: "God, do I have some dirt!" She ran her fingers like a comb through her disheveled hair. "Miss Ernestina McQueen was transferred."

Anne listened to the details of Ernest's disgrace with

shock. To her the conversation was strangely unreal . . . a grotesque distortion . . . like a reflection on a fun-house mirror. Surely she had to be dreaming what they were saying about Ernest. After all, would so many taxpayers contribute so generously to education if teachers like him were kept and teachers like Ralph Clearwater were fired. But what about her experience . . . all those years in school being mentally tortured . . . was that a dream also? She was sure it was when she saw Mrs. Daniels enter, coifed and dressed as expensively as usual, and heard her soothing voice address the teachers from her poised position in front of the stacks.

She was talking about the student panel, underlining with her golden voice certain key ideas. She elaborated on these key ideas so eloquently that the panel sounded like the *absolute* cure to all school problems. The danger of giving the panel the right to evaluate teachers or to decide on the curriculum or to set up school policies or to make decisions on hiring and firing was hidden with charm and tact. Like other teachers, Anne was calmed into passivity by the sound of her voice and the warmth of her smile. But when Anne heard the names of the two students selected for the panel, she suddenly bounced to her feet.

"*Who* did you say those students were?" Anne asked. She was sure her voice penetrated the consciousness of every teacher present. They all sat up on the edge of their seats, alert, looking at Anne, then at Mrs. Daniels.

"I've already *mentioned* their names, Miss Harte," she said, accentuating select words in her lady-like way.

"Please repeat them."

"Very well," she said. "Since you *insist*." But now the melody of her voice, the charm of her smile lost its splendor. "The two students are Rod Ramwell and Casey Clark."

Anne gasped in horror upon hearing the names of the two students and understood immediately the reason for selecting them. By teaching teenagers hate instead of right and wrong, by permitting them to get what they wanted by terror tactics instead of by productive work, the schools had succeeded at creating misfits who solved problems through violence rather than by reason, and now, after years of preparing them for this type of barbarism, the schools were ready to test the results. What would follow, if Anne didn't first turn the teachers and public against the panel, would be a terror campaign, led by Rod, with Anne his first victim. As Mrs. Daniels' and Anne's gazes locked together, her ingratiating smile which a few moments ago had won confidence had become unexpectedly demented and evil.

"Well, one thing is obvious, Mrs. Daniels," Anne said. "You certainly don't believe in being subtle about your motives."

"I don't know *what* you're talking about?" Mrs. Daniels said innocently, and her entire expression changed into an almost convincing look of innocence. "Would you like to explain yourself, young lady?"

"I mean, Mrs. Daniels, what good reason could you possibly have for appointing two thugs like Rod and Casey to the panel?"

"It's very simple, Miss Harte. Because I think they'll make *able* leaders."

"Have you forgotten what Rod tried to do to Mrs. Park?"

"According to the counselor's report her charges were unfounded."

"What about my charges? What about the charges of some of my students? Are they unfounded too? Is that why you've ignored them and given him and that gun-toting-sadist Casey Clark such power?"

"*Obviously*, Miss Harte, you *don't* understand how important it is to have teenagers like Rod and Casey on our side. Their ability to influence their peers can be *very* useful."

"Useful in what way, Mrs. Daniels? To teach their peers to get what they wanted by using violence and fear?"

"Right on, sister," one teacher shouted.

"Yeah, tell her like it is," another added.

Mrs. Daniels became uneasy and turned to Tom Slaughter for assistance. But Tom instead of springing to his feet, defending Mrs. Daniels as trained, was totally engrossed in his own thoughts. Ever since Tom's last conversation with Anne, he moved about the school preoccupied, as though he were wrestling with himself, with some deep problem which Anne's rejection had finally made him face. Mrs. Daniels, obviously disturbed by Tom's "strangeness", looked at him annoyed, then released her annoyance by saying with a lady-like fist to Anne: "I'm sure, Miss Harte, that you don't honestly believe that we . . . *concerned* educators . . . have any intention of teaching our students anything of the sort."

"But you forget, Mrs. Daniels, *you concerned* educators aren't thinking very clearly if you overlook the destruction to sound values such a panel will cause. What you're saying to the majority of students: You want recognition, then become mean and tough like Rod and Casey!"

The counselor unexpectedly spoke. "I believe," he said, "we spend too much time thinking about the negative and not enough time thinking about the positive."

Mrs. Daniels beamed with delight. "You're quite right, Mr. Little. More time should be spent counting our blessings!"

"Mrs. Daniels, at Church, thanks to you, we haven't any blessings to count."

"That's telling her Annie," one teacher shouted.

"It won't do you any good to protest," the principal said. "Whether you like it or not I must set up the panel and by Dr. Steele's guidelines. So you'll just have to accept the inevitable." She then added in her gloriously cultured voice. "We are now moving into a new age . . . "

"Indeed we are," Anne said gravely. "One where our schools . . . our very last hope for guaranteeing a healthy and free society . . . are being destroyed by administrators who want to create a society made up of ruthless thugs."

Mrs. Daniels glanced at her watch. "Well, I see our time's up," she said, and eyed Anne dangerously. "I guess that takes care of our meeting for today." She then walked from the library quickly, before anyone could detain her.

Anne turned to the teacher next to her. "How will I stop her? I can't let her . . . let that Steele . . . set up that panel. There's got to be a way of stopping them. But how? How?"

"You better think of something fast. Mrs. Daniels . . . as you know . . . can be a vindictive bitch!"

The newspaper reporter was scribbling on a pad, almost verbatim, everything Anne said, while the photographer sipped his coffee and gazed out the window of the teachers' lounge. The reporter who was young, just out of journalism school, seemed eager to get a good news angle, something which would make exciting headlines for his first by-line story. Since the panel was news, he concentrated on it and drew out Anne's opinion with question like: How was the panel selected? What was the reaction of the teachers? The kids? Do you think it will solve the problems?

Anne answered all his questions fully with insight. She told him about the reputation of the two teenagers selected, the attitude of administration, and what all this would do to public education. As she talked, he scribbled down everything quickly, in such haste that he neglected to shape his words legibly.

The photographer, on the other hand, seemed bored with the conversation. He was a veteran newsman who viewed life through a camera, looking always for the best angle to shoot. "Pictures," he had told Anne earlier. "That's what sells papers. Good pictures of people in action." He set his coffee cup down and broke his silence by turning to Helen, one of the young teachers who supported Anne's plan to go public with her grievance, and he asked her: "Where are those kids going?" He pointed to a thick mass of bodies trampling across the snow-covered field, paving a road through the snow.

Helen leaned over the back of the sofa, one foot touching the floor, the other bent and resting on the sofa. "Pranklin Street, I suppose." She was looking at the handsome photographer next to her, smiling almost too flirtatiously. The photographer didn't seem to notice. He was all business.

"What are they going to do there?"

"Probably break a few windows, rape an old lady. You know, fun things like that."

The photographer grabbed his camera, attached his telephoto lens, then opened the window and admitted the icy breath of late November. Leaning half-way out, he began to snap pictures in rapid succession. Afterwards, he closed the window, rubbed his hands together to warm them, then sipped his coffee. Helen tried to draw him out in conversation, but he had vanished safely into his own thoughts and couldn't be reached. Helen shrugged her shoulders, rose, poured herself some coffee, then stood next to Anne.

Anne heard the familiar sound of students in the hall. At first the sound was barely audible, but as the students neared the lounge, it grew louder like hundreds of feet stamping each time a little harder in place. As the students ran past the lounge, she could feel the floor tremble and see the coffee pot and wall pictures dance crazily.

The reporter stopped writing in his pad. "What's that racket?" he asked, his ears twitching.

"That's just the kids running through the halls," Anne said. "Sometimes when they're really bored they have gang fights with knives and all."

The photographer sprung to his feet. "That might make a great picture."

"I'm sure it would," Anne said. "Why don't you take a few?"

After the photographer and reporter left, Helen smiled. She obviously enjoyed their intrigue. It gave her the opportunity to rebel against a system which so thoroughly frustrated her. But unlike Anne she lacked the courage to do it alone. She needed others to lead her, and she now waited to hear Anne's next move with girlish impatience.

"Well," Anne said, "if that newspaper expose doesn't

get a few administrators jumping . . . nothing will."

"Oooh," Helen said, giggling. "I think we're so evil." Her eyes sparkled mischievously like a girl who was trying on her mother's nylon undergarments without approval. "I just love this idea of yours, Anne. It's so . . . so underhanded. Wait until Mrs. Daniels reads the paper. She'll be furious."

"I think Dr. Steele will be the one who'll really be furious. After all, the panel was his idea."

"Wouldn't it be fantastic if you were able to turn the community against them?"

"I hope so," Anne said. "It's about time someone raises hell and makes those administrators accountable for their decisions."

"You're absolutely right," Helen said. "Now let's go into the halls. I'm just dying to see what's happening there."

"You know, Helen. I never thought you were so devious."

"Honey, you don't know the half of it."

The photographer and reporter were talking to some teenagers near the auditorium when Helen and Anne located them.

"Hey, take my picture," one girl shouted to the photographer. "I wanna be in the paper too."

"All right," the photographer said, kneeling. "But do something. Don't just stand there, staring. *Do* something!"

The girl turned to a glass showcase nearby and flung her book at it. Just as the book hit and shattered the glass, the hall briefly blazed with light.

"Now take mine," one boy said, stepping in front of the camera.

"No, take mine," another boy said, shoving the first aside.

"Hey, nigger. Who do you think yer pushin'?" the first boy said.

"Don't-cha call *me* nigger!"

"What-cha gonna do 'bout it?" The first boy inflated his chest and pressed it against the other boy's chest. "*Nigger!*"

A fist flew through the air. It was quickly followed by

another and another. Teenagers swarmed around the fighters, ignoring the photographer, and screamed with delight. "Kill the motha-fuck," the crowd began to shout. "Knock the shit outa 'em."

The photographer pushed through the crowd and began to blind the fighters with bright blasts of light.

"We've got to stop him," Anne said to Helen. "He's getting those kids all worked up."

"Look at the brighter side, Anne. Think of the great front-page story it'll make." Helen then sniffed the air with exaggerated keenness. "Do you smell smoke?"

Anne sniffed the air. "Oh my god! It's coming from the auditorium."

Helen ran to the door and looked inside. "Good grief!" she said. "I better get help."

The photographer ran into the auditorium first, then Anne and the reporter. Soft red flames creeped up the blue stage curtains, turning them black almost instantly. A white smoke curled to the ceiling. Like a heavy cloud, it moved into the auditorium, bringing with it the offensive smell of burning cloth. Anne stared in horror at the fire, while the photographer ran around the auditorium snapping pictures. As Anne started to leave in search of the nearest fire alarm box, she saw Mrs. Daniels standing by the door, glaring furiously at her. Before Anne could say anything, Mrs. Daniels pivoted and walked briskly away.

The auditorium like the classrooms was cheerfully painted in keeping with the philosophy of making school a happy place. Rows of chairs were alternately painted in reds and blues and yellows and greens. Most everyone sitting in the colorful chairs near Anne and Helen were talking about the fire, about the fireproof curtain which now hung like uneven and ragged strips of black ribbon from a soot-covered ceiling.

Anne stared at the hardwood stage floor, partly destroyed to its cement foundation and felt guilty. It'll cost a fortune to repair the stage, she thought. And it was all her fault. Oh, why did she invite those journalists to school? It would have been so much better if she had gone to the newsroom. But no, she wanted them to come here . . . take pictures. And now this!

If the reporter had written an honest article, one which explained the causes for the problems here, she wouldn't have felt so guilty about the fire. Instead, he concentrated on the violence and destruction, excusing it with cliches about frustrated teenagers demanding a voice in school affairs, without once making reference to anything she told him. It seemed to her as if the newspapers weren't interested in the truth, only in sensational headlines exposing the violence to maintain high circulation. Realizing this made her feel used, even responsible for a fire which served no purpose except to confuse the community to the real causes behind the madness in the schools.

Anne knew, as long as the community remained uninformed about the facts, school conditions would continue to decay, unchecked, and educators like Dr. Steele and Mrs. Daniels would be able to strengthen their power-hold with dangerous "solutions". What made this so disturbing to Anne was that she felt so helpless now at reversing this. All those great dreams which had motivated her to accept the job were vanishing. How could she teach when many teachers and administrators discouraged it, when board members were bribed, when newspapers needed sensational headlines? Yet she knew she had to do something. She could never let them . . . the establishment . . . give the world to thugs like Rod. What chance would any decent, honest person have to survive anywhere if this happened?

Mrs. Daniels walked to the stage microphone. Upon seeing her, parents and teachers stopped talking and turned their full attention to her. Outside Anne could hear the click of heels come near the auditorium door. A few parents, after entering the auditorium, tiptoed to the nearest vacant seat. The tips of their shoes, soaked from the snow, squashed noisily against the tile floor, leaving behind tiny puddles.

Mrs. Daniels waited for everyone to settle in their seats, using the silence and the waiting to draw attention to herself and to the stage. Anne suspected that Mrs. Daniels was holding the emergency meeting here instead of in the more intimate surroundings of the library, because she wanted to focus attention on the fire damage and force everyone to pass judgment on it.

As she stood on the stage, so aristocratically aloof, there seemed to be a wide territorial separation between her and the crowd. But this separation shrunk when she spoke into the microphone. Her cultured voice rushed from the speakers, spaced in each corner of the auditorium, and enveloped everyone gently. "Many of you . . . after reading the paper . . . are deeply upset about the fire yesterday. Tonight," she said, carefully emphasizing key words, "I would like to examine the *causes* of it and hopefully offer a solution." She then paused and smiled. Her smile was so warm and ingratiating and like her voice so gentle that Anne could feel herself relax, even trust the woman. "But first let's *pledge* our allegiance to the flag and *sing* our national anthem."

After the opening, Mrs. Daniels said: "I know that most of you . . . like myself . . . are concerned about the violence at Church. But before we can discuss it, we must realize that *many* of Church's problems are adjustment problems which *all* new schools share in the beginning. Like *all* new-school-adjustment problems, *ours* are caused by a conflict of philosophies."

Her voice was smooth. Her words rolled from her beautifully cared-for lips effortlessly. How could anyone doubt the wisdom of a woman who spoke so well, looked so sincere? The crowd was mesmerized by her every word.

"Church . . . as you know . . . was built to *symbolize* a very important philosophy of education, a philosophy which recognized the students' *right* to be free. Of course, there are *certain* traditionalists here among the faculty who are opposed to such a philosophy. These traditionalists believe in repressing students, *depriving* them of their freedom! Right now at Church many of the problems we face are the result of these two extreme philosophies in conflict. So before we can end the unrest here . . . we, the concerned parents and teachers . . . must decide what we want Church to be. Do we want it to be *repressive* or *free*? The future of your sons and daughters . . . of Church . . . rests on your decision tonight."

The crowd broke their silence with gentle conversation. Everyone seemed to be considering Mrs. Daniels' eloquent isolation of the problem. Some seemed relieved to learn the problem could be solved so simply by merely deciding which direction Church should go. The problem didn't seem nearly as complicated as some had imagined. Should Church be the symbol of freedom or repression. It was very simple. Too simple for Anne.

Anne rose and said: "Mrs. Daniels, none of us here, I'm sure want to repress kids. Instead, we want them to grow into rational and independent adults who will be productive and happy, and masters . . . rather than slaves . . . of their environment. What we want to repress . . . if repress is the right word . . . is their violent and destructive behavior toward others and . . . for their own safety . . . toward themselves."

"Go to it, Anne," Helen said.

"As you may know, intelligent educators realized a long time ago that the best way to do this is to teach students respect for others' rights and properties, and to gently guide them toward satisfying their basic intellectual needs. But instead of doing this, you (and 'concerned' educators like you) have deliberately frustrated them in their quest for self-fulfillment and have permitted them the right to release this frustration in whatever way they choose. What you call freedom . . . which has resulted in this outpouring of disorder at Church . . . is nothing but enslavement. After all, how can anyone be free as long as he is at the mercy of his deviation and not his own will? Now to complete the job, to complete the malformation *your* freedom created, you have selected two of the toughest thugs at school to be leaders. In short, Mrs. Daniels, freedom to you is really a mockery of that concept, and can only lead to tragedy for anyone foolish enough to take you seriously."

No one seemed to be considering Mrs. Daniels' eloquent isolation of school problems anymore. They all seemed to be waiting impatiently to hear Mrs. Daniels' defense to Anne's charges.

Mrs. Daniels was obviously displeased with the ease with which Anne had turned the parents and teachers against her and nervously tapped the microphone, but stopped when the tapping reverberated throughout the auditorium like a monitored heartbeat. "I suppose *next*, Miss Harte, you are going to say I'm responsible for the fire." And she gestured with her arm toward the damaged curtains which hung like black ribbons behind her.

"Indirectly, yes," Anne said.

"No, Miss Harte. You're wrong. *You* started the fire . . . you and those journalists."

The crowd gasped in shock. Anne quickly responded with a loud denial, but despite her denial no one seemed to believe her.

"I suppose you're also going to deny inviting those men here."

"Of course, I invited them. But we didn't start the fire."

"Maybe you didn't *light* the match, but *you* and those men *did* set the fire by inciting the students to do it for you."

"If you believe it's that simple, then how do you explain all the violence and vandalism at Church before either they or I came to this school?"

"The answer to that, Miss Harte, *is* simple. The students here by their anti-social acts are demonstrating their *outrage* at being denied a voice in their schools. That's why the panel, approved by the school board, is important. But *concerned* parents, *some* teachers in our school *want* to repress the students, *want* to frustrate them." And she was looking straight at Anne. "They don't want them to have a *voice* in the school because they won't be able to *mangle* minds anymore with their Hitler-like teaching tactics."

"You're right, Mrs. Daniels," Anne said, defiantly holding the principal's gaze. "There are those in the system who want to mangle minds. They want to confuse and frighten kids in order to make them easier for man-hating thugs to rule. That's why the panel of students, made up of the toughest kids in the system, was approved by the school board. Surely you must realize that. You can't always be just working on that damn attendance chart in your locked office. There must be some moments of truth in your life!"

"Right on, sister," someone shouted.

"My daughter," a woman said, springing to her feet, "she come home yesterday with a black eye 'cause she didn't give 'er money to some girl. When I call'd you, you told me you was gonna have someone talk with the girl. Now today when my little girl come home from school her other eye was black 'cause that girl don't like my little girl to bust on her. I say . . . let's stop all this rappin' 'n' let's end this here violence."

"Yeah," the crowd shouted. "Let's end this here violence."

"I agree with that woman," one man said, standing. "We gotta put a stop to all this here riotin', then we can start talkin' 'bout educatin' our kids proper-like."

If Mrs. Daniels was disturbed by her lack of control over the meeting now, she didn't reveal it. Her voice was as calm as she was poised. "Very well," she said. "I'll see what I can do."

After the meeting, Mrs. Daniels approached Anne privately in the back of the auditorium. She was deceptively pleasant, and Anne had the disturbing feeling that Mrs. Daniels was concealing beneath her charming smile some Machiavellian plot. At first, she gave no clue to the motives of their private conversation. Instead, she spent a few minutes complimenting Anne on how well she handled herself tonight, how rational and articulate she was.

"That's why I want to recommend you for a supervisory job in the English department," Mrs. Daniels said unexpectedly. "I think you'll be quite successful *away* from the students, evaluating teachers. It's the *perfect* job for you."

"Is that why you are recommending me, Mrs. Daniels, because you think I'm qualified?" Anne said. "Or is it because you're afraid I may gain too much support opposing you?"

"No one *wins* opposing me, Miss Harte!" she said arrogantly. "You see, *I* represent the system, and the system can be *heartless* to its enemies. Your continued opposition to it will only cause certain influential people to become irritated with you. So I advise you . . . as an *older* and *wiser* woman in the ways of the establishment . . . *accept* my generous offer. It can be the beginning of a very worthwhile career for you."

"It's very kind of you to offer me such an opportunity, Mrs. Daniels. But I'm afraid I can't accept your offer. By accepting what you call a worthwhile career, I would also have to accept your values. Well, I can't do that. But thank you for at least the opportunity to refuse."

Mrs. Daniels suspected after her get-acquainted talk three months ago with Anne that Anne would never adjust to Church. Yet she never took the time to verify this suspicion herself; instead, she informally asked Tom Slaughter to do this for her. His complimentary report, though unexpected, convinced the principal that she might be wrong about Anne. It never occurred to Mrs. Daniels to question the accuracy of Tom's report. He was too ambitious, she believed, to be so foolish as to lie to her. She would have continued believing this, if the teacher hadn't stupidly exposed herself by asking those penetrating questions at faculty meetings. Mrs. Daniels knew then that Tom by preparing a false report on Anne was revealing his fondness for the teacher, a fondness which could undermine his usefulness at preventing insurrection. All Mrs. Daniels needed to disqualify her of a promotion next year was for one teacher like Anne to create the right disturbance in the school. Frightened by the possibility of this happening, she was ready to fire Anne, and would've fired her, as she had fired Ralph Clearwater, if Dr. Steele hadn't advised her to wait.

So she waited without knowing how long she would have to wait and cleverly tried to use charm and intimidation to keep teachers and parents under control. But despite her effort, Anne still managed to turn many parents and teachers against her. Worried over Anne's growing power, she tried to compromise her last night by offering her a promotion. But when she refused (and with such *nobility*) Mrs. Daniels knew then that she would never survive Anne's attacks and would lose her chance for a job downtown. She knew as punishment for her failure she would probably be quickly retired.

Fortunately, Dr. Steele wasn't disturbed by the newspaper article and the events last night at the meeting. He said it was exactly the type of attention he wanted for the school because now the public would know exactly what the school was like before the panel was set up. But most important, he said that the teacher had served her usefulness and would have to be quieted.

Delighted with his decision, Mrs. Daniels immediately telephoned Dick Webb's office and set up an appointment for a conference.

For years teachers had legitimate grievances with the school system. They had to work long hours, collect monies for numerous charities, support specific causes, attend church, and in general, be a paragon of moral and intellectual virtue (at least, as the system defined it). By pouring each teacher into such a mold of virtue, the system was able to shape them into a popular stereotype. The exceptional teachers who were unable to conform quit and took teaching jobs in private schools where their minds were left free or, if they had commercial talent, with private corporations. But the others (the majority) remained because they had no other choice. They had innocently allowed the system to shape them for too long, and before they could grasp what was happening to them, they were so mentally deformed that they were useless to anyone else. In this way, the Board of Education had created a need for unions, for Neil Page who eagerly became the president of the city's teachers' union ten years ago.

Many of the teachers remaining in the schools realized how limited their job opportunities were and were ready for Neil to organize a local chapter of the National Teachers' Union. They wanted to shorten their working days, lighten their work load, break free of cumbersome classroom and professional restrictions, and enjoy a few of the benefits which a free society reserved for its citizens. For them, teaching in the public schools was their life (whether they liked it or not), so they signed up with the union in hopes of grabbing some of that power and freedom which Neil promised them.

Like most employees who wanted security, they expected what no sane employer would offer unproductive workers: job tenure, promotions and salary increases by seniority rather than ability, and an attractive retirement plan. By promising them this, Neil had appealed to their corruption (their greed for unearned rewards), and was able to get nearly a hundred percent support for his chapter. Like a shrewd gangster, he used this support against the Board of Education by threatening strikes and other costly demonstrations if it didn't capitulate to his demands.

Although the Board was pressured into recognizing the union, it never gave up its control of the schools, and Neil Page was never allowed to believe it had. The power was ultimately in the hands of the system, and as long as he worked within the specific limits of his power and never said or supported ideas which were inconsistent with those leading the country to destruction, he was able to remain president of the union. He knew this unquestionably, for it was made clear to him by those powerful government men and union leaders. Since he liked this illusion of power (the throngs of worshipping union members, the complimentary newspaper headlines, the respect and attention of the community), he learned to live within the limits of his power. He knew if he didn't he would be swiftly replaced. As he used teachers for his power, he was being used by the system to maintain its power. Consequently, despite the press reports on his hard bargaining stand during contract negotiations, important decisions were made for him during a series of private, closed-door conferences which he was never admitted to. He was only allowed to make certain public moves, mouth certain demands for the benefit of the newspapers and his union members. Everything else was decided well in advance. In short, he was an actor with a very definite script to follow.

For this reason, he didn't know quite what to say to Anne Harte when she saw him about her grievance. There were many teachers like her who had expressed concern about giving power to a student panel. From the beginning, he realized it would be an unpopular decision, one which could cause considerable anger among teachers. Since he was told explicitly that he had to go along with this decision, all he could do (all any sensible union president was permitted to do) was to repeat the cliches which the Great Thinkers in Education were telling him to repeat and persuade enough members to support the panel by promising them for their cooperation a large pay increase in the new contract. But as he listened to Anne talk (listened to the pure reason in her presentation) he knew a voice as clear and strong as hers could never be silenced like the others by promises of more money.

Although he pledged to her his support with all the fiery concern reserved for public appearances, he knew the final decision wasn't for him to make. After she left his office, he called Dick Webb and requested his advice on how to prevent her from becoming an embarrassment to the union and the school system.

The storm clouds dissolved the upper stories of the skyscrapers with its gray mist. Little flakes of snow swirled in the air, as people scurried in and out of the office buildings, bowing their heads to protect their faces from the sharp wind. Anne stepped from the cab and felt the cold air pierce her armor of wool and suede, chilling her to the bones. She ran through the snow to the Board of Education building shivering. Some of the snow which had collected on her boots slid onto the already wet tile floor inside and enlarged the already large puddles.

She took the elevator to the third floor and wondered if maybe she had been too hasty in refusing the promotion. A supervisory job would have given her the opportunity to encourage and to support teachers, something most supervisors neglected to do. It was a joke (even though few teachers took it lightly) how some supervisors would use their position to intimidate teachers with their sadistic games. Some would criticize them unmercifully, reduce them to tears and guilt, then leave the class triumphantly, as though their only mission in life was to inflict as much misery as possible on teachers. Although several supervisors who visited Church had a reputation for being fair and understanding, and even for trying to help with suggestions and materials, the majority seemed unconcerned about helping teachers and only seemed to exist to make teaching more difficult.

Yes, she would have made a good supervisor if good supervisors were what the system wanted. But she was sure that it didn't. If it had, there would be less indifference among supervisors to support teachers. The same forces, she suspected, that compromised teachers were compromising supervisors, and for that reason, if she had accepted the job, she would have been as frustrated at it as she was now at trying to teach. Under the circumstances, she had acted wisely. Her only regret was that she might lose her job because of her decision. Unless she could convince Dr. Webb that she had just reason for her behavior during the past months at Church, she would be fired immediately. With Christmas vacation only three weeks away and her obligations for college loans totaling nearly $15 thousand, she began to suspect that she had acted just a little too hastily at refusing the promotion.

The receptionist had just finished painting her nails emerald green when Anne approached her. After blowing her nails to quicken drying, the receptionist looked up at Anne and asked the usual questions: Who do you want to see? Why? Your name? Do you have an appointment? She then reached for a pen and wrote down Anne's name. Afterwards, she told Anne that she would tell the assistant superintendent of personnel of Anne's arrival as soon as he returned from lunch in the dining room downstairs. Anne sat down near a table. Moving quickly ahead of her through a maze of filing cabinets which broke the large rectangular room into sections were aides and administrators who like at Church seemed more interested in the coffee percolator, water cooler, and restrooms than the work piled on their desks.

Bored by the sight of them, Anne removed a woman's fashion magazine from a table and indifferently glanced at the pictures. The few times that she had her hair done stylishly and had worn sleek, clinging evening dresses as in the magazine, instead of feeling elegant and in vogue, she had felt cheap and obvious, and returned to more conservative clothes and hair style with relief. Seeing these fashionably dressed models now leap charmingly from the pages bored her, and she closed the magazine. She then reached for a general-interest magazine and tried to read the lead article on the crisis in the classroom. The emphasis on violence (with colorful examples and pictures) rather than on the cause and cure for the violence upset her, and she quickly closed that magazine too.

Once again her thoughts slipped back to Church, and she wondered if Mrs. Daniels would succeed at having her fired. In an effort to defend her "lack of professionalism" (as Mrs. Daniels called it), Anne tried to organize her argument for her behavior during her short time at Church, but was unsuccessful. All that she could think about at this moment was how foolish she was to fight the system. Any notion that grievances, when properly processed, would lead to meaningful communication between teachers and officials was irrational on her part to hold. Her awareness of all the corruption in the schools convinced her of this.

Then why was she here? Why didn't she accept being fired and just leave? There were other jobs. She acted, when she agreed to this hearing with the assistant superintendent of personnel as if her entire life depended on *this* job. She didn't like to think it did, but she knew in the abstract it did. If Mrs. Daniels won and teachers like Anne were dismissed for trying to do an honest job, who would be left to educate the young? Teachers like Betty Savage, Joy Franks, Ernest McQueen? What about the teenagers (the good and able ones)? What would happen to them if thugs were given full freedom to repress them with fear and might? Would this be the type of world she would feel safe in? No, she had to defeat Mrs. Daniels through the force of reason. She couldn't allow her and educators like her to continue to destroy lives and spread fear through their blatant hatred for everything decent and honest and rational.

She was pondering some of these thoughts, examining them from every reasonable position, while waiting thirty minutes for Dr. Webb to return from his late afternoon lunch.

Many of the office personnel were leaving, trying to hurry home before the blizzard. The receptionist had completed a second coat of polish on her nails, two cups of coffee, and an unusually large amount of cigarettes when Mrs. Daniels, Neil Page, and a distinguished-looking, gray-haired man breezed past Anne. They were chatting about what a congressman at the luncheon had said was needed at all schools, both private and public, to save them: more federal money and controls! Ten minutes after they breezed past Anne, they summoned her into the conference room.

The distinguished-looking man who was Dr. Richard Webb sat at the head of a large rectangular table opposite Mrs. Daniels. Neil Page sat to Dr. Webb's right and Mrs. Daniels' left and directly across from Anne. Although the union president was personally interested in defending

Anne, he now showed no interest in the case. Instead, he chatted about the congressman with Dr. Webb and Mrs. Daniels without even pausing long enough to acknowledge Anne's presence. As far as he was concerned, she could've been another empty chair in the sterile-white, stucco-walled conference room.

Anne tried to wait patiently for the conversation to end, but when it showed no signs of ending, she became restless. She glanced out the floor-to-ceiling window beyond Dr. Webb at the flakes of snow outside, hitting and dissolving against the warm glass. "I think," she said, interrupting the conversation, "we should start the conference. I'm afraid there's going to be a blizzard and I'm sure we don't want to be trapped here all night together."

The union president stopped talking and stared across the table at Anne as though surprised by her presence. Mrs. Daniels and Dr. Webb also turned toward her, obviously perturbed by her interruption.

"You're quite right, Miss Harte," Dr. Webb said. "We should get started right away." He then folded his hands on the table, after gently pushing his glasses closer to his eyes, and said to Anne in a tone that annoyed her: "Mrs. Daniels has brought some serious charges against you, young lady. I suppose you have a defense?"

Anne held back her annoyance and sat perfectly erect. She then calmly presented her case as the union president had advised her, trimmed to the essence. She explained that she nor the newsmen had any connection with the fire, that all the newsmen were guilty of was recording the facts, and she for inviting them to school. She believed that this was minor in comparison to the offense which Mrs. Daniels had committed: the total mismanagement of the school. She cited as examples the problems in the halls as well as the hall checks, vandalism, gang fights, and robberies.

As Anne spoke no one revealed any indication of listening to her. But as soon as Anne finished talking, they became bright and alert, as though refreshed from a nap; then Dr. Webb and Mr. Page turned to Mrs. Daniels and with almost exaggerated interest listened to her put everything Anne had said into proper perspective. Although Mrs. Daniels occasionally made no sense and mispronounced key words (due to too much alcohol at the luncheon?), Dr. Webb and Mr. Page didn't seem to notice. Instead, they revealed by their expression that everything she said made complete sense to them and was the most incisive account of a teacher's unprofessionalism that they had ever heard.

"No," Mrs. Daniels said, after telling how Anne had neglected her responsibilities as a teacher (citing Mr. Ward's teaching evaluation, the bake sale incident, the disruption of faculty and parent-teacher meetings, and the costly fire in the auditorium). "No," she repeated. "It isn't *I* who am guilty of neglecting my duties. It's teachers like Miss Harte who neglect my duties for me. That's why I *insist* she is fired!"

"Thank you, Mrs. Daniels," Dr. Webb said, acting impressed with Mrs. Daniels presentation. "Of course, you and Miss Harte realize that I would like to study all the facts carefully before making any decision. It has never been my habit in matters so grave to rush to a conclusion without first weighing both sides carefully. But just as soon as I reach a decision, I'll notify you both in writing."

Anne left the conference room while the others remained to finish their conversation about the luncheon. She was certain as she descended to the main floor, that she would be fired, that the excuse of studying the facts first was just that, an excuse to create an illusion of fairness. She shuddered, when she realized how easily and seemingly fairly, the system thinned the public schools of competent teachers.

Dr. Steele Appointed School Superintendent

Dr. Marshall Steele, after eight months as acting superintendent, was today appointed superintendent of schools officially replacing Dr. Fritz Spender, fired last spring for payroll extortion.

During the press conference, announcing the appointment, a school board member cited the impressive success of the student panel, especially at Church Junior High School, as the primary reason for selecting Dr. Steele for the permanent position. "Students are no longer roaming the halls there, creating disturbances," the board member said. "Now that they have a strong voice in their schools they actually *want* to go to class."

Board members, unanimous in their praise of Dr. Steele, were thoroughly convinced that the student rioting which caused nearly a half-million dollars in damage to just Church wouldn't have ended if Dr. Steele hadn't convinced the board of the practicality of approving the panel. "There is no question in our minds," a board member said. "Dr. Steele understands the real needs of the students and is the sort of sensitive educator we need running our schools."

Amendment

Chapter 13

Mrs. Daniels made it quite clear to Rod and Casey that their first concern as members of the student panel was to "convince" students of the practicality of returning to class. "I don't care if you *break* their necks to do it," she said confidentially. "But do it . . . NOW!

Both Rod and Casey looked forward with pleasure to obeying Mrs. Daniels' orders. To have the principal turn to them during this emergency and request their assistance was a confirmation to them of their physical and mental superiority to the others at school. Flattered, they took their power the only way they knew: by spreading fear!

The first few hours, after Casey and Rod began bringing order to the school, none of the students understood what was happening. There was no explanation, no assembly, no bulletins. Unexpectedly, Rod and Casey would appear amidst the crowd of bored, restless teenagers and would command the teenagers to return to class. If anyone were slow or reluctant to obey their commands, they would pound him with their fists until he crumbled to the floor in tears and pain. After stripping him of money and jewelry, they would leave him in the hall, bleeding, as an example for the others. A few such beatings were all it took for the teenagers to run at the sight of Rod and Casey to the nearest classroom for safety. "Open up," they shouted, banging on the locked classroom doors. "Let me in!"

Some teenagers, though, were courageous and refused

to be bullied by the panel and its exclusive gang of toughs. Inflamed with defiance and self-pride, they organized against the panel and fought back. But they weren't any match for Rod's or Casey's well-armed gangs and were often subdued with clubs and tear gas. Afterwards, they would be dragged to the office, where Mrs. Daniels would fill out the necessary papers to have them bused to another school.

A few teachers, disturbed by the violence, tried to organize the teachers to strike in order to demonstrate their disapproval of what was happening. But when they met to discuss a strike, most of the teachers objected because a strike was untimely. Christmas was near (only two weeks away). If they went on strike now, they would receive no salary, maybe even lose their paid 10-day vacation, and, for some, possibly go into debt because of all their spending on Christmas gifts. Maybe in January or February. Besides, they should wait, see what happened first. Perhaps in a few days everything would settle down.

Disillusioned by their attitude, these few teachers saw Neil Page about the problem, and he calmed them with promises of "looking into the matter." The majority, on the other hand, thought the panel was really a good idea. It was making those "delinquents" more respectful of authority. Why the kids were now actually *doing* their work, one teacher remarked, pleased. Of course, the teachers agreed that this was because they were too scared of what might happen to them if they didn't. But then, what was so awful about that? After all, the teachers only wanted them to master a little knowledge. So what if the teachers occasionally threatened to report them to the panel. Scaring them like that was sometimes necessary to keep them interested in their studies.

One teacher, disturbed by their attitude, bravely said that maybe some of them enjoyed frightening the kids, maybe they liked punishing them for all those months of rioting and assaulting. The others laughed nervously, then said that was nonsense. Besides, in a few days all this confusion would be over, and they would be able to teach.

To hasten order about fifty students were transferred from the school. A few teachers believed the community pressure which Anne Harte had brought about was responsible for Mrs. Daniels' quick, clean-up of Church. With teachers in the classroom where the responsibility of order was shifted to them, Mrs. Daniels was free of any further community pressure. If anything went wrong, she could blame the teachers. These teachers were certain Mrs. Daniels would have many opportunities to do this (if she chose). For three months, the teenagers had been free to run wild. Suddenly they were expected to become docile. Although during the first few days they were, out of fear of what Casey and Rod might do to them, by the end of the week (after learning their rights at an assembly) they quickly changed and came to class with a determination to will their way. If the majority of students chose to play cards or dance or listen to records, the teacher had to permit it.

Some teachers who once approved of the panel objected. They began to find it impossible to cope with the problems which student power created. They were told on the one hand to give full consideration to students' requests and on the other hand to maintain a learning atmosphere in the classroom. Most teachers discovered quickly that maintaining a learning atmosphere wasn't possible as long as they had to bow to the irrational demands of students. To complicate this, students were given the right to rate teachers, very much as supervisors had, and if the teacher received more negative than positive ratings, he could be fired. Consequently, many teachers did what they had to under such circumstances: They ingratiated their students and hoped by becoming their "friends" their careers would be left intact.

To relax themselves and to forget their classroom problems, teachers would amuse each other during those cold December days before Christmas with the morning bulletins. Once the bulletins were heavy with cumbersome details about special duty assignments, abstruse quotations from famous educators, and reminders of PTA, faculty or departmental meetings. Now they were spiced with outrageous new policies enacted by the triumvirate (the name which most teachers gave collectively to Rod, Casey, and Mrs. Daniels). The policy creating the most comment among the teachers was the one which permitted the students to wear whatever they wanted to school. One girl chose to test this by wearing a see-through blouse without a bra. The following day others wore similar blouses. One girl decided to take this freedom a step further and disgusted several teachers by coming to class in an unbuttoned cardigan sweater, exposing her well-developed breasts for all interested boys to touch.

Perhaps the most amusing ruling was that teachers couldn't hold classes after the bell rang. If anyone forgot to end the class immediately when the bell rang, they would be called before the panel and warned. If it occurred a second time, they would be held after school and forced to write 500 times: "I must not keep my class after the bell rings." Since no one taught because the students voted against teaching, none of the teachers were worried about being kept after school. Still a few teachers objected to this ruling and tolerated it only because they lacked the tenure (which only two or three teachers at Church had) to protest it openly without being fired and losing their 10-day vacation salary.

As Christmas neared, everything became an issue for the students. Assemblies would be held daily to discuss some of them. Led by Rod and Casey, these discussions would rage for hours. Should black history and Swahili be taught in lieu of American history and English, or should the former be electives? Should homework be banned, grades simplified to passing or failing, and students automatically promoted regardless of achievement, or should standards be established? Yet despite the avowed purpose of these debates, which was to settle controversial issues, decisions were seldom reached. The students were having too much fun expressing themselves to care much about what they said or accomplished.

There were only two issues which the panel absolutely settled. The food served in the cafeteria was the first. Cokes had to be substituted for milk, and the only potatoes would be French fries. Rod voted for beer, cheered by the students, but Mrs. Daniels vetoed this request. Nevertheless, the triumvirate agreed that the dietician had to prepare a menu in advance and submit it to the panel for approval. When the dietician argued against junk food by insisting that growing teenagers needed a balanced and nutritious diet, the panel told her if she didn't want to be fired she had better obey. The dietician who was putting a son through college decided to forget what she had learned in school about nutritious foods and do as the panel advised.

The other issue concerned a longer lunch period in order to allow the students to have a dance in the gym after eating. This especially pleased the staff because the teenagers didn't want any adult chaperons. The only person objecting was the janitor because he had to clean the gym afterwards of broken bottles and candy wrappings and cigarette butts, but no one listened to him. Occasionally a teacher would hear rumors of someone being gang-raped or beaten. Since the victim wouldn't verify these rumors, fearful of reprisal, the rumors were never investigated and were soon forgotten.

Perhaps the only thing at Church which continuously interested teachers was the sudden change in the science teacher's behavior. The science teacher, unbeknownst to the other teachers, was persuaded with a portable television to vacate the science laboratory. Rod gave her no reason for this request. He merely told her that she would be happier watching her favorite soap operas in a small, unused office than in trying to teach. Since she loved her soaps and would often take sick leave just to see an important episode, she gladly accepted the television and entangled herself emotionally in the neurotic problems without asking why Rod was so generous. She was too weary of trying to stop her students from mishandling lab equipment, from playing with gas jets, and from torturing the guinea pigs to concern herself about the reason. Besides, why burden herself with thinking when television could do it for her. So she hissed at the sight of the evil drug dealer selling hallucinogenes to innocent teenagers at Breezy Meadows High or cried with grief every time that wonderfully sweet Beatrice Love talked about her brutal rape by that mental patient without once feeling guilty at "earning" her salary watching the soaps.

By the end of the week, though, this all changed for her when the teachers, teasing her about the offensive smell of decaying flesh coming from the lab, asked her jokingly: "What are you doing in there, cremating kids?" Jolted into thinking, the science teacher became concerned that maybe Rod was experimenting with something which could be dangerous. Determined to find out for certain, she unlocked the science lab with her spare key and peeked inside. To her horror, she saw two men in white aprons, their faces hidden by gas masks, and their hands covered with rubber gloves, heating test tubes filled with chemicals which at boiling point emitted a bluish vapor. Frightened by what she saw and nauseated by the foul death-smell of the boiling chemicals, she quickly retreated from the room and bumped into Rod. She knew when she saw the evil anger in his look that she had discovered what she wasn't supposed to discover.

"You just say one word 'bout this," he warned her in a low, dangerous voice, "just one word 'n' I gonna see that you's flatter than them tiles."

Without speaking, she backed away from him, then hurried to her private classroom where she tried to forget what she saw by turning her attention to the soaps. But her conscience wouldn't let her forget, and she nervously paced the floor, wondering what she should do.

Many of the teachers began to discuss the strange way the science teacher was behaving whenever they teased her about that smell coming from the laboratory. But they stopped when they heard rumors about one boy in the community ripping out his eyes and another boy repeatedly stabbing himself in the heart after taking a new drug called Space-Out. A teacher, disturbed by such violent acts, tried to link the new drug, so easily made in makeshift labs, with the strange behavior of the science teacher and the offensive smell in the science lab.

"Oh, don't be silly," one teacher said in an effort to deny similar thoughts which she and other teachers indirectly were sharing. "The science teacher is just exhausted and a little nervous, like the rest of us. After her 10-day Christmas holiday in the islands, she'll be her happy and cheery self again. You wait and see."

The attendance officer once believed that she was doing a Great Humanitarian Service by using her skills of persuasion to keep students in school until sixteen. But that was a few years ago, after being saturated in innocent thinking at the State University. In the past year especially she no longer felt any inner drive to persuade reluctant parents to send their children to school. Her argument about the need for an education in a highly industrial and technological society seemed to break down whenever she entered the schools and saw first-hand how educators were teaching healthy and eager minds to fail in such a society. What could she say to parents who like her knew about this evil in the public schools? You're right. The public schools are destroying minds and should be closed? Or should she turn truants over to the juvenile authorities, as she was taught, and in serious cases even have them placed in foster homes or reform schools?

Some parents didn't care what she did. As far as they were concerned their sons and daughters were a nuisance, someone to feed and cloth. "Take 'em 'way if you like," they would tell her. "Serve 'em right!" Others cared because if they lost custody of their children, their welfare payments would be reduced or canceled. In cases like this, the officer felt she was doing the child a service by preparing a strong recommendation for the courts. Anything would be better for such children than their present homelife. At least they might have a chance in a different environment. But what about those others, those concerned and loving parents who already provided their children with the best they could afford by working hard and even sacrificing for them? What could she say to them when they were afraid to send their children to school, were too poor to put them in private schools? She couldn't hide the truth from them about the schools. Their eyes and ears were wide open, and they knew what was happening there.

What about the innocent parents who believed teachers and the newspapers and blamed their children for what was happening in the schools? What could she say to these parents when they punished their children for not being good and doing what the teacher said? Should she tell these parents that what the teachers wanted wasn't always for their children to be good? It wasn't any mystery to her why children rebelled against their parents and the establishment, and even destroyed themselves with drugs. How could it be any different when educators were torturing children in a mentally and physically harmful environment?

Sometimes the attendance officer wished that principals like Mrs. Daniels weren't so obsessed with maintaining 100 percent enrollment. It made it impossible for her to be kind and look the other way when teenagers skipped school. The community like many principals, through its citizen spy system and police department, often showed the same zeal in fighting truancy as these principals. Their entire focus, it so often seemed, was in keeping children in school without any desire to find out why the children were truants in the first place.

Public school education, she believed, wasn't working. This point was made clear to her repeatedly whenever she heard about a boy or girl being beaten at school, whenever she saw teachers strip a child of all self-respect with their vicious tongues, and whenever she listened to the reasons for a judge sentencing a teenager to reform school.

Sometimes to blur the ugliness of her job, of the human misery she was spreading by working to be a Great Humanitarian for the Board of Education, she would get drunk after work, and stay drunk, especially during the weekends. One of these days she would quit, she kept telling herself. One of these days she would tell the entire world why. But she never did. Could it be that she too was evil?

Anne was surprised when Dr. Webb didn't fire her. Convinced his decision was based on an objective study of the facts, she courageously resisted what was happening at Church and tried with persistence and good lessons to teach. But this all ended abruptly for her when she attempted to stop a classroom fight. The student spectators, angered by her interference, reported her to the panel. At a student panel conference, Mrs. Daniels who used the charges against Anne to reprimand her told her that Dr. Webb hadn't fired her for her unprofessional behavior in the past because the student panel felt she deserved another chance; but because the panel was *once* lenient with her didn't mean it would be a second time, especially for something so grave as *touching* a student! Disturbed at learning the truth, and especially at watching Rod stare at her as if she were a stripper, disrobing, she felt totally defeated and returned to her classroom without any desire to teach again.

Like most achievers, Anne resented being in such a situation of helplessness in which she couldn't function to the limits of her ability. She wanted to rebel, but was now afraid if she did she would be fired and would lose her paid Christmas vacation. For 10 days of salary, she was now selling her soul, and she hated herself for this because she knew such a decision by being pragmatically wise was against everything in which she believed. But her student loan obligations and her living costs made it economically impractical to do anything else until she found another job.

Her unhappiness with her decision to stay for two more

weeks was made unbearable when she realized that some of her once promising students no longer had that special fire of ambition which made teaching them such a joy, and had given up all hope by turning to drugs. Occasionally Anne would see track marks on their arms or observe strange behavior in which they acted out highs and lows in obscurely symbolic ways. On one occasion she had to summon for help to stop a boy from beating his head furiously against the wall. On another occasion, she had to have several students hold back a girl from flying out the window like a bird. At such times, Anne was convinced that this was what an ambitious government wanted in order to have an excuse to increase its controls over its citizens' lives. After all, what other explanation was there for the Federal Drug Prevention Agency spending so much money on drug education that increased rather than decreased drug use? She had sat through enough such films at school to know that the purpose of such films wasn't to discourage, but *to* encourage the use of drugs. What made these movies so effective was that they would first dwell on the despair of the entire black experience by arousing frustration in the viewer, then afterwards vividly show how some teenager coped with this frustration with drugs. Although there was a moral attached to the film, it was easily overlooked by the vivid portrayal of a "junkie's high life". A similar end was achieved by drug companies with their visually attractive posters of drugs which they used to "combat" drug addiction, or the Federal Drug Rehabilitation Program which "cured" addicts by transferring their dependence from one drug to another!

Was it any wonder that, according to FBI reports, serious crime among teenagers rose 25 percent over last year? What made this so disturbing was with this rise in crime was a rise in leniency for criminal acts. She knew by making criminal laws more lenient than civil laws, the country was taking a major step toward totalitarianism. But then, wasn't that the purpose of all this: to reduce a great and powerful industrial country like America to slavery?!

Her other bright students who didn't use drugs were subtly being destroyed by the games they played. Perhaps the most popular game for them was school. One boy or girl would be the teacher and would ask the students to solve a riddle. Since no one could guess the answer because of its absurdity, the "teacher" would punish the students (which seemed to be the purpose of the game) by giving them pages of math problems. In this way, they were conditioning each other, as teachers had conditioned them, to view an objective and precise science like mathematics as punishment. Disturbed by the negative teaching value of this game, Anne tried to intervene and teach them a learning game which could achieve positive results. But she stopped and never tried again when they completely ignored her.

It wasn't long before those students became as incorrigibly corrupt as Rod and Casey. They would take anything of value which they could carry and would destroy anything which displeased them, and if she dared to correct them, they would brazenly deny it all by accusing her of "puttin' lies on 'em." When bored, they would accuse Anne of making racist statements and would laugh with savage pleasure at seeing their classmates attack her with books and erasers. Once in awhile a student would brandish a knife under her chin and another, after disarming the first student, would offer her protection for a price. If she refused, which she always did, the blackmailer would usually make life unbearable for her.

Trying to talk to these students about right and wrong was useless because they were convinced that being evil was the only way to survive in life. Although Anne learned from her experiences with her learning center, that many such problems would disappear with a wise teaching plan, she knew also that some problems, created by Rod's and Casey's example, couldn't be solved so easily. These problems needed a change in philosophy of education at Church from one which rewarded dishonesty and conformity to one which rewarded honesty and individualism. But trying to reverse this negative philosophy, promulgated by educators like Mrs. Daniels and Dr. Steele, was like ramming against a bureaucratic wall.

To ease her frustration, caused by her helplessness at combating the evil forces at work in school, she became compulsive about keeping the room orderly. After each class, she would use kitchen cleanser and a sponge to wipe away the obscenities scribbled in magic marker on the desks and try to make the room look cheery and ready for learning. Perhaps tomorrow, she hoped each day at three, her day would be pleasant. Perhaps tomorrow, she could teach them something of lasting value. But her tomorrows were like her yesterdays. Her hope of someday reaching that sunny summit of success seemed what it was at Church: an impossible dream! At such times, she would count the days on the calendar until Christmas or study the help wanted ads for job openings. Since she was too exhausted at the end of each school day to go on job interviews, she usually went home and tried to forget by telling herself after next week, it would be over and she would then have the time and energy to search for a job which would take her away from this madness.

Of the 25 promising students that Anne had once taught during her lunch and planning periods only one remained loyal to her. That one was Birdie Smith. All the others were defeated by the treachery of the system without any clear understanding of the cause. All they understood was studying, learning, and being competent or good in their work wasn't the way to survive. There was a wiser way, a way paved by Rod and Casey.

Forcing hard-working, productive Americans by heavy taxation to finance this degeneration of their children was one of the most evil schemes sold to a free nation. Such a scheme, if carried to its intended extreme, would waste the wealth of its citizens on expensive education programs, and, at the same time, destroy what a nation needed most to thrive: intelligent, independent, educated youth! Anyone trying to make this system work was in her opinion as evil as the masterminds of the scheme. What made this realization for her so painful was that by doing nothing at school to combat the spread of this evil, she was as guilty of contributing to the moral and intellectual decay of students as the Great Thinkers of Public Education.

One point was now quite clear to her: these Great Thinkers understood exactly the purpose of their scheme. They needed teachers like Betty Savage to freeze their students' intelligence for easy manipulation at moronic levels, teachers like Joy Franks to brainwash their students with war slogans for quick excitation, and teachers like Ernest McQueen to spread hate through "love" by seducing minds and bodies with promiscuous and sadomasochistic sex. They needed all this in order to prepare the country for a world where the irrational was rational and the rational was irrational, for a world in which the state through the aid of thugs like Rod and Casey had all the rights and the individual had none.

Education, she was beginning to believe, could only be successful as a private business, supported voluntarily by consumers who approved the methods and programs, with one school competing against another for the best teachers, the best students, and the best programs and methods. At least then, a parent would be able to choose for himself that school, that ideal which he felt was right for his children without being robbed through heavy taxation to finance government-controlled schools. This, she was sure, was the only way to eliminate the dry rot of a huge, evil bureaucracy, dedicated to reducing inquisitive minds to non-thinking Pavlovian animals, and to free the citizens to become independent, whole men and women.

Anne wondered how long it would take Americans to awaken to what was really happening to their children, and if they did awaken, what their awakening would be like. Would they feel helpless and out of control, a sort of Space-Out hysteria where jumping from windows or stabbing oneself repeatedly was the only possible solution? Or would they feel that government-controlled education was wrong and had to be ended? Anne knew only time would provide the answer. But every minute wasted, every opportunity neglected would make it harder for Americans to free themselves and their children of the evil destroying them. The propaganda of the media, of the schools, of all the institutions which had an interest in skrinking the conceptual powers of the mind to the size of a molecule would render them helpless and incapable of climbing the heap of concrete-bound issues to a clear understanding of what was happening to America: of the totalitarian state which was adroitly and quickly being created!

Already America was taking another major step in this direction, which the government was advancing with huge grants to private universities, organizations and prominent "thinkers" for special research in the behavioral sciences. This trend by giving special assistance to a select few "intellectuals" and certain organizations and universities for any research that advanced undemocratic ideas was providing an already powerful, Washington-based government with the needed data for ultimately enslaving the public. Because of the "respectability" of the institutions and individuals involved, this trend was beginning to achieve the expected results. Anne's experience recently at trying to get the truth published rather than the opinions of certain well-known educators was only one of the many obvious signs. She knew if this trend continued unchecked, it wouldn't be long before it would be impossible for the truth to be heard, and like totalitarian countries, the government would take complete control of the minds and bodies of its citizens. This, she thought ruefully, would be an awful price for taxpaying Americans to pay for their generous gift to the government for assuming the responsibility of "educating" the young.

But she tried not to think about this. Each day at 6 p.m. after Anne had recovered from school by taking a nap, Birdie would arrive at Anne's apartment for special tutoring. Although Anne would have preferred to tutor Birdie at school, she knew this was impossible, not only because of the noise and confusion in the classroom, but also because of the time limit for each class. Confining classes to rigid time schedules didn't, in Anne's opinion, give consideration to those who needed more than 50 minutes to master a lesson. The only choice Anne had was to schedule classes after school. At least in the comfortable setting of her apartment, Birdie was able to relax and work uninterrupted.

To make Birdie's visit informal and pleasant, Anne would bake fresh cookies and would serve them with hot chocolate like an eager-to-please mother indulging her 15-year-old daughter. Occasionally Anne would buy a little gift, a print blouse or some new shade of lipstick just for the pleasure of making Birdie happy. But instead of wrapping these gifts in colorful paper with a big bow, she would hang the blouse in the closet or leave the makeup on her dressing table with all her other personal effects. Then, before or after the lesson, she would lead Birdie to the table or closet on the pretense of showing her how to apply makeup or how to select the right color clothes for her complexion. After she tried on the clothes or applied the makeup, Anne would then tell her how much nicer it looked on Birdie than on Anne and asked her . . . as a personal favor . . . to keep the makeup or the garment. In case Birdie refused Anne would always have some excuse ready (the blouse was too big in the chest or she was allergic to that makeup). It didn't matter exactly what she said as long as it was plausible and didn't make Birdie feel like a recipient of charity. Since Birdie needed these little "luxuries" she seldom refused them. But there was always a hint of embarrassment which she communicated. This became especially evident today. As she sat on the Hollywood bed, crossing her feet at the ankles, she glanced at the blouse lying next to her. Her expression seemed to reveal that she regarded the gift as an obligation which would have to be repaid, an obligation which could undermine her struggle for independence. Anne knew then as she observed Birdie that she would have to limit her gifts to teaching. Providing her with the skills to achieve her dreams was the greatest gift that she could possibly offer her.

Anne would have never guessed that the old Birdie who once had robbed her would mature so much in such a short time. It took courage to confess the robbery to Anne (for Anne had no clear memory of the thief) and personal sacrifice to pay back the stolen $7 from her part-time job. Seeing the new Birdie before her made her believe that the old Birdie had never really existed, but was only a thin disguise hiding the innocent and sweet girl waiting to be discovered. Yet despite this significant metamorphose, Anne still worried about her. Already at fifteen she was pregnant. If she continued on this familiar road, paved before her by so many other teenagers, what would her life be like at 20 or 25? What would happen to that dream which she always talked about?

Although this dream was reasonable, it now seemed unreasonable at this time in her life. She maintained the naive attitude that all she needed was to learn to read and type, and suddenly she would qualify for a job which would amply support her and her baby. She didn't realize that learning to read and type wasn't enough for a successful career with all the American-middle-class extras. Even if she did acquire a give-away, affirmative-action job, how long would it be before she realized that it was a gift for being economically deprived and black, not for being competent in her work? How would she react then? How would any intelligent, sensitive person react then? Would she become bitter and angry and revert to her old self, so carefully conditioned by poverty and racism, and give up her dream? Or would she remain dedicated to her dream and strive to achieve the competency needed to hold her job on ability? The fact that her many adversities and her father's tragedy hadn't destroyed her dream was a testimony to her strength and courage. But how long would this courage and strength last, improperly nurtured?

To guide her to think clearly about her future, Anne had told her to study the help wanted ads for salaries and job requirements for typists. She even encouraged Birdie to call a few employers and discuss the jobs with them. Then she suggested she find out what apartments, groceries, clothes, as well as various nursery schools cost. As an alternative to working, she asked her to talk to welfare mothers and find out from them how much they received, maybe even call the welfare office to see how much she would get. In short, Anne tried to guide Birdie to examine clearly her future before she had committed herself to it.

As Birdie now sat on the Hollywood bed, she revealed by her expression the sadness which came from a sudden awakening to reality, and Anne knew that the purpose of her little exercise had achieved its end. "Have you made a decision about what you're going to do about the baby while working?" Anne asked, curious to see what Birdie would say.

Birdie hesitated and ran her fingers lightly over the new blouse lying beside her as though it were too precious to hold. Without looking up from the blouse, she said: "My pa gonna watch 'em."

"Do you think he should?"

She glanced at Anne, obviously aware of the purpose of the question, of the irrationality of expecting an alcoholic to take care of a child, and shook her head.

"Then what are you going to do?"

Birdie bit her lip and stubbornly tried to hold back the tears which were beginning to flow. "I guess I just gonna put 'em up for adoption."

"Is that what you think is best?"

She nodded. "I's just too young to be like them women I talk to." She paused and took a deep breath, as she prepared herself to voice the most important decision of her life. "I don't wanna be like them, Miss Harte. I wanna have a nice life, live good and comfy in a place just like this. But I guess to do that you gotta be smart, get a good education. Well, I can't do that if I gotta take care of a baby. So . . . so I just decided to give it to somebody who can support it good. Maybe later when I have a little money in the bank. Maybe then I can have a baby and raise it right. But now, well, now I gonna get smart, smart like you, Miss Harte, and study to be a doctor or lawyer or somethin'." She looked down at the blouse, embarrassed by her ambitions, by the great dreams she was beginning to have. "But first I gotta learn to read good. So I ask you, Miss Harte. Ask you as I never ask'd nobody before. Will you teach me all you know? Make me smart like you?"

Anne smiled and gently squeezed Birdie's hand. "Of course I will, Birdie. I'll teach you as much as I can."

Rod spent nearly an hour in the Adult Book Store watching pornographic movies. Most of the movies (at least those he watched) were of women gagged and tied to beds or chained to the walls being whipped by men in black-leather pants, vests and masks who culminated their orgy of blood and pain by raping the women. Although Rod had seen many such films with horses and spiked dildos substituted for sexually well-endowed rapists, his only moment of real sexual excitement came when he saw the women defeated before their captors, their wills totally crushed. He spent nearly $5 dollars in quarters watching the cycle of events from the beatings to the rape for the excitement of that one moment. Afterwards, he left the book store like an animal ready to kill for the pleasure of that one moment.

His gaze which restlessly scanned the prostitutes on Pranklin Street halted when he saw a girl in mini skirt, high boots, and a soiled white fur jacket, leaning against the door of a boarded store front. Her face was covered thickly with makeup which made her face stand out like a mask with two full, blazing red lips, marred by an open pea-shaped sore. The girl stared at him through un-focused eyes. Although she was about fourteen, she looked much older like a woman conquered by drugs and men, too worn out to give her body even for the right price. He backed away, disgusted by the empty shell staring at him, the motionless and spiritless girl leaning for support against the store, and he turned away. As he turned, he saw Anne Harte leave a drug store. Seeing her, he quickly forgot the girl. He thought only of Anne, of the sexual thrill of violating her will, and of reducing her to his power. He hurried after her, staring at her hips, which swayed from side to side, breaking gently the straight lines of her suede coat. He knew this time, unlike before in her classroom, he would not fail in his mission!

Anne tried not to panic when she heard, then saw Rod follow her down a deserted hall at school. Since she had threatened him with the scissors he had maintained his distance and had stalked her silently. She didn't know if he were afraid to approach her again because of what she might do in retaliation or because he was deriving a sadistic pleasure from teasing her. She did know, though, that the moment he grew bored with his game, and she showed the slightest weakness, he would attack.

To avoid him whenever he was near, she would seek the company of teachers, the safety of the office or her locked classroom. In this way, she was able to prevent any confrontation with him. But today on this last day of school before the Christmas holiday, she had nowhere to go quickly for safety. As she hurried along the deserted hall at Church, past the broken glass showcases, past the obscenities and sex symbols on the walls, and under the openings in the suspended ceiling where white tile blocks once were, she listened as Rod's footsteps behind her grew louder and closer.

Billions of dollars spent on education, she thought. For what? So that one teenager . . . one angry and dangerous teenager . . . could threaten her safety in a way which no one in any civilized society should have the right to. For a moment, she wanted to run through the hall to the teachers' lounge at the other end of the building. But she refused to reveal panic. "Remain calm, Anne," she kept telling herself. "Show him you aren't afraid."

Without quickening her pace, she walked toward the lounge. At the same time, she listened carefully to his heavy footsteps in order to judge his distance behind her. As his steps grew closer, she glanced at the doors ahead and wondered if she should chance entering the gym during lunchtime when all the teenagers were there amusing themselves.

He was directly behind her. She could feel the heat of his body, see her shadow ahead of her suddenly disappear into his when he grabbed her hips and pressed his body against her in a mock intercourse. Angered, she broke his hold by swiftly turning. She then slapped him. She put all her anger into that slap, and when she dropped her hand, burning from the violent contact with hard flesh, he smiled and told her that she should be nice to him. He reminded her that he could have her fired if she weren't nice. He then bragged about how Mrs. Daniels listened and obeyed when he warned the principal about firing Anne. Losing such a nice teacher, he said, repeating his conversation with Mrs. Daniels, could upset the kids, make them mean. Maybe Anne should listen and obey too and give him what he wanted. Maybe next time he wouldn't ask politely.

"Well, if you think that's going to make me change my mind," she said, letting her hatred for the monster which the school helped create rush out, "*forget it!* I'm still *not* interested!"

"That don't make me no difference. 'Cause there is ways of makin' you interest'd."

"Haven't you learned yet that I can't be persuaded by any of your tactics?"

He laughed. It was the mad laugh of someone who believed he had the divine right to take anything he wanted. "Maybe I ain't gonna try to persuade you. Maybe I got me another idea this time."

He then grabbed her and forced her against the gym doors. His unzipped leather jacket exposed his form-fitting shirt open to the navel. Around his neck was a gold chain. Attached to the chain was a clenched black fist which, as he breathed, moved toward and away from her. Inside the gym someone began to play a record. The sound was loud, unintegrated musically, as if various instruments took turns making noise while a drummer pounded heartbeats. To this noise, a man spoke (sung?) in a coaxing, sexy voice an obscene song about love.

As Rod stared at her, visually stripping her of her armor of winter clothes, he could have been speaking (singing?) those same words. Annoyed by his look of familiarity, she defiantly dared him to step closer, her last defense against a madman. He responded to that dare by bending down to kiss her. She jerked backwards and felt the doors behind her open. Then in panic, she broke away from him and ran into the gym, past the teenagers wrapped together on top of mats, past the smokers taking deep inhales of foul-smelling cigarettes, and past the dancers jabbing each other suggestively with their bodies in time to music. She continued running toward the back exit. Near the exit she tripped on a mat and fell on her stomach. After she rolled over and as she was about to rise, she saw Rod standing over her, smiling. His smile (a mixture of hate and lust) resembled nothing human now. It was too savage to be anything human. Yet she had seen that smile before. It was the same smile she remembered on her classmate's face before he raped her six years ago.

She glanced at the exit about ten feet away. She knew if she could reach the door she would have a good chance of making it to the street and to safety. Watching him cautiously, she inched backwards on the mat. But as she sprang to her feet, he leaped on her and threw her to the floor. He then held her down while he tore off her skirt and undergarments. Faces swarmed around her, a wall of faces, staring down at her, as they watched with delight as Rod began to satisfy his lust.

Parents Challenge Permissiveness As an Alternative to Discipline

Parents of school children are angrily challenging educators on the wisdom of no—control—on—the—child philosophy by bluntly stating that permissiveness as an alternative to discipline isn't working. According to the parents, children aren't innately good (as many parents had long believed) and mustn't be allowed to "do their own thing" any longer. Their change in philosophy, some educators believe, is a result of the scandal last year at Church Junior High School.

At Church, allowing students "to do their own thing" resulted in them using the gym for sex orgies and the science lab for manufacturing a deadly drug. The drug in this case was the potent hallucinogenic Space-Out which had caused seven deaths and over 25 cases of permanent psychosis to users.

Concerned about these recent events, eminent educators with grants from the federal government to finance their research have gathered data to support the view that children aren't innately good and don't have a natural curiosity for knowledge. Their research, which is a compilation of studies in schools during the permissive era, has led them to conclude officially that freedom is dangerous and inevitably results in evil and self-destructiveness.

Despite the overwhelming evidence, presented by the Federation of Educators, the National Teachers' Union and eminent educators in universities throughout America to validate this view, some educators still don't agree and believe the studies are one-sided contrivances. Miss Anne Harte, the former Church English teacher allegedly raped by a student during a sex and drug orgy in the gym last year, is one such educator. Her pamphlets and magazine articles, and her soapbox talks downtown during her breaks from her job as waitress at the Imperial Gardens Restaurant stress that "It isn't freedom that breeds evil and self-destructiveness, but immoral and criminal repression of a child's psychological and intellectual needs". Perhaps her most outspoken convert to this point of view is the former assistant principal at Church, Tom Slaughter. Mr. Slaughter along with two teachers at Church quit their jobs last December to "demonstrate their disapproval toward the sins of public education and to dramatize their support of Miss Harte's views."

With them as allies, Miss Harte has been winning backing from parents throughout the city to introduce a voucher system which they will put before the voters in November. The voucher system, which

(See p.7)

Premissiveness challenged

has created much controversy among educators, if put into effect will give a credit for the money an individual citizen is taxed for public education. This tax credit or voucher can then be spent to put a taxpayer's children or anyone else's children of his choice through any school he likes to the credit limit of what it costs the government to offer comparable education. Miss Harte feels such a voucher system would place public schools in competition more fairly with private schools and would force them to up-grade standards in order to hold students. Her ultimate goal, one which has made many educators think of her as a "crackpot", is to bring about a constitutional amendment in which the government will be prohibited from involving themselves directly or indirectly in the education of children.

To gain voter attention for her cause, Miss Harte has filed criminal charges against the alleged student panel member accused of raping her, as well as the Board of Education. For her case next week, her attorneys have perpared a 30-page report, documenting her charges against the Board of Education "of willfully contributing to her rape by corrupting the intellectual and moral health of students and teachers."

Most school board members are justifiably dismissing Miss Harte's case against the Board of Education as an "outrageous publicity stunt to tarnish the concept of public school education." These members believe her evidence against the school system is too weak to win a legal case and her educational goals too controversial to gain public sympathy. Like many local citizens, they believe the best solution to the problems in the schools is to end the permissive era and once again return to rigid standards and a back-to-basics teaching program, and not a Montessori education of moral and intellectual objectivity as Miss Harte proposes. Most of the elected school board members have learned from the beatings, robberies, drug manufacturing and trafficking, and sex orgies that they can only guarantee the moral and intellectual growth of children through complete censorship of their activities. According to Mrs. Loretta Daniels, former principal at Church and now assistant superintendent of personnel, "It is obvious Miss Harte hasn't matured enough professionally to learn the same lesson from past mistakes."

anquaɑe

Author's Note

Writing this book wasn't easy. Although I completed the story about ten years ago, my characters never came alive for me. The primary reason was that my thoughts of what was happening in the schools didn't agree with the "experts", and I found our conflict in opinion difficult to explain. Of course I could have ended this conflict and concluded (as the "experts" surely wanted me to conclude) that my inability to agree with them was because I was dense. Fortunately, I wasn't that brainwashed by 28 years in the schools as a student and a teacher to believe this. Consequently, I just put the book away and waited for that moment when I could see my story more clearly. That moment came after reading Ayn Rand's article, "Comprachicos" (*The New Left: The Anti-Industrial Revolution*, Signet). This article as well as her other books, especially her two famous novels, *The Fountainhead* and *Atlas Shrugged*, helped me understand the reason for my disagreement with the "experts".

With a clearer understanding of how "experts" think, I was ready to return to my book. Since I lacked any strong idea of what a good teacher was, I had to find the answer to that in Beatrice Hessen's article, "The Montessori Method" (May-July 1970 issues of *The Objectivist*, available through the libraries). In her article, Mrs. Hessen gave me the needed introduction to my heroine and to the two conflicting philosophies of education as exemplified by the Montessori and Progressive schools. For more information, I read Dr. Maria Montessori's books (especially my favorite, *The Absorbent Mind*) and Dr. John Dewey's writings on education.

For an introduction to the philosophy of pragmatism, I turned to Dr. Leonard Peikoff's article, "Pragmatism Versus America" (May 6 and May 20, 1970 issues of *The Ayn Rand Letter*). This article was an excerpt from his book, *The Ominous Parallels*, published by Weybright and Talley, Inc. Unfortunately, I wasn't ever able to obtain a copy of the book (out of print?).

Other sources included:

Dr. Banesh Hoffman's book, *The Tyranny of Testing*, which introduced me to the lack of objectivity in tests; Miss Joan Beck's book, *How To Raise a Brighter Child*, which provided me with some ideas parents can use to develop intelligent children; Dr. Milton and Mrs. Rose Friedman's book, *Free To Choose*, which gave me the solution to my novel (also Miss Rand's article, "Tax-Credits for Education", *The Ayn Rand Letter*, March 13, 1972); Michael M. Mooney's book, *The Ministry of Culture*, which reinforced my thinking on how the government influences ideas; Allen Drury's novel, *Capable of Honor*, which reveals how some journalists deliberately distort truth to manipulate their readers; and Miss Frances FitzGerald's book, *America Revised*, which provided me with a disturbing look at the text book business. Fundamentally I don't agree with Miss FitzGerald. While she has done a good job at researching certain facts, her interpretation of these facts leave much unanswered. In my opinion, the best solution to the problem would be to get government out of education. This would bring to an end the enormous power of Boards of Education to influence publishers with their huge book orders, and it would force publishers to be more accurate in content if they wanted to meet the largest school market. Of course, there were many more writers and thinkers who were helpful. Many of them have been forgotten by name. Some of their outrageous and, in a few cases, inspiring statements are all that I can remember.

While I fully respect the Montessori approach to education, I do not endorse all schools with the Montessori name. Those interested in this type of education for their children should read *Dr. Maria Montessori's Own Handbook* (as well as her other books) and should visit the schools in the area. They then will be in a better position to evaluate the educational practices of these schools.

Joe David
February 11, 1981
Alexandria, Virginia